CAPEVILLE

THE DEATH OF THE BLACK VULTURE

MATT MIKALATOS

CAPEVILLE
The Death Of The Black Vulture
Copyright © 2016 by Matt Mikalatos

Printed in the United States of America
First Printing, 2016

ISBN: 978-0-9977699-0-6

Cover Design by M. S. Corley
http://www.mscorley.com

Editing by Lisa Parnell
http://lparnellbookservices.com

Book Formatting by Kevin G. Summers
http://www.happycatstudios.com

Published by Pulp Hero Books

www.Capeville.net

In Memory of Nate Woodford
One of the first and best fans of the Black Vulture.

TABLE OF CONTENTS

PROLOGUE

FIFTEEN YEARS AGO

Chester the Jester cocked his head to one side, and the bells on his tasseled hat jingled in the cold night air. A puff of surprise came out of his mouth, but his thumb didn't waver from the orange button on the detonator. His barest twitch could set off the explosives packed like bats on the underside of the bridge.

The Black Vulture felt grim satisfaction to have caught his old nemesis off guard. He repeated his offer. "Don't look so confused, Chester. I give you my word. Turn yourself in, and I'll retire. I'll hang up the cape."

"It's a trick." Chester shook his head, and again the faint jingling of the bells rang out over the dark waters of Levitz Bay. "The Black Vulture is tireless. You'll never tire, let alone re-tire."

The Black Vulture flexed his hands, one at a time, keeping them limber. He had been stiffer the last few years. It took more work to keep in shape. Climbing up the suspension cables after Chester, keeping a handhold as he hurried up the main cable, thick as a small car, had exhausted him. He thought he was fast enough to tackle Chester and take him over the side of the bridge, but only if he had a distraction. Even so, the villain might detonate the explosives. He watched out of the corner of his eye to see if the bridge had been completely evacuated. No.

1

People milled around below, out of their cars, standing on the deck and watching the two men high above their heads. His mind ran over the situation, looking for a way to end this without any loss of life.

The man in the jester suit grabbed a cable with one hand and leaned out over the water, peering into the inky blackness below. "Could I have forgotten someone? Is one of your super-powered friends hiding nearby?"

"No."

"King Jupiter is under house arrest. The Governor and Caesar are dealing with the civil war on Mars. Chrononaut has been suspended from this entire decade. The Flying Squirrel is retired. Percepta, the Pacific, the Thunder family, Wise Owl, Rocket Cowboy, the Foreigner, the Mighty Flea... none of them can help you."

Policemen were hustling people off the bridge. "It's always been just the two of us, Chester." He took a step toward the Jester, his gloved hand crawling along his belt, looking for the right tool.

Chester laughed, and his high, thin voice echoed out over the water. "All these years... I commit a crime, and you stop me. I plan the parade and you rain on it. I cook a gorgeous meal and you throw it in the swimming pool. I start a joke and you –"

The Vulture's booted feet slammed into Chester's chest. Chester fell backward, toward the water, but the Vulture grabbed him by his multi-colored tunic and yanked him back. He wrenched Chester's fingers open and the detonator fell, tumbling through the dark air before being swallowed up in the distant water. He slammed Chester against the main cable. The Jester rolled at precisely the wrong moment and slipped over the edge, toward the water, his thin hands squeaking across wet metal. The Jester let loose a cackle of laughter more suited to a hyena than a human being, his fingers slipping off the edge. "You ruin the punch line! I set a bomb, you drop the detonator in the bay! Ha ha ha ha!"

The Black Vulture grabbed his wrists, preventing him from falling. "You left something out, Jester. You murder people. Do you know how many you've killed in the last twenty years?"

The Jester frowned. "Oh, my dear scavenger bird, I don't keep track. They're all part of the show."

"I know their names, Chester. Every single one. Seventy-three people."

Chester rolled his eyes. "Is that all?"

The Vulture growled, a low, rumbling thing that threatened to tear out of his chest and into the depraved man hanging below him. "I should have killed you years ago."

"I've often wondered why you didn't," the Jester said reasonably. He struggled to look over his shoulder at the cops moving people off the bridge. "They're all going to die, you know." He looked back up at the Vulture, his eyes sad. "That's part of the joke, my desert bird. Everyone dies."

"Not tonight."

The Jester sighed. "You really are retiring, aren't you?"

The Black Vulture turned his head away. "Let's get you to a squad car."

The Jester grabbed the Vulture's wrists and yanked him close. The Vulture struggled backward, barely keeping his balance, keeping Chester from pulling him over the edge. "I did this all for you," Chester whispered. "If you're done with the costumed life, so am I. It wouldn't be any fun without you." Spring-loaded knives snapped out of the Jester's sleeves, cutting into the Vulture's forearms. Startled, he released his grip, and the criminal tumbled, hitting a lower cable, which sent him spinning back toward the deck. He slammed into the ground, hard.

The Vulture leapt, trusting that the exo-skeleton built into his costume would absorb the force of his fall. The impact still hurt, though, a bone-jarring jolt radiating through his entire body. He collapsed, but he could still hear Chester's maniacal laughter. He pushed himself to his knees and Chester kicked him in the head. He fell onto his back.

The Jester tore his jacket off, revealing a harness, which he attached to a long bungee cord on the ground beside him. "I planned ahead, my feathery friend. That detonator was a prop. My bombs are on a *timer*."

The sound of a speedboat popping across the dark waves below echoed up to them.

Chester stood at the edge of the bridge. He climbed onto the protective barrier.

The Vulture was on his feet now, groggy but moving. He heard the clattering of cops headed toward them.

Chester tilted his head. "That's my ride, and just in time." He pulled out a pocket watch and smiled at its face, as the Black Vulture sprinted toward him. "One hundred and twenty seconds until 'retirement.'" With that, he kicked the coiled bungee over the side and jumped out backwards from the bridge, just as the Vulture leapt, tackling him in mid-air.

They tumbled in free fall, the Vulture's view shifting from Chester's face to the black water, and the bobbing light of the speedboat below. He tightened his grip, crushing Chester to him, hoping that the bungee would hold both their weight.

Chester screamed with laughter. The bungee stretched to the bottom of its reach and then shot upward again. The Vulture's blood rushed to his head in a dizzying, pounding moment, and his muscles groaned as he struggled to keep his grip on Chester, to keep from flying into the water. He fired a shot from his grappler, the puff from the tiny explosives sending the hook hurtling upward. As the hook connected to the underside of the bridge, he cut Chester's bungee.

They spun out of control. He nearly lost Chester, but managed to tangle his hand into the harness. The grappler's winch pulled them to the bottom of the bridge in roughly forty seconds. Chester said nothing, and the Black Vulture felt a momentary pride despite his anger. He had never scared the Jester into silence before. The explosives hung like overripe fruit in the recesses of the deck above, just within reach.

The Jester's eyes never left the bulbous rows of explosives. At last, the Jester spoke. "I have an override... in the boat."

"Tell your goons to use it, then."

"They don't know the code!" Panic. His eyes darted around, looking for a way out. "The people on the bridge. You have to choose... capture me or stop the bomb!"

A strange, furious calm descended on the Black Vulture. "There's no override switch, Chester. It's not your style."

"You have to let me go!" Chester's voice broke and he nearly sobbed. "It's rigged to explode if you try to defuse it."

The Vulture had a sudden urge to tell Chester everything. Why he was retiring. About his pain over the years, the people he had lost, including Courtney. He thought about the baby. Regret washed over him as he thought about his own son, how damaged their relationship had become. Mistakes paraded through his mind. Some had faded with time. Some had been corrected, and some could never be undone. It was strange. He felt--not affection, exactly, not for someone who had murdered so many--but a familiarity for Chester. They had spent years at each other's throats. That was something they shared.

"Ten seconds!" Chester struggled in his grip.

The Vulture almost dropped him. Would that be a mercy? The lights of his city winked at him. Saying farewell. He had done some good, he thought. He remembered a man and woman and their son who he had protected from a mugger, years ago, outside a movie theatre. He remembered the look of wonder on the boy's face, the grateful shout of the man, the way the woman slumped faintly against her husband as they exited the alley together. Who knew how different that child's life would have been without the Black Vulture? But now, on his last night in this role, maybe his last night in this life, he had failed. How many people were on the bridge? Three hundred? Five?

He could barely hear Chester over his own thoughts. A wind picked up, coming from the city, stronger than it should be for this time of year. A flicker of red danced in the distance, but too late, he knew it was too late. A tug on his hand turned the Vulture's attention back to Chester.

Chester had unsnapped the rings connecting his harness. He slipped out of it, and the change in weight caused the Black Vulture to bob on his grappling line. Chester fell away from him, shielding his face from the coming explosion. The Black Vulture thought of the people on the bridge and all the others he had failed in his life, Chester included. This was the end, then. One mistake and it was all over.

He felt the impact in his back and ribs, felt his own bones cracking from the force, felt the air escape his lungs. The light -- so bright it washed the world into a blank page -- hit him before the heat, and the heat far ahead of the deafening sound and he wondered how that was possible but by then he felt himself falling through the air like a star, like a planet falling through the void, like a bird hurtling toward its prey and his last thought was that he wished he had done more, somehow, with what had been given him.

CHAPTER 1

GRADUATION DAY

John Ajax sailed his bike off the curb with a victorious whoop, landed it in the middle of the street, popped a wheelie and swerved past a dented blue truck. Eighth grade was finally over, and an unbelievably vast ocean of summer days stretched out ahead of him. Nothing to do now but throw his backpack under his bed, grab some ice cream, slouch to the sofa and play Tread Battalion 2.

The air tasted like summer and exhaust and hot pavement. He cut a diagonal across an intersection and a white minivan honked lazily at him. He popped onto the curb and turned toward home. The whole world seemed familiar and strange at the same time. He had seen this stretch of sidewalk a million times, but never as an eighth grade graduate. A *high schooler*.

A dog slid out of a shadowy alley and onto the sidewalk. Its grey and white fur gave it the unmistakable look of a husky, but its hair was ratted and a deep, hairless scar ran over its forehead and slashed across its snout. When John looked at the dog, it stopped moving and turned its head away. John stopped pedaling and watched it more carefully. Every time he looked away, the dog moved closer. John's neck hairs stood on end. Was it... *hunting* him?

He stood on his pedals and zipped down the sidewalk, cutting toward the white walk lights whenever he hit an intersection. The dog followed close behind, and twice it nearly got flattened when it jumped into traffic. John got caught at an intersection while the green turn arrows were lit, which meant no walk signal. A weird guy leaned against a streetlamp at the intersection, and John figured being near someone -- even a weird someone -- would be good if the dog got too close. John rolled to a stop at the corner.

The dog came padding up the sidewalk and stopped a half block from John, its tongue lolling out and sides heaving. The man against the lamppost had short-cropped that hair covered a sweaty scalp. Even in the summer heat he wore long jeans and a black leather jacket. He had a black number thirteen written across the left side of his face, coming down from his forehead, over his eye and cheekbone and ending on his lower cheek. Whether it was a tattoo or magic marker, John couldn't tell. The man squinted at the dog, then at John, pinched off his cigarette and flicked it into the street.

"That your dog, kid?"

"No." John looked at the scarred husky. Its ears perked up. Number 13 stood a step closer than before, a lopsided sneer on his face.

The man scratched at the thirteen on his face with his right hand. "You John Ajax?"

John shook his head, keeping his eyes on the man. The light changed and he put his foot on his pedal. "I've got to get home, Mister."

Number 13 grabbed John's handlebars. "I'm not going to hurt you, John." He said it like an actor reading a script for the first time, like he wasn't used to people believing him.

What should he do? Leave his bike and run for it? Yell for help? Before John could think of another option, the dog barked ferociously and ran toward them, startling Thirteen and John both. The man's grip on the handlebars loosened and John tugged away and pedaled furiously across the street. He cut across traffic and barreled down the street toward home.

The dog kept close behind him, growling and barking, its white teeth inches from John's tire. It pulled even with his legs, so John poured on more speed, worried about being bitten. He cut down an alley, speeding past Dumpsters and illegally parked cars. A homeless man looked up from his cardboard shelter and John yelled, "Careful, there's a crazy dog out here!"

The homeless man shrank back into his box, stroking his beard, and shouted after John, "Looks like a wolf!" He pulled a flap down over his box and mumbled, "Wolves in the city. Never a good sign."

A chain link fence blocked the end of the alley, a Dumpster pushed against the building next to it. He pedaled up fast, skidded to a stop and jumped on top of the Dumpster. He grabbed his bike and, with a grunt of effort, slung it over the fence. The dog didn't break pace, but ran and leapt on top of the Dumpster. John swung his backpack and caught the dog in the chest, sending it flying into the far wall.

He tossed his bag over the fence and followed after it. The dog, still on the other side, growled and snapped at him. John pulled his pack on and picked up his bike. He leaned against it and took a deep breath. What was going on? A stranger and a dog chasing him on his way home from school? The dog growled one more time, then sped back the way it had come.

"Nice move, John."

He recognized the voice immediately. Number 13. He turned. Thirteen stood in the middle of the alley, his arms crossed. He looked precisely the same as before, with one difference. The number thirteen on his face had been replaced with a number seven.

"What happened to your thirteen?"

Number Seven laughed. "So, we've met already, have we?" Seven cracked his knuckles, then dropped his fists to his side. "Since you're running I can only assume you rejected our deal."

"I didn't even hear your deal." John tried to edge around the guy, but the narrow alley prevented it.

Seven grabbed John's wrist. When John pulled away, he gripped it tighter. "You're coming to meet my boss. He has plans for you. And, considering his history with your parents, he thought it would be safer to send me to pick you up."

John twisted his arm sideways, yanking his hand free from Seven's grip. He kicked him, hard, in the kneecap. Seven fell backwards, gasping. Seven's skin stretched and bubbled, then pulled apart as a second man yanked himself free from Seven. A disgusting sound, like a foot being pulled out of mud, echoed through the alley, and two nearly identical men stood in front of John. One with the number Seven on his face, and the other with no number.

Seven groaned. He pointed at the new man and said, "You're thirty-two."

John edged away from the two men. No way. No way this was happening. Since the Jester blew up Kane Bridge and the Rubicon Protocol came into being it was illegal for people with powers to be anywhere but Capeville. Capes shouldn't be in regular society.

The new man pulled a marker from his pocket and drew a three and a two on his face. He turned to John. "Your parents have been hiding things from you, John. We can tell you the truth about them, about everything."

"What are you talking about? And why aren't you in Capeville? Caesar is going to find you, and he's the most powerful superhuman on the planet."

Seven coughed, laughing. "Caesar is dead. No one has seen him in years. The Black Vulture is dead, too. I'm not worried. We're going to kill every cape out there, John. And you're going to help us. If Caesar shows up, we'll kill him, too." He used the wall of the alley to regain his feet. He turned to his double. "There's a momentary weakness and confusion associated with the multiplication. Write the number on your face. We have to keep track of which number we are for when we re-assimilate."

"I already did it," Thirty-two snapped. "Pull it together, Seven."

John ran, coasting his bike alongside. He put one foot on a pedal and swung on, already well out of reach by the time they yelled for him to stop. He ignored what they said about his parents. His parents were weird, but they had never lied to him.

The guy with powers made him nervous. They had studied power manifestations in health class. This type was called replication. This guy had a pretty good version of it. John had heard of people who could multiply but not replicate their clothes, so every copy was naked. Or people who could replicate, but every copy had decreasing amounts of mass, or muscle, or intelligence. His whole life John had been kept out of the "power" circles, far away from the "capes." His dad didn't like them, and his mother worried incessantly about John developing an unhealthy interest in it. Then there was his crazy grandfather, who hated the powers enough that he had written books about it. In fact, he had pretty much single-handedly shaped public opinion into the Rubicon Protocol. There were no "super hero" posters up in John's room, no documentaries of the famous heroes or villains or freaks.

John took a sharp right and wondered if they knew where his house was. They must at least have an idea, or how would they know where to wait for him after school? And they knew his name. And his parents. Who would hate his parents? The guy said that his boss had issues with his mom and dad and John couldn't even imagine it. He took deep, calming breaths as he pushed his legs to the limit. Shane's house was nearby, he could probably hole up there. But Shane's mom didn't get home until late, and the doors in most of the house were glass. Anyone who really wanted to get him could, and he knew for a fact there were at least thirty-two people after him.

"Hi there. Are you John Ajax?"

Number Four. John rode off the sidewalk and pedaled harder, just out of Four's grip. Four yelled "We have a runner!" and the street burst to life with identical men. Three of them came around the corner and ran after him, just as a fourth burst out of a floral shop and grabbed for him, nearly catching hold of his backpack. Up ahead, five more spread into a phalanx and advanced on him with triumphant grins. A couple of them jumped across alleys from the rooftops, watching him.

John changed direction, but they were behind him now, too. They formed a loose circle with John at the center. He looked for help, but there weren't any cars coming. Could they have blocked traffic somehow? He looked at the shops. Men with numbers on their faces blocked the doors. A woman in a clothing store yelled into her phone, he hoped talking to the police. Several of the men grabbed his bike and another yanked him roughly off it.

Number Three walked up to John, flanked by Five and Six. "You're smart, John," he said. He gestured to the mob surrounding John. "Smart enough to see that you're going to get hurt if you fight us."

They all started talking at once.

"Don't you want to know the truth, John?"

"We're not going to hurt you."

"This would be easier if you came willingly."

"You're not normal, John, you're like us, we can help you."

"Things are heating up, John, and you're going to have to pick a side."

John held his hands up for silence, and the numbers obliged him. "I am a little curious," he said. They smiled. "Your replication process -- we studied this in school -- it's involuntary, right? It's triggered by something you can't control."

"He's observant," Number Nineteen said.

"It's a pain response," Number Three said. "Whenever we're hurt, we multiply."

John smashed his fist into Nineteen's nose, grabbed his handlebars, jumped over them and drove his feet into Five's chest, knocking him into Two and Three. He picked up the bike and swung it, fast, in a complete 360, the tire knocking into multiple men on the way around. He elbowed another in the gut, swept the feet out from under the next guy and watched as they all fell back, their skin stretching as their doubles burst into life. He fought his way through the crowd, and every time a fist or foot or elbow connected, a copy fell back as it produced another. John almost made it to the edge of the crowd when someone grabbed his feet, and he fell forward, caught by the arms of three more men. John struggled wildly against them, but there were too many. With one last, savage, thrust he whipped his head backwards and caught the man behind him in the nose. He noticed with satisfaction the crack, followed by the sound of groaning and the wet-mud sucking sound of the replication.

"I ought to cripple you before I take you back to the boss." He had the number one on his face, and he stood directly in front of John. John tried to yank his arms free, but the copies held him tight. "That was clever, forcing me to replicate. It's disorienting, and it almost worked."

John spit in his face. Number One took his hand and wiped it off with a slow, meditative gesture, then looked at the spittle on his fingers.

"I'll remember that, John." He threw a hard, fast slap at John's face, and John's head snapped back. John scowled at One, but said nothing. One shrugged. "Tie him."

They twisted his arms back, hard, and rough ropes bit into his wrists. John struggled to make it a difficult process for them, and mostly succeeded, but within a minute his hands were tied so tight that he couldn't move his arms, and a painful burning sensation travelled from his wrists to his shoulders. They pushed him onto his belly, the hot pavement stinging his face.

Number One crouched down next to him, a grin on his face. "I'm Frank Hydra, kid. You can't escape me. Remember that next time."

The sound of police sirens came bounding down the cement canyons of the city. John turned his head toward the sirens, but couldn't see the squad cars.

"Pick him up and let's get moving," Hydra said. John turned his head, looking for a way out. He saw the wild dog, crouched low to the ground and creeping through the forest of identical legs. John's heart leapt into his throat as he watched the dog head his way. Its scarred muzzle and sharp teeth almost panicked him. He struggled to stay calm.

Number Eight shouted something, and the dog skittered forward, claws clicking on the pavement. It leapt into the air and smashed into Number One's chest, causing another copy to pop out of him before he hit the cement. He landed on his back, the dog's teeth firmly encircling his throat.

John rolled over, curled his legs up and rocked himself onto his knees. In less than a second he was on his feet and running toward the sirens, his hands still tied behind his back.

Numbers swarmed after him, hands grabbing at him.

John lashed out with his feet and head, trying to slow them down.

Eighteen grabbed John by the shirt collar, yanked hard and knocked him to his knees. He pulled a switchblade from his pocket and held it to John's neck. He leaned in close, his whisper barely loud enough to be heard over the sirens. "Boss said, worst case scenario, I make sure you don't make it home."

Then Eighteen choked, grabbed at his head, and folded in on himself like a napkin. All around him, the numbers fell to the ground, folded and disappeared with a small puff of displaced air. John looked back at the dog.

The dog released One from his grip, shook his coat out and trotted nonchalantly over to John. Number One lay still and silent in the middle of the street. Unconscious, or dead? The dog growled and grabbed hold of the ropes that tied John's wrists, and with a few deft bites tore them off.

John got to his feet. The dog sat placidly beside him, tongue splayed out to the side, his mouth turned up in a doggie grin. John stopped beside Frank Hydra and felt for a pulse. He sighed, relieved. He would live, although an angry set of teeth marks decorated his throat. John grabbed the discarded ropes and tied Frank's wrists together, tight. The sirens came closer, and John lifted his bike from the pavement. His legs were shaking, but he managed to get up and riding again. He turned down the street and headed for his house, the dog trailing behind him. Summer had taken an unexpected turn. He wondered if Frank Hydra's boss was the sort to give up easily. He suspected not. With a chill, he remembered that they knew where he lived. He pumped harder on the pedals. He needed to warn his parents.

CHAPTER 2

SUMMER PLANS

"Mom!" John flung the door open so hard it smashed into the wall, leaving a hole where the doorknob hit. He flung his backpack down by the door, slipped on the newly waxed floor, fell onto his back, slid past the bar stools in the kitchen and smashed into the back wall. His mom raised an eyebrow from where she stood in the kitchen, mixing a batch of cookies, her half apron tied around her waist and her hair perfectly coifed.

"Hello, John. Did you close the front door?"

He hadn't. In fact, the dog stood in the open doorway, looking past John's discarded bike and into the neighborhood. "Mom, this guy stopped me on the way home from school and –"

His father stepped into the room, his slacks perfectly pressed, his shirt starched and his tie expertly knotted, his hair in a perpetual frozen surfer's wave over the crest of his forehead. He wore a cardigan, and held a pipe in his right hand. John didn't know why, but his parents dressed like 1950's television parents. He didn't realize it was weird until a couple of years ago when he started going to his friends' houses more regularly. He thought all those old television reruns were just what life was like in a family. His parents were decidedly "Leave It To Beaver." His friends had never even heard of the show, but he lived it. It explained, in retrospect, why all the kids had thought he was weird for wearing slacks and a button down shirt to school every day. Not any more, of course, he'd been picking his own clothes since fifth grade, and he had purposely washed any weird clothes on the hottest settings possible and convinced his mom to give away the shrunken results.

Dad cleared his throat and said, "Mom did a great job waxing the floors today, didn't she, son?"

Mom's smile gleamed as she stared lovingly at Dad. "Thank you, darling."

"Dad, there was this guy on the way home from school who was –"

"There, there, son, we can talk about it over lunch. Mom made a special lunch in honor of your last day of school." Dad grabbed John and pulled him to his feet. "Let's get your things put away, shall we?" He put his arm around John's shoulder and steered him into the hallway, where the well-worn husky stood just inside the doorway.

John prepared himself for his dad's ballistic yell, but instead Dad crossed quickly to the door, shut it, locked it and pulled the window shades. He knelt down and grabbed the dog by the scruff, and looked into its eyes. A genuine smile spread across his face, and his eyes twinkled. "Hey, Dogface! Long time no see!" He scratched behind the dog's ears until its hind legs started twitching and thumping against the floor.

"You know that dog, Dad?"

"Hmm?" His father's face slipped back to its usual look: charming, unflappable, vaguely amused. "No, of course not, Johnny boy." He called into the kitchen, "Tara, set another plate for lunch, we have company." He put a hand on John's shoulder. "You better go clean up, John. Lunch in five."

"Dad, I really need to talk to you about this guy --"

"During lunch, son. Go wash up."

"Yes, sir." John walked up the stairs, slowly, watching his dad and the dog. His dad stared after him with that same frozen smile until the moment he was out of sight. John paused on the stairs, counted to ten and leaned back. His father was bent over the dog, speaking in an earnest, low whisper. John walked into his bedroom. His bed was made, his floor picked up and vacuumed. A duffle bag sat on his bed. He zipped it open. It was stuffed full of his clothes, neatly pressed and folded. What was going on? He went into the bathroom and washed his hands and face mechanically. His cheek smarted where number One had smacked him.

He combed his fingers through his hair. His mom had set out some clothes for him. He hated it when she did that, treating him like a first grader. But today, instead of some strange outfit from the 1950's, she had set out a pair of jeans and his favorite Tread Battalion 2 t-shirt, the one where the red tank was bursting through a brick wall. He knew she hated his video game shirts, so she was sending a message. She felt bad about something and was trying to make it up to him. He pulled the clothes on. He yanked the curtains back and leaned against his window pane.

The neighborhood looked normal. Quiet, even. Some young kids jumped in a lawn sprinkler down the block. A cat lounged in the back yard of his neighbor's house. Nothing weird. Nothing unusual. No sign that a wild dog might follow you home, or that a man with powers might try to kidnap you in the street. John assumed the cops had picked Hydra up, maybe busted him for violating the Rubicon Protocol. No one seemed to have followed him home. He shrugged and picked up the duffle bag, and walked quietly down the stairs.

As he came closer to the dining room, John paused and listened to his parents' hushed voices. His mother said, "It's time to tell him."

"There's no question they've found us, Tara, but if we can give him a normal life for even one more summer then I think that's --" The dog barked. "He's in the hallway."

John stepped into the dining room. His parents sat at the table, smiling. Steaming steaks hot off the grill, baked potatoes, salad, french fries, hamburgers, spaghetti... his mom had created an enormous smorgasbord. Strangely, the dog sat at the table as well, a plate and silverware and a cup set out for him, as if he were one of John's friends come to visit.

"You look handsome, dear," his mother said as he set the duffle bag down and slid into his seat. She grabbed his hand and squeezed, and his father took his other hand. The dog grinned.

John pulled his hands away, and they dished up their food. John wanted to ask about the dog, but the whole day was tilting sideways and he didn't want to upset things farther. John put a steak on his plate, and some french fries. The dog barked for spaghetti, which he slurped up greedily, the sauce flying all over the table cloth.

"Mom..."

"Shh. It's fine, dear. It will come right out." She gave him her *watch what you say in front of the guests* smile.

His father cleared his throat. "Son, we have something to tell you and you may have mixed feelings about it."

His mother clucked her tongue. "Oh, Walter. He'll have a wonderful time." The dog barked, and she poured milk into a bowl for him. He lapped it up, the milk spilling to join the tomato sauce on the tablecloth.

"Son, we've talked to your grandfather, and we think it would be best if you went to spend the summer with him."

John collapsed into his chair. "Dad. Grandpa is weird. And mean. I don't like visiting him. I sure don't want to spend a whole summer at his house." And he lived, for some crazy reason, in Capeville, with all the capes and people with powers.

It didn't make any sense that his grandpa lived there, either, because he hated capes. Grandpa had convinced the public and the government that capes should be quarantined, put in a ghetto where they could be watched. Capeville. John didn't relish the idea of running into Frank Hydra or any of his super powered friends there.

"Your grandfather is a good man, and we owe him a great deal."

"He's never done anything for us. Whenever he visits he bosses you and mom around and he's never satisfied with anything... my grades, my room, my attitude, nothing. He acts like a drill instructor from a movie."

John's dad laughed, and he politely dabbed the corners of his mouth with his napkin. "Between you and me, John, I think they based those drill sergeants on Dad." He drummed his fingers on the table. "Nevertheless, your mother and I promised we'd send you for the summer. Your grandpa said he could get you a summer job. You could meet some new friends, start saving money for college."

His mother leaned over. "Or for taking girls out on dates."

"Mom!"

His dad twirled an upraised finger in the air. "Or you could save up for one of those video games you love."

John piled more fries on his plate. The dog watched him longingly, so John threw some on his plate, too. John ate a couple of fries, watching the dog. He couldn't figure out why his parents would let the dog sit at the table. "I have plans this summer, Dad."

"Video games?"

"Yeah... and hanging out with my friends."

"You mean, playing video games with your friends?"

John laughed. "Sure, Dad. That's not all we do, you know. But it's the last summer before high school. It feels like everything is about to change and we want to enjoy the last couple of months."

John's dad leaned close to him and took hold of his shoulder. "Sometimes things change faster than we like, son."

John watched his face, embarrassed. He had that feeling his dad was about to launch into an awkward talk about his childhood or puberty or something. His best bet was to end the conversation. "Okay, fine. I guess. I'm not super happy about it, but I can still play Tread Battalion and Omega Point with my friends online. Tell Grandpa the video games are non-negotiable."

His mother smiled. "When you're not working, dear." She swept into the kitchen and returned with a giant tray of cookies and a half gallon of ice cream. She started scooping ice cream between the cookies and handing them out. "I packed a bag for you."

"When do I leave? Next week? Are we driving?" Three Christmases ago they had driven to Grandpa's house. Capeville was a unique place, and John had loved it, to be honest. He wouldn't tell his parents that now, but Capeville had a certain draw. You saw lots of people with powers there. John wasn't sure why his grandpa, the cape hater, would live there, but it was pretty nice. Capeville was an artificial island as big as Hawaii. Caesar built it, along with a super bridge that went all the way out to the island. It took a full day to cross the bridge, and everyone said it was one of the most high tech bridges ever built. Caesar built it in a day and a half.

John's father threw a plane ticket on the table. "Flight is in an hour. As soon as you eat your dessert we'll be on our way."

John choked on his ice cream. "An hour?"

"Your grandfather sent the ticket."

John put his hands flat on the table. "What is going on? First that guy tried to kidnap me on the way home from school... a guy with powers, Dad! Then you let the dog sit at the table. Then you tell me I'm headed away for the summer. In an hour! When did you decide this?"

His mom raised one eyebrow. "You have such a wonderful imagination, John."

John's dad laughed. "Attacked by a guy with powers. Your grandfather will love that story."

"No, really. He had numbers on his face, and every time I punched him he would split like an amoeba and his name was Frank Hydra."

His dad frowned, and he hit the table with his hand. "That's enough, young man."

"No, really, Dad. Ask the dog!"

They all three turned to look at the dog, who returned their look for a minute and then stared out the sliding glass door. He whined piteously and wouldn't look at any of them. Finally, his mom said, "I think we should drop this whole unpleasant conversation."

"Mom. Dad. I am not going to drop this. These people, whoever they are, they know where we live. They know what route I take home from school. They know my name. I'm worried they'll come here looking for me and that you'll get hurt. I'm worried they'll follow me to Grandpa's."

John's dad sighed, and he moved his hand across the wave of hair on his forehead, his fingers surfing it all the way down to cover his face. "I think the jig is up, Tara."

His mom smiled. "At last." She got up from her side of the table, and came around to John, pulling his head close to her in a hug. "You're so smart, Johnny. We've tried to keep you sheltered from all this." She reached down for the steak knife beside John's plate and held it up by his neck. "This is going to hurt, John. Deep breath."

John went stiff and struggled to get away from her, but his dad grabbed his arms, pinning him in place. "Mom! What are you – aah!"

The knife bit into his neck, and his mother made small, reassuring noises, then pulled away, a BB-sized device between her fingers. Red lights flashed in it, and she threw it to the table. Dad smashed it with his water glass until all the lights went out. "Rubicon tracker," he said to his son. "We can talk freely now. Don't want anyone tracking you after today."

"Rubicon tracker," John said, staring at the sparking remnants of the device on the table. "Mom. That's for people with powers."

"Yes. Or people likely to develop them." His mom clucked her tongue, then looked at John's dad. "Do you think that's how they found us, dear?"

"Someone must have hacked the database. The Shadow Director won't be pleased about that."

The doorbell rang. "Company," the dog said. "Not nice company."

John stood up and knocked his chair backward onto the kitchen floor, his hand covering the wound on his neck. He stared at the dog. Then the busted tracking device. Then his parents.

"Close your mouth, dear," his mother said. "It's impolite to stare."

His father took hold of John's arm. "John, grab your bag and the airplane ticket and head into the garage."

John reached out and took the plane ticket without really looking at it and stuffed it into his back pocket. "The... dog..."

The dog bounded over to him and put his paws up on the table, then reached one out to John. "Dogface. Nice to meet you." John stared at the paw until the dog said, "Shake!" John shook his paw and the dog said, "Good boy! Ha ha ha. I love saying that to people. Now grab your bag, kid, you got a plane to catch."

The doorbell rang again, and John slung his duffle over his shoulder. His mom came into the hallway, her pink 1950's dress flouncing as she walked. She leaned over and gave John a kiss on the cheek and told him that she loved him and to be good for Grandpa. Dad gave her a kiss as well and when they parted she said, "Plan Seventy-three?"

"That seems safest, dear."

She nodded pertly, reached into the hall closet, pushed on the back wall, and stood back while a panel slid aside. She reached into the dark recesses of the closet and pulled out a gigantic, shining silver rifle. It was smooth, with a flat barrel and a glowing line down the side. John had never seen anything like it. His mother hefted it up in one hand and walked demurely in her high black heels to the front door. She smiled winningly back at her boys and winked.

Dogface laughed. "It's a pleasure to see you back in business."

The doorbell rang again and she called sweetly, "Coming!" Dogface trotted up alongside her, and with the hand that wasn't holding a giant silver rifle, she shooed the boys away toward the garage.

John's dad grinned as he pulled John into the garage, and they hurriedly jumped into dad's battered Crown Victoria. "Seat belt, John." John pulled it on. John's dad cranked the engine, watching a spot on the garage wall. John didn't see anything out of the ordinary. Until a green light behind the wall came on bright enough to shine through the wallboard. "Now, John... we get to have some fun!" John's dad hit the gas and the car rocketed out through the garage door, tearing it to shreds. John's head bounced against the door as his dad whipped it around. John caught a glimpse of a police car in front of the house, and his mother opening the front door as the startled officers reached for their sidearms. They shouted at John's dad to stop the car.

John's dad let out a victorious war whoop and stomped on the gas, just as John's mom pulled the trigger on her rifle. A bright green light lanced out at the police car, and it popped straight into the air fifteen feet, then crashed to the ground before catching on fire, sirens blaring and lights blazing. John grabbed the armrest on the door, trying not to shout. As they tore out of the neighborhood, John heard another explosion behind them. He wormed around in his seat. A black, roiling column of smoke rose over the neighborhood. A theory popped into John's head. The secrets. The giant laser gun. The crazy thug chasing him after school, the Rubicon tracker.

"Dad? Are you and mom... super-villains?"

John's dad laughed maniacally and hit the gas.

CHAPTER 3

SECURITY CHECK

John's dad cranked the car around another corner, and the wheels squealed in protest. He laughed joyfully while John pointed out the deadly black cloud of smoke hovering approximately where their house stood. Or, maybe, used to stand.

"Dad? I asked you a question... are you and Mom super-villains?"

Another burst of laughter from his father. "What are you going to ask next? If your mom is a time-travelling burglar?"

"That's not an answer, Dad!"

A cat walking in the middle of the road nearly met its fate on the front grill of Dad's cruiser, but it jumped out of the way, a screeching, irate puffball. More sirens wailed in the distance. John added things up, holding on for dear life. His parents had secrets. Clearly. They had laser guns hidden in the house. They were friends with a talking dog. They weren't actually the 1950's family of the suburb he had thought that they were. On the other hand, it's not like they had tons of money sitting around. And someone had put a Rubicon device in his neck. In his neck! Gross. His mom had cut it out without any trouble. His parents had never stolen anything that he knew of, and were kind and generous and friendly. He couldn't imagine them trying to take over the world, or knock over a bank, or threatening to destroy a city. On the other hand, the whole 1950's family thing could be them trying to fit in with regular society. Maybe they were just bad at it. And they were running from the police.

"I can hear those wheels turning!" His dad grinned. "Hang on!"

His dad cranked the wheel, and the car burned rubber as they slewed across traffic and headed back the way they had come, not getting on the highway, as John expected, but sticking to the surface streets. "Dad. I deserve an answer. Are you super villains or spies or what?"

"Safer if you don't know for now, John. We'll fill you in after this summer. They'll be watching the highway. Shouldn't occur to them to check the small planes airport by the river."

A police motorcycle pulled up alongside the passenger window, the driver pointing a gun at them. "Dad, the police want us to pull over."

His dad yanked the wheel toward John, and the car smashed into the motorcycle. The officer jumped off and landed on the hood of the car, his helmet flying off behind him. He had the number 17 written on his face.

Seventeen shattered the window with his gloved fist, and John, more by instinct than anything else, punched him in the chin. Seventeen's head hit the ceiling of the car, bounced against the window frame and then followed the rest of his body down to the pavement, skidding alongside the car for a moment before bouncing along behind them. Several more bodies popped out of Seventeen.

John's father let loose with another victorious whoop and slapped John on the shoulder. "I guess all those martial arts classes paid off!" He laughed. "I'd give anything to have seen you lay into old Frank Hydra this afternoon."

"What, now you believe me?"

"John, your mom and I knew you were telling the truth. But since they fit you with that tracking device a few years ago, we've thought it best to keep quiet. Dog-face told us about your afternoon, and it sounds like you did great. Now, look behind us and make sure we're not being followed."

No cars, motorcycles or anything else seemed to be behind them. No multiplying bad guys. No cops. No capes. He told his dad so, and his dad reminded him to check the sky for fliers. Nothing there, either. The regional airport splayed out ahead of them, a few dilapidated buildings, a couple of small hangars and a stretch of field that had been converted into a landing strip decades ago.

"Am I really going to Grandpa's house?"

John's dad glanced over at him, a worried look on his face. "John, do what Grandpa tells you. He's difficult, but he has your best interests at heart. We'll call if we can. Okay, we're coming up to the door. I'm barely going to stop. You jump out and I'll keep driving."

"Dad!"

"What is it, son?"

John couldn't think how to say what he wanted to say, and he felt a seed of anger growing inside him. He couldn't believe his parents lied to him. They'd been lying to him for years. But at the same time, this could be the last time he would see them. For all he knew his parents were headed for some secret super-villain lair. Typical families weren't evading assassinations and fake cops. "Take care of Mom, okay?"

His father smiled. "Be careful, son."

John's dad slowed the car to thirty miles an hour, reached over and threw John's door open. John unlatched his safety belt.

"Cross your arms and tuck your head in close." His dad slowed slightly, then pushed John out the door. John hit the ground hard, rolled a good distance, and smacked his head lightly on the curb. Between the waxed floor and his dad shoving him out of the car, his parents had given him more bruises than the bad guys had. John got to his feet in time to see his dad throw the duffle bag out of the car, lay rubber around the corner, and disappear into the suburban streets.

John brushed himself off and retrieved his bag. His head ached, and he'd cut his elbows pretty good on the pavement. The air still smelled like summer and freedom, but now with the strange, unaccustomed smell of danger and burnt rubber.

The wooden door to the airport squeaked when John opened it. It wasn't even automated. John had never flown out of this place, and when he walked inside he wondered if anyone else had, either. The main room was the size of the downstairs of his house, maybe a thousand square feet. Two exit doors, marked "GATE ONE" and "GATE TWO" stood on opposite sides of the room. A bathroom with two symbols on it -- one with two legs and one with a skirt -- sat in a recessed corner, and a water fountain loitered near the bathroom door, rusty and unloved.

John knocked on the bathroom door, and when no one answered he pushed his way in and slid the meager chain lock in place. A single toilet, crowded out by towering boxes of toilet paper, airplane parts and old magazines, sat lonely in the corner. A shiny metal patch doubled as a mirror, and John studied his bloody elbows, washing them off with paper towels. He splashed water on his face. He leaned back on the sink, testing it first to make sure it could hold his weight, then took out his airplane ticket. It listed CPJ as the destination, and the airline as Fighting Fifty-Five Air. A logo of two red fives with boxing gloves blazed across the center of the ticket.

Someone knocked at the door and it shivered in its frame. John quickly put his ticket in his back pocket and unlocked the door. A bored-looking airport employee in a brown airport shirt looked in and said, "It's time to clean." John nodded and got out of the way. Standing near the bathroom he could see the whole waiting area. A chunky kid ate a candy bar while his hair curled around his face like some overzealous octopus, a blue backpack slumped against him, his back against the wall. A thin girl about his age, with mocha-colored skin and dark hair, sat in a wheelchair by Gate One, his gate. Another bored airport employee, this one with his arms crossed, leaned against the wall behind the girl in the wheelchair. A man sat near the center of the room, reading a paper. This seemed so clichéd and common from spy movies that John purposely watched to see if he ever turned the page. He didn't. A lump formed in John's throat. He backed toward the bathroom and rapped on the door. The airport employee shouted it was being cleaned and John said, "I'm about to be sick." The door flew open and the employee jumped out of his way.

John grabbed him and pushed him back into the bathroom. He slammed the door shut behind them, and the guy fell into a terrified karate pose. "I know ninja skills!" he shouted.

"Shh! Listen. There's this guy out there trying to kidnap me and I need your help."

"You want me to call the cops?"

"No, he's --" He's part of some secret organization that has no problem with impersonating cops. He's likely a vicious murderer. He has super powers. John's mind whirred, trying to come up with something believable. "He's a cop."

The employee frowned at John skeptically. "The guy with the number tattooed on his face? No way." John's face must have gone white at the mention of the number, because the employee suddenly looked like he believed him.

"Listen, kid, I don't know what's going on. If you need to call the cops, you can borrow my phone. But you can't pull people into the bathroom and threaten them." Another knock rattled the doorframe, followed immediately by impatient jiggling of the handle. The airport employee raised his eyebrows. "You gonna let me out or am I being kidnapped?"

John undid the lock and turned the handle. The chunky kid stood outside, still eating his candy bar, the wrapper splayed down like a banana peel. He glanced in quickly, looking from John to the employee and back again, a carefully neutral look on his round face. He took another bite and said, with his mouth full, "What's the problem here?"

"No problem," John said hurriedly.

The kid tilted his head sideways and chewed thoughtfully. "I can help, you know. I'm a super hero." He pushed his way into the closet-slash-bathroom, pulled the door shut and locked it behind him. The box tower by the toilet wobbled, but the employee steadied it with his hand. The kid folded the wrapper carefully up over his candy bar and slipped it into his pocket. He thrust out his hand and said, "I'm the Gecko."

John took his dry, papery hand. "John."

The employee sighed. "Guys. Can I get back to work?"

The boys exchanged glances, and the Gecko pushed himself up against the wall, trying to make room for the employee to get out. John tried to get around the mop bucket and employee but it wasn't easy, and eventually he had to step up on the toilet seat to let him pass while the Gecko wedged himself against the sink. The employee shook his head and made his way out, making sure to yank the door shut on his way.

John stared at the perfectly ordinary looking kid in front of him. "Do you really want me to call you the Gecko? Wouldn't you rather I called you by your real name?"

"Nah. Secret identity. I have to protect my loved ones and stuff. Even my parents, I guess. That's what my uncle says, anyway."

"But I already know what you look like."

"It's not like you can look up 'The Gecko' on the Internet and find my address."

"How can you be a super hero? I thought anyone with powers had to stay in Capeville."

"It's only illegal to be outside of Capeville if you use your powers. You can go anywhere you want if you agree not to use them while you're gone."

"And put a tracker on," John said.

The Gecko shrugged. "Sure. If they know you're on the mainland they'll put a tracker on you." He relaxed and put his back against the peeled paint on the bathroom door. "Where you headed, John?"

John jumped off the toilet, and quickly pushed the tower of boxes back against the wall. "Capeville."

"Oh yeah? Me, too." The Gecko rearranged his backpack. "I could tell you were in trouble. My gecko sense went off."

"You have a gecko sense? It warns you of danger or something?"

"Just kidding. It was the way you kept edging around the bathroom and casing the waiting area. It's that guy with the number on his face, right?"

"Yes! That guy has been trying to kidnap me. He's a replicator. How did you know?"

"I figured it wasn't the pretty girl in the wheelchair."
The Gecko snapped his fingers. "I saw her boarding pass.
She's on our flight, too."

John shrugged. "Isn't everyone in the waiting room on
our flight?"

The Gecko kicked the box tower, which sent it col-
lapsing down around them, shirts spilling over them like
a muddy brown tide of cotton. The Gecko threw one to
John and told him to put it on. "Okay, new friend John.
Here's my plan. I distract the bad guy, you pretend you're
an airport employee and get Wheels on that aircraft."

A tinny, static-filled voice crackled to life throughout
the airport. "If you have the good fortune of joining me
on the flight to Capeville, we're loading up now. There
should be three of you. We're in a bit of a hurry, so let's
move along, soldiers. Gate One. Now boarding."

The Gecko grinned. "Count to ten, then go get the girl
and get on board." He plopped his backpack at John's feet.
"Take this."

The Gecko flung the door open and shouted, "Gecko
power! Evil doers, beware!" The door swung shut again,
and John heard chairs flipping over and shouts from airport employees, and the Gecko shouting, "You! Number
Face! Your number has come up and now you have to face
me! Ha ha!"

John counted to ten. The brown shirt hung on him like
a dress, and he doubted it disguised him much since he
had the Gecko's backpack on, and his duffle bag hanging
off one shoulder. He pushed out the door into the bedlam
caused by his strange new friend. The Gecko clamped
onto Hydra's leg while Hydra cursed and tried to shake
him off. Airport employees clutched at Gecko's arms, trying to pull him off, and everyone was shouting. John kept
his eyes down and walked quickly past the knot of struggling people.

The girl in the wheelchair didn't turn her head or say anything as he approached, although her eyes followed him. John's face grew hot when he felt her eyes on him, but he kept walking, came up behind her and said, "Miss, let's get you on your plane."

She didn't move other than to say, "It's not a plane, it's an aircraft." John shrugged and grabbed hold of the handles of her wheelchair, which bit him with an electric shock.

"Static," John said. He laughed despite the situation, rubbed his palms on his jeans and took hold of her chair, wheeling her out the glass door and onto the tarmac. As they exited, he heard Hydra call his name. John turned. Hydra, still trapped by the Gecko, slapped himself hard in the face, twice, and two copies popped into existence. The Gecko immediately grabbed them both with his hands, his feet still twined around the first Hydra. John leaned over and told the girl, "We're going to run."

But where? John didn't see a plane anywhere, just a strange round thing. It looked like an inner tube the size of a house lying on its side, with a gigantic fan blade in the center. It had a glass observation deck arcing around one side and a ramp leading to the deck. The whole contraption rested on giant rubber tubes filled with air. John moved hesitantly toward it. The girl nodded, barely moving. The Fighting Fifty Five logo covered one side of the craft, and as soon as he saw it John poured on the speed.

A fat old man with a wreath of white hair, khaki pants, black boots, a too-small brown leather jacket and a jauntily tipped hat loomed at the top of the ramp. He saluted as they came aboard. "Welcome to the J.W. Webb Flying Donut, soldiers. I'm Captain Francis Anytime of the Fighting Fifty-Fifth." He took John's ticket and punched a hole in it. "You can call me sir."

"Yes, sir."

He took the girl's ticket and punched it. "Welcome aboard. You can call me Anytime." She smiled, and John's stomach flipped when he saw her straight, even teeth and the dimples in her cheeks.

"Miss, your seat is there along the wall, and soldier, you can sit beside her."

John rolled her over to the wall. "My name is John," he said. She smiled and his knees almost buckled.

"I'm Katherine." John stuffed his duffle under his seat and threw the Gecko's bag onto the next seat over. John looked back at Captain Anytime. Anytime pulled a pocket watch out, stared at the face, then looked back toward the gate. The Gecko stretched out between four copies of Hydra, holding two with his hands and somehow clutching the other two with his bare feet.

"Captain, sir, any chance we can get on our way?"

Captain Anytime looked at him with steely blue eyes. "Trouble, eh, soldier? Well, you're with the Fighting Fifty-Fifth now, and your troubles are our troubles. Get Katherine strapped in and I'll get this donut airworthy."

"You'll have to lift me into my seat," Katherine said.

John blushed again. Katherine looked like she had just heard an amusing joke, and she motioned John closer. He stepped toward her. She was wearing a cream colored skirt, and a black, sleeveless shirt which clung to her body and showed off her brown, well-muscled arms. Her arms circled his neck and he awkwardly slid an arm under her legs. His hand and forearm tingled when he touched her cool, smooth skin. His other hand went to the small of her back and he lifted her gently from the wheelchair and set her down in the chair beside his. She smelled like vanilla. He tried not to look at her while he moved the wheelchair to the side and locked the wheels. She thanked him, that same amused glint in her brown eyes.

A coughing sound came from the wall behind their seats, then a loud thrumming that grew to a high pitched hum, the giant fan in the center of the aircraft starting up. Captain Anytime hurried into the cabin and started to pull the gangway in.

The Gecko ran across the tarmac, his improbable mess of hair bouncing in the wind and his fat legs moving faster than John thought possible. Two Hydras followed close behind him. "Captain! Lift off, sir, lift off! Leave the ramp down!"

Captain Anytime let loose with a hearty laugh. "Mr. Gecko!" He hurried past John and Katherine. "Fasten your belts, soldiers, we're headed straight up." John jumped into his seat and snapped his belt into place. The Flying Donut shuddered and lifted from the tarmac.

They were lifting straight up, the monstrous fan at the center of the donut pushing them off. John grabbed his armrests. They were already six feet off the ground when the Gecko jumped. John didn't think he would make it, but one of his hands fell flat against the ramp, and it stuck like it had been glued there.

One of the Hydras grabbed hold of the Gecko's foot, and the Gecko shouted, "No!" Hydra dug his fingers into the fabric of the Gecko's pants and started to climb up him as the Flying Donut shot skyward. Wind burst in through the entry door, blasting John in the face. Katherine's hair whipped around her head. "John!" The Gecko's voice sounded panicked. "I need a sidekick."

The Donut bounced in a bit of turbulence. John unbuckled his seatbelt.

"Hurry, John," Katherine said quietly.

He ran to the door. The wind whistled through the doorway. He fell to his stomach and put his hand down toward the Gecko.

Hydra had climbed onto the Gecko's back, and was pushing his way up by putting his feet on the Gecko's waist. "My pants are falling off, John! You've gotta help!"

"Stop worrying about your pants and grab my hand!"

"I don't need your hand, John. I'm using my gecko powers to stick to the Donut. I need you to kick this guy off. Hurry! My pants!"

John took a deep breath. The only way to reach Hydra was to go out the door. A metal ring was welded into the doorway, and John grabbed hold of it. Katherine shouted for him to be careful, and the thought of her distracted him, but only for a second. He told his heart to stop trying to get out of his chest, tried not to look down at the dwindling airfield below and swung out, feet first, at Hydra's face, holding the ring tight. His feet connected and knocked Hydra backwards. Hydra nearly fell, but he snatched John's foot at the last moment.

"If I fall, John, I'm taking you with me!" Hydra shouted over the sound of the wind and The Flying Donut's engine. "I've got a hundred more bodies. I'll be fine. But what about you, John? Think you can survive a fall from this height?" Far below, the river twisted like a glistening snake and the checkered city blocks were far enough away to look like a chessboard.

John's grip on the metal ring slipped. His fingers burned. The airfield below looked like a colored square. They entered a cloud and all was obscured in fog. He tried to reach up with his other hand, but his arm was pulled sideways. He couldn't reach. They lifted out of the cloud, and John's fingers slipped further.

Hyda's fingers tore into his jeans and John kicked frantically at him until he felt his other foot connect with Hydra's chin. Hydra fell backwards, flailing for a grip. Hydra caught the Gecko's pantsleg, but only for a moment because the pants tore and Hydra fell, clutching a giant swatch of cloth in his hand. John only saw him for a moment before the clouds swallowed him. The Gecko crawled past John and into the Donut, then grabbed John's hand and pulled him in.

Together they closed the door, the Gecko spinning the wheel to lock it. John slumped to the ground. The Gecko nudged him with his toe. "John. Do you have an extra pair of pants?"

John rested his head against the hatch. He knew his pants wouldn't fit the Gecko. "No. Sorry, Gecko."

Katherine asked if they were both okay. John nodded weakly, trying to catch his breath and slow his heart rate. The Gecko bowed to her gravely and then inched past her, making sure to keep his backside turned away. He grabbed a blanket from his seat and wrapped it around his waist just as Captain Anytime appeared from the cockpit.

"Nice skirt, Mister Gecko."

"Shut up, Captain. Sir."

Captain Anytime laughed heartily and punched his fist into his palm. "Now, that liftoff took me back to the glory days, lady and gentlemen."

"I almost died," John said, panting.

"I saw that!" He beamed at John, put his thumbs in his belt loops and carried on as if today was a perfectly normal day. "A few comments before our flight. Due to the nature of our cargo we'll be using the minimum number of electrical devices on this flight. Your reading lights won't work, and I've shut down most of the instruments in the cockpit. Flying blind!" He laughed and looked happily out the window. "It's exhilarating. So, sit back, relax and we'll be in Capeville in a few hours." He lifted John to his feet, slapped him on the back, and shoved him toward his seat. He moved toward the cockpit, then paused and looked back over his shoulder. "Mister Gecko. I can't wait to tell your uncle about your skirt." He slammed the cockpit door, but they could still hear his echoing laughter. Katherine snickered, and then a big grin spread across her face and she started to giggle. Her laugh infected John and soon they were both laughing, looking at each other and then at the Gecko, who scowled at them, which set them off on another hysterical laughing riff. John's stomach hurt, and then his throat and he couldn't stop. He wondered if it was because of the panic a few minutes before, but then he remembered Hydra tearing Gecko's pants off and started laughing again.

John pulled off the giant airport employee shirt he had taken from the bathroom and tossed it to the Gecko. The Gecko looked out the window and mumbled, "I'm thankful none of you know my real name."

CHAPTER 4

THE YEARBOOK

The Flying Donut lifted through the clouds, bound for Capeville. It moved with a smooth, fluid motion, like riding a wave at the beach. Unlike a plane, John could see the whole space in front of them, not just a small oval of sky. The floor to ceiling windows made him feel like he was on a balcony overlooking the entire world. The Gecko lay slumped in his chair, breathing heavily, his eyes half closed. Katherine had fallen asleep, and a strand of her hair slipped down across her eyes, moving softly every time she breathed. Her hair came to her chin in the front, then followed the angle of her jaw. Her dark hair looked almost like night, and the setting sun over the clouds washed the whole cabin with golden light. John wanted to tuck the hair back behind her ear, and almost without thinking he reached out.

An inch from her head, a blue-white spark leapt between them, and John pulled his hand back reflexively at the shock. Katherine opened her eyes and looked up at him. He blushed, tried to hide it and looked away. He kept his face turned toward the Gecko, watching the slumped, dumpy super-hero breathe until he counted to a hundred. He turned slowly back toward Katherine, hoping that she wouldn't be staring at him. Her eyes were closed, but her lips turned up faintly at the corners.

John rubbed his hands through his hair and tried to find something to occupy his mind. He couldn't take another minute of looking at Katherine without talking to her. He pulled out his duffle bag, which his (super villain?) mom had packed, and zipped it open. Maybe she had packed some snacks or something. But no, it was only crisply folded clothing. He stuck his hands all the way under the pile of t-shirts and shorts and his hand brushed something hard. He grabbed hold of it -- a book of some sort -- and pulled it out. He pushed his bag to the floor and sank into his seat, his hands wandering over the cover of the book. It was a scrapbook, brown leather with the words MY FIRST YEARBOOK printed across the front.

He flipped it open and immediately recognized his mother, younger and with a broad smile, her golden hair falling in mostly perfect curls... mostly perfect because some of them were wet with sweat and pasted to the side of her face. She sat up in a bed, wearing a thin gown, looking at the camera with a mixture of wonder and pride, cradling a tiny, mewling baby. John's dad was pushing his way over mom's shoulder, not even looking up at the camera, his eyes fixed on the baby and his sappy grin shining out despite his ridiculous mustache. Beneath the picture his mother's perfect script announced *John's First Day!*

The following pages held more pictures with mom and dad, them taking turns with John, smiling at each other, at the baby, at the camera, at nothing. One picture showed dad sacked out in a chair, holding John protectively in the crook of his arm. John shook his head. Just like mom to send baby photos when he went away for the summer.

In the next picture a whole crowd of people pushed into the frame. John didn't recognize them, or most of them at least. His parents stood on the right side of the frame. His grandfather was turned slightly away, as if he was trying to get out of the picture, thinner and stronger than John remembered ever seeing him, and without a wheelchair, too. An older man pulled on Granddad, bringing him back into the picture. Strangers filled the rest of the frame: fit, young, beautiful people mostly, friends of his parents he guessed. One serious man, who must have been six-and-a-half feet tall, lurked toward the back, and someone had posed a manikin with a robot face in the back row as well, and one spot on the photo had gone bad, leaving the impression of a blurred face where no person stood visible. His mother's firm hand beneath the photo said Another Regular Get Together At Dad's.

After that, newspaper clippings and magazine articles from the year of John's birth fought for space in the yearbook. A virus swept through the Middle East, killing sheep but no people. The election of the new president, who vowed to end the Sino-Russian conflict. A list of the ten most popular movies and songs from that year. An item about a Hollywood star who married a stuntman, and another about a dog who saved a bunch of school kids who had been lost in the desert.

Most interesting to John, his mother had also included a large segment of paranormal events. A robot from the 1850's called the Governor left Earth to fight in some sort of Martian civil war, and came home with a trophy he called the Galaxy Box. Caesar had been with him, the article said. A criminal called Chester the Jester destroyed Kane Bridge, killing hundreds of people, including three police officers and a costumed vigilante called the Black Vulture. A long magazine article about super heroes retiring, with particular attention paid to two favorites, Ms. Universe and The Flying Squirrel, who had retired within three months of one another. Both of them had huge fan networks, and their announced retirements brought protests around the country, and a riot had even broken out in Boston. And while some super groups disbanded, like the Ninth Street Regulars, others launched the same year, like the Chinese super team, The Autumn Tigers. A New York Times chart tracking new heroes, retired heroes, captured villains and the most wanted super criminals filled one page. The last page included an opinion article with the headline, "You Can't Trust A Masked Man" with the basic point being that someone who requires anonymity to do good things is, by definition, hiding something and is therefore dangerous.

John read the article, which seemed unnecessarily vicious, and then noticed the picture at the end. The author was his grandfather. Pasted next to that article was a letter to the editor from the next issue which read, in part, "We wear masks to protect others, not to hide ourselves. Our loved ones, our neighbors, our co-workers deserve the protection of our masks." The last note from his mother read, Sometimes Secrets Protect the Ones We Love. And then, under it, Caesar Has Crossed the Rubicon. He closed the book and held it in his lap.

Secrets. His parents had plenty. His mom kept a giant silver gun hidden in the house. His father drove a decked out super car, in addition to being friends with a talking dog. Strangers attacked his house, his parents tried to protect him by sending him to live for the summer with his hateful grandfather. He read the note again, about secrets protecting loved ones, but he didn't feel protected. He felt betrayed. He should have a say in all this, on whether he got pulled into this strange world where multiplying criminals try to kidnap him after school. Or, for that matter, maybe he would have wanted to know what was going on years ago, so he could protect himself. What if Hydra had managed to get him after school? Or at the airport for that matter?

John flipped through the yearbook again. Then again. Then a fourth time. He read the articles carefully, looking for clues. He stared at the people in the party picture, but he didn't know anyone but his parents and his grandfather. He wondered if his mother included articles like the one about the civil war on Mars because it was interesting or because it meant something to her. He tried to cobble together a timeline, but it wasn't easy. He noticed, for instance, that Ms. Universe retired five weeks before the end of the Martian civil war, but so what? He flipped through it again. He tried arranging things according to his birthdate, but it didn't matter. The Flying Squirrel retired six months before John was born. The anti-paranormal article came just a few days after the explosion at Kane Bridge, which was also before he was born. It was weird, actually, that his mom had collected articles from before he was born. Caesar and the Governor had returned from Mars a few months before his birth. Seemed like most people collected articles and top ten lists and photos from after their babies were born, not before. He closed the book and tapped his fingers on the cover, thinking. It was as if the articles had nothing to do with him, but if so, why put them in his baby book?

The door to the cockpit burst open and Captain Anytime blustered into the cabin, waking the Gecko and Katherine. "We're preparing for descent, my friends! I kept making announcements on the intercom, but I forgot I had the power turned off. It might be bumpy flying blind, so put your belts on!" He slammed the door again, and Katherine laughed. She rubbed her eyes and smiled at him. He looked away, then kicked himself for not smiling back. He didn't know what to do around her.

The Gecko stood and stretched, then pointed at the yearbook. "What are you looking at, John?"

"Shouldn't you put your seatbelt on? "

The Gecko shrugged, and ran his hands through his messy mop of hair. "Nah. My fingers and toes can stick to anything I touch. I can grip the floor tighter than your seatbelt can hold you to the chair." He touched the tips of his fingers to John's book, and the book lifted up by the cover when he pulled his hand away. "See?"

"What is it?" Katherine asked.

"Nothing," John said quickly.

The Gecko shrugged. "Some sort of weird baby book about John." He showed a picture to Katherine. "Not the best looking kid, was he?"

She looked up at John. "I think he's adorable."

John blushed for real this time. Katherine cooing over his baby pictures would be the most embarrassing outcome John could imagine for this flight. On the other hand he wasn't wearing a makeshift skirt like the Gecko. Katherine held her hands out for the book, but the Gecko kept flipping through, nodding his head occasionally. He stopped for a long time on the picture of John and his family and all the strangers, looked at it intently, then turned the page, as if he had seen nothing important about it. He read the anti-paranormal screed from John's Grandpa. He snorted and said, "Man, this guy hates capes."

Katherine cocked her head. "What does it say, Gecko?"

"That anyone who wears a mask can't be trusted, that's all. That they're terrorists, or worse, and should be 'shot down like criminals, which is what they are.' I'm surprised anyone ran this." The Gecko scowled at the yearbook for a long time. "I'd like to meet this guy," he said finally, and he handed the book over to Katherine.

Katherine, instead of flipping through baby pictures (for which John was grateful), carefully read the article by his grandfather. "He is harsh," she said. "But I see his point. Why wear a mask if you aren't hiding anything?"

The Gecko snorted again. "I suppose you think I'm hiding something?"

"You're not wearing a mask," Katherine said reasonably.

"Yeah, but I won't tell you my name. And if we met in other circumstances, I would have worn my mask. Wearing a mask doesn't mean you have something to hide, it tells people what you're hiding. It says, look, I'm not going to tell you who I am, you'll have to figure that out by looking at my actions. Not my name, or the color of my skin, or my disfigured face. It's the people *without* masks you can't trust. They're hiding something, too, they just won't admit it."

Katherine said. "Don't you think some people hide behind masks because they don't know if they're doing the right thing? That they're afraid they're making a mistake?"

The Gecko shrugged. "Not me. I'm the Gecko with or without the mask. The mask is just to protect people... the people close to me who aren't willing to sacrifice everything for justice. Me, I'd be glad to go all the way if it meant saving the world. If it meant saving even one innocent person."

"I'd never wear a mask," Katherine said.

John shook his head. "Everyone wears a mask. My parents have been hiding my whole life. They're wrapped up in masks. We're all hiding something." He looked out the window. A long, bright strip stretched out in a line in front of them. The Capeville Bridge. Up ahead, a bright spot in the distance shone up at them, getting closer every moment. "I'm hiding something, too. That crazy guy who wrote the article about paranormals? That's my grandfather. That's the guy I'm going to live with today."

The Gecko shrugged. "Most people hate something. That guy hates me and my kind. Won't stop me from saving him from a runaway bus, if the time comes."

John looked at the Gecko. John could see he meant it. For the Gecko it didn't matter what someone thought of him, it only mattered that he do the right thing. John looked down at his hands for a long time. Katherine didn't say anything, but after a few minutes, her hand slipped into view, grabbed his, and squeezed. Then she pulled it back into her lap. John looked up at her and their eyes locked. "You're right, John. We all have our secrets."

The Gecko clapped John on the back. "Learning who to trust, that's the trick."

The city came into view, and it looked like something designed by a World's Fair exhibit in the 1920's. Startling white towers rose with curved tops and stripes of blue lights. A gigantic statue of Caesar, nearly the size of the Statue of Liberty, stood near the Bridge. His left arm was at his side, his hand curled into a fist, and his right was up over his head, his hand clutched around the neck of a giant dragon, its maw stretched toward his face, snake-like coils and tail looping around his arm. His eyes looked vigilantly toward the far horizon, and all of this was lit with bright white light. Yellow lights wound through suburb streets, and occasional small black ponds of shadow revealed lakes. The city pulsed and glowed with light, beautiful as a pocket full of gems spilled in black sand. The tallest buildings were clumped tightly in the center, and as the buildings moved from the center of the city they grew gradually shorter, giving the whole place the shape of a great circus tent, light pouring out into the sky and calling the bored, the pleasure seekers, those desiring wonder to come and see.

The Capeville airport, nestled up against the shoreline, came into view as they rounded the statue of Caesar.

Captain Anytime took them right past the great statue's face, and John and the Gecko pressed their faces against the glass, drinking it in.

"What's that dragon?" John asked.

The Gecko snorted. "It represents the Golden Dragon, Caesar's greatest enemy. It seems like any major villain works for the Dragon, somehow. Most evil plots boil down to some minor step in his master plan. Some people think Caesar has disappeared as part of his never-ending battle against the dragon." He shrugged. "I don't know. I've never seen either of them, it's all rumors from the old guard."

John thought about that, and watched the chiseled face of Caesar, the most powerful hero in the world. Maybe Caesar would help him if Hydra came after him again. And that was the second time someone said Caesar was missing. Hydra had said the same thing when John tried to scare him off by mentioning Caesar's name. Was he naïve to think that Caesar was still out there, watching out for people like him?

Captain Anytime's voice came from the cockpit, warning them to take their seats for descent. A perfectly smooth landing followed, the monstrous fans in the center of the Flying Donut whirring at high speed before gently touching down.

Katherine leaned over to John. "Here's my phone number," she said, and she slipped a small, folded piece of pink paper into his palm. "You should call me. If you get bored at your Grandpa's house."

Captain Anytime came running into the room and popped open the door hatch. A small army of men in white lab coats came marching up the ramp, clipboards at the ready, led by an African-American man with small, round glasses and bright silver hair perched on his head like a wig. He bent over and gave Katherine a kiss on the cheek and said, "Have you kept still, Katherine?"

Katherine frowned. "Of course, Father."

"Don't even speak! You know what happens when you move too much." Katherine's father turned to look at John. "I hope you didn't think her rude. Katherine has a rare illness, and any physical movement, even something so simple as writing a note or speaking to someone can have disastrous physical results."

The Gecko popped over. "She didn't say a word."

Her father beamed. "That's my girl." His assistants unsnapped the brakes on her chair and they wheeled her down the ramp and out of John's life. John looked at the slip of paper in his hand and showed it to the Gecko.

"How am I supposed to call her if she's not allowed to talk?"

Captain Anytime swooped in behind them and grabbed them both in an enormous headlock, one under each arm. "Boys! If you need me, you call me. Day or night! I'm itching for battle! The wind in my hair! The guns blazing! The smoke of battle!"

The Gecko struggled out of the headlock. "You don't have any hair, Captain. And you had to pull all the guns off The Donut a long time ago."

Anytime chortled and let John go, mussing his hair. "Don't listen to Mr. Gecko, soldier. I may not have hair, but I do have a few tricks up my sleeve if it comes time for war." He grabbed John by the shoulders and shook him. "Promise to call me if you need a flying donut."

John laughed. "Okay, okay, I promise."

He shouldered his duffle bag, and the Gecko did the same with his bag. The two of them walked down the gangplank. So. This was Capeville. It didn't look that much different than an ordinary airport, though a strange array of communications antennae sprouted from the control tower, and of course the Flying Donut sat on the tarmac.

John also saw what looked like a Viking ship alongside a commercial jet, and a rocket ship from the 1950s.

The Gecko hurried him along, into the airport and down to baggage claim. John didn't see his grandfather anywhere. They walked out along the sidewalk, watching the cars creep by the curb. "Maybe he didn't know what time your plane got in," the Gecko said.

"He bought the ticket."

"Maybe he's waiting to hear from you."

"I sent him a text." John sighed. "Knowing him, this is some weird test to see if I can find his house." John crossed the street to the taxi stand. "I'll grab a cab."

The Gecko looked around, arms crossed. "I haven't seen any trouble, John."

"Nah. You should go home." He shook the Gecko's hand. "Thanks for all your help."

"No problem. Welcome to Capeville."

"How do I call you? You know, if I want to hang out with you and Katherine?"

"I'll be in touch." And with that, the Gecko disappeared into the airport. John slid into the cab and gave the driver his grandfather's address. He realized as they pulled away that he didn't have any cash to give the driver, but he figured he could get some at his grandfather's. As the cab turned onto the highway, John leaned his head against the window and looked into the sky, hoping to see a super hero flying up above, but all he only saw white towers and blue lights and dark skies. His phone buzzed and he flipped it open. It was a text from his grandfather. "Something came up. Cash for a cab on the kitchen counter. DON'T TOUCH ANYTHING."

John flipped his phone shut. Secrets. His parents. His grandfather. He slipped the phone into his pocket. Maybe, he thought, I didn't get that last text. Maybe I'll need to explore the house a little, looking for money to pay the cab driver. John felt a stirring of intuition, a sudden feeling that he had been lied to his whole life, and he was on the verge of discovering some lynchpin fact in the true story, that all the lies would come crashing down and he would know everything. He wondered how long he would have until his grandfather came home.

CHAPTER 5

GRANDFATHER'S HOUSE

John's grandfather lived in a housing development with wide streets, wide cars, short-cropped grass and bright streetlights. The cabbie pulled up in front of the house, a flat, ranch-style place, with two windows out front and one concrete step functioning as a porch. John slung his bag over his shoulder and told the cabbie he'd be right back with some money. The cabbie grunted and left the meter running.

John hadn't been to the house in a few years, but it looked like he remembered: as if it was for sale. His grandfather paid to have the lawn and house meticulously cared for, but it looked cold and professional. It was a house, but not a home, and there was never any evidence that someone lived in it. John bounced over the cement step and pushed on the door. Locked. Of course. Because Grandpa made everything as difficult as possible. John debated breaking the kitchen window. That would teach the old man a lesson.

Instead, he pulled the thin cord on the side gate and swung it open. He walked through the side yard, the palm-sized river stones his grandfather used for gravel clacking together under his feet. He skirted the pool. The sliding glass door didn't budge. He pushed again, then once more, then lightly kicked the door and grunted in frustration. He leaned his back against the glass and looked out into the back yard. It was a warm night, he could probably just camp out by the pool until Grandpa got home. Of course, the cabbie would have to leave without being paid. What a mess. At least no one had followed him from the airport. He shivered at the thought of super-powered goons finding him here, alone, outside the house.

Something moved on the other side of the yard.

He froze. A shadow moved near the swimming pool, close to the tree which hung over the house. The shadowy figure stood, silent and still, near the tree. As John peered into the darkness, his eyes adjusted and he could see a man in a tight-fitting green outfit. He wore a mask and thick goggles. John couldn't see a gun, but that didn't mean there wasn't one.

John palmed a river stone and tested the weight. He looked casually around the back yard, trying to seem nonchalant, and then whipped the rock at the shadowy figure. It flew in a bright arc across the pool, glinting in the momentary moonlight, and smashed into the shadow's head. The shadow flipped backward with a surprised grunt, legs and feet flying up into the air and following the rest of the body down to a heap on the ground. John ran around the pool and leapt for the shadow's body, but the shadowy man scrambled from the ground and into the tree. Not before John grabbed his foot, though, and, with a mighty yank, pulled him down again.

John kicked him once, hard, in the side and the shadow rolled over, shouting, "John, John, it's me!"

John stood there, panting, fists clenched. The shadow rolled to its feet and moved into the light. On closer inspection, John could see that the green outfit was, in fact, dark green tights with a thick green jacket over a yellow shirt. A black silhouette of a lizard climbed up the front of the shirt, and yellow boots and gloves nearly finished the outfit. A mask, which looked like it had been fashioned from an old aviator's cap and a pair of motorcycle goggles, clung to the shadow's head, covering an unruly sea of hair. The stranger held his hands out and kicked one foot to the side. "Ta-da!" he said, almost laughing. "It's the Gecko."

"You jerk!" John punched him in the arm. "You scared me. I thought you were staying at the airport."

The Gecko's face took on an expression of mock pain. "Moi? A jerk?" He brushed the dirt off his outfit. "I didn't throw any rocks at least."

John grunted. "Ha. Good throw, right?"

"Great arm."

"How did you get here at the same time as me?"

"Trade secret."

John's eyes lit up. "Can you fly?"

The Gecko looked at him disdainfully. "Do you remember the whole episode on the Donut where a bad guy pulled my pants off while I hung on for dear life? Does that sound like someone who can fly?" He shook his head. "I followed you on the Gecko Cycle."

John watched the Gecko for a long moment. "Couldn't you have given me a ride, then?"

"I wanted to make sure no one was following you. And I had to change out of my makeshift skirt into my spandex."

John pointed at the house. "I'd invite you in, but the doors are all locked."

The Gecko made a noncommittal noise and walked over to the house, putting his fingers against the sliding glass door, which didn't budge. "He didn't give you a key, I guess."

"Obviously not." John picked up another rock. "We could break the window."

"Not a good idea in Capeville. Never know when some cape will rig his back door with killer robots or something."

John thought about this for a minute. His grandfather wasn't a cape. He hated them. But he was in a wheelchair. So, it made sense that the front door would probably be locked, he couldn't use it because of the step. Why hadn't he put in a ramp? Thinking about it, his grandfather probably couldn't reach the string to open the back gate, either. Or push his chair through the gravel on the side of the house. "Let's try the garage," he said. The Gecko shrugged and followed him.

The cab driver looked up when they came around the house. John waved to him, and he went back to talking on his cell phone. John bent down by the garage door and pulled on the silver handle in the center. It didn't budge. He put his hands on his hips and stared at the door.

The Gecko cleared his throat. "Open sesame," he said.

John rolled his eyes. Actually, his grandfather wouldn't be able to pull on the garage door from his wheelchair. John crouched down to put his head at his grandfather's level. Just to the left of the garage he could see a small indentation in the wooden frame of the door. He ran his finger along it and found a small button, which he clicked. The door rolled up and revealed the pristine, empty garage. "And, we're in!" He turned and gave a thumbs up to the taxi driver, who didn't return the favor.

The interior door opened easily. They entered the dark house through a sunken living room. John flipped on some lights, and they walked up a ramp into the kitchen, where a small stack of money waited on the counter. The Gecko offered to walk it out to the cabbie, but John stopped him. "Let's pretend we didn't see it, and take a look around."

"What, you don't trust your own Grandpa?"

They walked through a short hallway. On their right was the guest room, John's room. He stuck his head in. The bed was made and pushed up under the window. The closet door was opened a crack, and John could see it was empty. "Nice digs," the Gecko said.

"Yeah, it'll be fine." There was a small television next to the door. "I wish I'd had time to grab my video game gear."

"What do you like to play?"

John pointed at his t-shirt. "Tread Battalion 2 is my favorite, but I like Omega Point, too. You?"

The Gecko shook his head. "Not a lot of time for video games. My uncle is always training me. If the Rubicon Protocol ever gets reversed I need to be ready to use my powers in the real world. In the meantime, there's plenty of opportunity to do good things here in Capeville."

John sat down on his bed. "What do you know about my grandfather? On the Flying Donut you seemed to know something."

The Gecko shrugged. "Everybody in Capeville knows about him. After the massacre at Kane Bridge, your grandfather wrote all these articles about how capes brought more harm than good. It turned society sour toward us. Somehow he convinced Caesar, too. No one's sure about that piece. But once Caesar decides to do something, nothing can stop him. He built Capeville and started rounding capes up as soon as the government signed the Rubicon Act into law."

"Rubicon Act? Is that different than the Rubicon Protocol?"

"Caesar and some of the capes who agreed with him called it the protocol. The law in the U.S. that made it legal was called the Rubicon Act. Within a year or so, all the capes were gathered here in Capeville."

"Like a reservation."

The Gecko nodded. "Or a prison." He walked to the closet and opened the door, quickly scanned the empty interior, then shut it again.

"Why are you still here if you think it's a prison? You were on the outside. Why did you get on Captain Anytime's flying donut and come back?"

The Gecko grinned. "My uncle tried to send me out into the 'real world' to keep me safe. There's a rumor going around that someone's building a doomsday device here in Capeville, and that they're planning to blow up the city, maybe kill a bunch of capes. My uncle -- he's the original Gecko -- he doesn't want me to 'play super hero' and try to find the people doing it." The Gecko sucked in his gut, stood up straight and put a sour look on his face, waggling his finger as he said, "'This isn't a game, young man. This is none of your business. These people are dangerous. Let the authorities handle it.'" He deflated, puffed out his cheeks and looked out the window. "There's a reason the world needed super heroes. Heroes adopt responsibilities that are greater than themselves. The doomsday device is none of my business, but I'm going to do everything in my power to stop it. My uncle should understand that, but he doesn't."

John rubbed his chin. "What do you know about the doomsday device?"

"Rumors mostly. Supposedly an old-timer is involved, someone who has stayed quiet for a few years. Buying up explosives, recruiting people, that sort of thing. There's a rumor some people are after a force field generator, but I don't know why."

"Maybe they could use it to keep people away while they set up the bomb or something."

The Gecko shrugged. "Sure. But this is a class one force field, the kind that can keep anything out. Probably even Caesar. Why would you need that to set a bomb?"

John didn't have an answer for that. "You didn't show up here just to check in on me, did you? You're investigating my grandpa."

The Gecko leaned up against the wall. "Your grandfather hates capes so much that he gets us corralled into a ghetto on an artificial island. Then he moves here. It doesn't make much sense. It's the sort of question you have to follow up."

John tapped his front teeth with his finger. What was his grandfather doing in Capeville? John had never understood that. "We're not going to find anything in the guest room. Let's go check his room."

John led the way down the hallway, then turned left into his grandfather's room. Sheets hung low on the wall, tacked up with staples. The Gecko pulled one off. Underneath were maps of Capeville, gridded and marked with red pen.

The Gecko put his finger on one map. "This map is all the seats of government, the police headquarters, the fire departments. Look, there's the statue of Caesar down by the bridge."

John studied the map. Red marker crisscrossed the paper, circling important landmarks, crossing out other places. A few red lines seemed to trace major highways and roads. His heart dropped into his stomach. "Looks like terrorist targets."

The Gecko rubbed his chin. "Could be." He looked at another map. "And what's this? Hiding spots for the device maybe? Sewer entrances, public parks, empty lots."

John pointed to a street on the south side. "He's marked it here. It's circled a hundred times. He's written something next to it that I can't quite make out."

The Gecko leaned in close. "Sunnybrook Retirement Home. Okay, we should check into that. Anything else strange, John?"

John looked around the bare room. A bed. A small bathroom, walls covered in maps and sheets and a closet door. He looked more carefully at the closet door, and ran his fingers along the frame. "The hinges on this closet are on the inside."

The Gecko walked over and looked at it. "So?"

"So, hinges are usually inside front doors, bedroom doors, places like that. Where you don't want an outsider getting in. Closets, though, the idea is that you don't want someone stuck inside, so you put the hinges outside, so you can take them off if you have to and pull the door off. Hinges outside means a closet. Hinges inside means... a room. Or an entrance."

The Gecko put his hand on the door. "An entrance to what?"

A loud clunking sound came from the front of the house, followed by the sound of the door creaking open. John jumped, and the Gecko quickly threw the sheet back over the maps. "We have to hide," the Gecko whispered.

"Where?"

They could hear him wheeling down the hallway. "John? Are you in here?" They looked at each other, and the Gecko motioned for him to say something. John shook his head.

He whispered, "How do I explain to my terrorist grandfather that I have a costumed superhero in his secret lair?"

The Gecko quietly moved to the closet door. He motioned for John to hurry over. His grandfather's voice came from the hallway again. "John, I know you're here, the taxi driver told me you're looking for money."

The Gecko pulled on the closet door, but it was stuck.

Grandfather spoke again, his voice hard and cold. "I told you not to go snooping around in the house. If you're in my room... you'll regret it."

"There's nowhere to go," the Gecko said. "The door is locked."

John shook his head and tried furiously to think of something to say to his grandfather. Before he had seen the maps, he would have just said they were looking for money for the cab driver. But now... John wasn't sure what his grandfather would do if he suspected John was lying.

"Let me try," John whispered, and he grabbed the door and it yanked open so easily it slammed into the wall. John and the Gecko both gasped. It opened on a small room, like an elevator. A faint light came from within, and on the back wall there were two buttons, red and green. There was no time to think, they both pushed into the room and John pulled the door shut.

"Where are we?" The Gecko asked.

"I have no idea." He pointed at the buttons. "Should we press one?"

They could hear his grandfather in the bedroom now.

"I'll do it," the Gecko said. "It might be dangerous." He pressed the green button, but nothing happened. Then the red. He shrugged. "Broken?"

John pushed past him and pressed his own finger onto the green button. A sharp bite, almost electrical, stung his finger. There was a jolt and then the feeling of a slow slide, as if the elevator box was on wheels and silently coasting in neutral on a slight hill. They picked up speed, moment by moment, and then John's stomach pushed up against his spine, a feeling of extreme acceleration. They steadied themselves against the walls. A loud sound thrummed through the elevator.

"I'm gonna puke," the Gecko shouted.

As if in answer to this declaration, the sound died down, and the elevator steadied. They both held their hands against the walls, panting. It was eerily silent, except for their breathing. "I don't hear my grandfather anymore," John said.

The Gecko pulled himself up straight. "Open the doors."

John hesitated. If his grandfather was still out there he was going to interrogate them about what they had seen in his room. On the other hand, after that strange feeling of acceleration, who knew what would be on the other side? There was no telling who had owned the house before his grandfather. It could have been a super hero or a super villain. The door could open up in Antarctica or outer space.

There wasn't an obvious button for the door, and it wasn't opening by itself. Finally, John decided that if the green button did whatever the green button had done, maybe the red button either undid it or opened the door. He took a deep breath, and pressed it. No shock this time. But the door slid open, just like an elevator. Which was strange because it had swung like a closet door a moment before.

They stepped out of the elevator. They stood in a long, white hallway. Far down the hallway stood a tall manikin dressed in a red robe, trimmed in silver, that fell all the way to the ground. It glided toward them, its robe ruffling out behind it as it approached.

It stopped in front of them, a plastic, unchanging stillness on its face. "Welcome," it said. Its lips didn't move and its voice was cold and without inflection.

"Where are we?" John asked.

The manikin turned and began to glide back the way it had come. "Follow me," it said. John and the Gecko exchanged looks, but they followed. It stopped outside a large, wide door, about twice as large as a garage door. A thin metal arm came out from underneath the robe and inserted itself into a tiny slot on the wall. The door began to slide up into the ceiling. The manikin turned toward them again. It didn't turn its head, the whole manikin turned at once. "You are in your secret lair."

John tried to figure out what the thing was talking about, but its plastic face revealed nothing. "My secret lair?"

"Yes," the manikin said. "The secret lair of the Black Vulture."

CHAPTER 6

THE VULTURE'S NEST

The door slid the rest of the way into the ceiling, but John couldn't take his eyes away from the unmoving face of the manikin. He narrowed his eyes. "Did you just call me the Black Vulture?"

"Yes. Genetic scanning from the door handle confirms your identity." It turned toward the open door. "And this is your secret lair, which in your past incarnation you called the Vulture's Nest."

"My past incarnation?"

"Yes." The manikin glided past the door into a large, hangar-like space. John and the Gecko followed it past a huge black plane, a motorcycle, a helicopter and a car. All of them had the stylized black and red symbol of the Black Vulture on them. The far wall was made of glass. Through the clouds below they could see Capeville. John could see the back of Caesar's statue, the metal cape flowing behind him, and the long bridge stretching out toward the mainland. The buildings below stood in bright light, a city that liked to show off.

The Nest had to be flying somehow, and hidden from view. John certainly hadn't seen it floating over the town. They followed the manikin into another room, about the size of an ordinary garage. There were Plexiglas cases with strange guns and newspaper articles about the

Vulture's victories over a variety of enemies: Chester the Jester, Ice Box, the Fox, and many others. There were a few articles about the explosion at Kane Bridge and Caesar's vendetta to remove every cape from regular society. "This way," the manikin said, and headed through another, smaller door.

John lingered by the bridge articles. "The Black Vulture died in that explosion."

The manikin turned an impassive face toward him, its robe fluttering. "The Black Vulture ceased to exist fifteen years ago."

John tapped one of the articles. "Who collected these, then?"

The manikin turned away. "I did."

"This stuff is amazing," the Gecko said, his face pressed against a display with some sort of throwing knives and grappling hooks. "Why didn't you tell me you're the Black Vulture?"

"I'm not," John said.

The manikin spun around, and six slender arms burst from beneath its robe, each one tipped with glowing ends. "Defense programs initiated. Likelihood of erroneous genetic identification from door handle test? 17% and rising."

John grabbed the Gecko's arm. "I'm new to this whole super hero thing, but are those lasers pointed at us?"

The Gecko shook his head. "I don't think those are lasers. Looks like disintegrators."

"That's not good."

"No."

The manikin's glowing arms brightened. "You have thirteen seconds to identify yourselves or depart from this facility."

"I'm John Ajax."

"Twelve seconds."

"And this is my friend, the Gecko." They stepped back from the manikin, which tracked them carefully.

"Nine seconds."

"Run for the elevator," the Gecko said. "Come on!" He grabbed John and yanked him down the hallway. They sprinted, but they could still hear the manikin's countdown.

"Five seconds."

"We're not going to make it!"

"Three seconds."

They were still several yards from the elevator, and the heat from the manikin's disintegrators washed over their backs. John spun toward the manikin, putting himself between it and the Gecko. "I'm the Black Vulture!" John shouted. "Override! Halt! Stop! Cease! Desist! Don't fry us!"

The manikin's arms didn't retract. On the other hand, John and the Gecko hadn't been disintegrated. There was a whirring sound as another arm came out, this one with a long syringe attached. "We're not dead," the Gecko said.

John pointed at the syringe. "Is this better than disintegrators?"

The syringe struck at John, stabbed him in the shoulder and instantly retracted, before he could even shout at the quick pain. The syringe arm disappeared under its robes and then, after a few seconds, all the disintegrators retracted. "Identity confirmed. You are the Black Vulture. John Ajax is the Black Vulture. Updating security protocols."

John rubbed his shoulder. He eyed the manikin carefully. He'd have to make sure not to say something to set it off again. "Glad we got that straightened out. So. All this stuff is mine, then?"

"Correct."

The Gecko grinned. "This is amazing, John. We've got the start of our own super team right here. This is more gear than my uncle has, not that he would ever let me use any of it. All you have to do is sneak into your uncle's bedroom closet every once in a while and you'll be part of the next generation of capes!"

"I don't have any powers," John said. They walked back into the hangar, past all the vehicles and trophies. In the next, smaller room, there were various Black Vulture costumes, all set out on display like in a museum. They were in order of appearance. The oldest was little more than a strip of black cloth for a mask and a formal evening cape. Apparently the first adventure of the Black Vulture had been impromptu. Various other costumes moved on from there, from simple, utilitarian work pants and belt with a canvas shirt all the way to the next-to-last costume, a heavily reinforced Kevlar vest with greaves and joints built into it for movement. The final display case was empty.

"Your previous incarnation also had no powers," said the manikin, "making him unique among his fraternity of heroes. But he always had the respect of his peers, and his enemies feared him."

"Where's his last costume?"

"It... was not recovered." Beyond the costumes were two gurneys, one of which held what looked like a normal human teenager with his chest opened up and wires and cables spilling out from inside. The manikin covered him with a sheet. "I am making myself a new body," it said. The next gurney held another Black Vulture costume, but this one looked heavy, like armor. "The prototype Vulture armor," the manikin said. "Initial testing is incomplete."

It passed into a third room, and the boys followed it. This last room had banks of giant screens, each tuned to a different news program, police link or security feed.

Several screens were flashing through images so quickly that John couldn't even tell what they were pictures of. "What's going on in here?"

"I am running diagnostics on criminal elements in Capeville most likely to be involved in a rumored doomsday plot to destroy the city and kill most superhumans. This is how I became aware of your presence in your grandfather's home and the need to extricate you using the Vulture Nest's unilink technology."

The Gecko leaned against a computer screen and touched a few of the feeds, moving pictures around with his fingers, watching how responsive the images were. "You must be using satellite technology to watch his grandpa's house?"

"No. I am using self-conscious nano-extensions. They are independently self aware, but their observations are fed to me as if by my own senses. The process is roughly similar to your own ephaptic coupling."

John shook his head. "What did you say?"

The Gecko slapped him on the back. "He said that he's got tiny robots keeping an eye on your grandfather."

"And is he a terrorist?"

The manikin turned its body toward John. "This requires definitional clarity. Your grandfather is breaking the law. His activities are dangerous and could bring harm to others, including yourself."

"But is he the one who --"

Red lights started flashing on multiple screens, and a siren screamed to life in the room. The manikin bent over a bank of flashing lights and several long, thin arms burst from beneath its robe, making it look like the underside of an umbrella as the struts tapped on screens and moved switches. "An attempted robbery on Lakeside Avenue. The criminals are bearing weapons. There are ten soldiers." It pressed a few more buttons. "There is a

93% chance they are part of the doomsday crew, and a 74% chance that what they are stealing is an essential part of the device itself." It paused. "Capeville authorities will arrive within six minutes. I can transport you to their location within one minute." On the screen men in heavy grey armor and black helmets carted rifles twice the size of firewood. One of them was setting up a large device with an energy screen in front of a bank.

The Gecko laughed and pulled his goggles down over his eyes. "Are you going to send us in that crazy elevator?"

"No. Egg drop will be more efficient in this case."

"I'm not so sure about this," John said, but the Gecko was already up and moving.

"You don't have to go, John. It's illegal, after all, to wear a mask in Capeville. If we get caught, we'll go straight to jail."

"I didn't say I wouldn't go, I said I wasn't sure about it. I'm not about to let my grandfather blow up Capeville. If he wants to smear the family name and kill people, there should be at least one Ajax standing in his way."

"Good. Then we should go to the hangar, right?"

They moved to the hangar, and the manikin gestured to the next-to-last outfit of the Black Vulture, the proto-type armor laying out on a gurney. "I would suggest this would be the safest costume for your use today, sir." The armor was for a guy twice his size, and John said so. The manikin seemed distressed by this. "I regret to inform you that the only costume that will fit correctly is the pro-totype armor."

"Let's go then," John said. The manikin raised the gur-ney and it pivoted into a vertical position. John backed into the armor and metal tentacles slithered out and cov-ered his arms and legs, lifting him into the suit. The front of the armor closed over him, his face the only part ex-posed to the air.

"When you close your visor, sir, the armor will activate. Most features are, regrettably, disabled. However, the unit should give you increased resistance to damage as well as superior strength."

The Gecko slapped him on the shoulder, but he couldn't feel it. "You're taller now, too. You're the size of an adult."

The manikin glided across the room, leading them to a black egg-shaped vehicle the size of a VW Bug. A series of thick metal arms held the egg in place. A hatch stood open on one side. John banged his head against the hatch, forgetting he was taller now. He bent down to enter, followed by the Gecko. A series of flashing lights, dials and buttons covered the inside, and there was one seat connected to the console. John said, "If I take the seat, Gecko, are you going to use your suction fingers to keep you safe?"

The manikin said, "I can install the second seat in a matter of minutes."

"No time," the Gecko said. "I'll stick to the inside, like John suggested."

"I would advise against that. The egg drop is a one-destination transport that functions essentially like a cannonball. The ride can be ... bumpy."

The Gecko jumped on the side of the egg and clambered inside, sticking to the slick black panels as if they were covered in Velcro. "I'll be fine."

John stooped down and lowered himself into the chair, the strange feeling of augmented motion created by the servos and shocks built into the exoskeleton making it feel like he was moving through water. He strapped himself in and pushed down his visor. A display popped up inside his visor that said, "LAUNCH EGG DROP? Y/N?" The door closed, sealing them inside the egg.

"You ready, Gecko?"

The Gecko padded closer to the console, where a darkened glass viewport gave them a view of the outside world. "I live for this stuff, BV."

"BV?"

"Black Vulture. I can't be calling you John once we hit the outside." He cracked his knuckles, and then stuck his hands back onto the surface of the egg. "And I just want to say, BV, don't be intimidated by my wacky quips and quick wit when we're fighting the bad guys. It just comes natural to me."

John laughed. "Alright then. Prepare to launch." It took him a second to figure it out, but if he focused his eyes on the "Y" it started to glow. The display changed to say, "COMMAND ACCEPTED" and the egg exploded out of the hangar, spinning crazily. They spun so fast that the Gecko lost his grip and flew toward the windshield. He smashed against it. The crazy spinning of the egg revealed quick glimpses of ocean and city as they hurtled toward land. The Gecko's cheeks were flattened against his face and he let loose a long, roller-coaster inspired scream.

The egg bashed against the corner of a building, then spun in a new, slightly off direction. For one brief second John saw the armored men outside the bank in the distance. The bank looked like an art deco toaster, turned sideways. A bone-shaking impact threw the Gecko onto the floor, and John's head whipped in the restraining seat. Smoke and dust rose around the egg, obscuring the view outside the window. "OPEN HATCH? Y/N?"

John groaned and focused on the Y. The door slid open, but the egg was sideways on the ground. John released his seatbelt and dropped to the bottom of the egg, next to the Gecko. "You okay?"

"A little motion sick," he said, and then puked all over. "Sorry. Hope that doesn't upset your robot." He got to his knees. "I feel better now. Let's go kick some butt." He crawled out of the egg and tried to get to his feet, stumbled and fell. John went after him, the exoskeleton practically the only thing keeping him up.

John helped the Gecko to his feet. The Gecko shook his head like a dog getting out of the pool. "Check it out," he said. The egg had landed on two of the armored men, smashing them.

John hurried to make sure they were all right. He pulled on the helmet of the nearest man. The entire head came off, and John dropped it, screaming. "I didn't mean to do that! This armor makes me way stronger than I thought."

The Gecko picked up the head and looked at the face. Wires hung out where the neck should be. He tore off the front of the helmet, revealing nothing but metal and wires. "Relax, BV, they're robots. Which means we don't have to pull our punches when we fight. That's good news."

John tried to catch his breath. "That's great. We'll have to talk to that manikin back about his aim when he's launching the egg."

The dust was settling, and three armored robots stood in a rough semi-circle around them, guns staring at them like evil eyes. "What are you doing here?" one of them asked.

"We're here to save the people of Oz," the Gecko said.

"What are you talking about? Put your hands up or we're going to fill you with holes."

The Gecko jerked his thumb over his shoulder at the two robots under the egg. "Looks like we killed the Wicked Witch of the West already. Now we're gonna dunk you jokers in a bucket of water."

One of the robots laughed. "What does that make you, Mr. Superhero? Dorothy?"

The Gecko's hands balled into fists. "How dare you. My name isn't Dorothy. It's... THE SPECTACULAR GECKO!" The Gecko leapt backwards, stuck to the egg, jumped into the air and landed on the shoulders of two of the robots. He used his sticky fingers to knock their heads together, dove backwards from their shoulders, grabbed their guns with his sticky feet, rolled on the ground, and popped up holding a rifle in each hand. "Excuse my reach," he said, and pulled the triggers.

Both robots fell to the ground with a loud squee, and the third robot took three steps backwards, firing blindly at John and the Gecko. John rolled to the side and ducked behind the egg, while the Gecko leapt onto the top of the egg and scrambled over it. The Gecko grinned at John. "Pretty good, huh?"

John nodded. "I should have taken care of that third one while you were taking out the other two." A laser bolt skimmed the egg, flashing just past John's head. He ducked lower.

The Gecko shrugged. "It's your first battle. You'll get the hang of it." He glanced down and saw the wreckage of the two robots they had smashed on entry. "Okay, two down from the egg, two more a second ago. What did the manikin say? Six guys?"

"Ten," John said. "Ten guys. So there are six more out there." The lasers had stopped. There was shouting in the distance. John stuck his head around the corner. They had landed in the middle of a street, the buildings on either side all retail or industrial, none of them more than six or seven stories high. Still, it made a sort of canyon, and five robots were loading a floating box about the size of a dishwasher onto a flatbed truck. The robot that got away was with the others and pointing back their way.

"They talk pretty well for robots," John said.

"We need to split up," the Gecko said. "I'll draw them off, you slow the truck down. Slash the tires, smash the engine, whatever it takes. We don't know what's in the crate, so do your best not to jostle it."

"What could possibly be in there that we wouldn't want to jostle?"

The Gecko laughed. "It might be full of bricks of cash or gold, in which case no problem. But what if it's something for the doomsday device, like uranium or something?"

"They wouldn't keep that at a bank, Gecko."

The Gecko winked. "Trust me, BV. Just to be safe."

John shrugged. "Whatever you say, Gecko. You run and I'll count to five before I head for the truck."

The Gecko waved and happily bounced from behind the egg, ran up to the nearest building and threw his body against it, sticking like fresh cooked spaghetti. He shimmied up the side and shouted, "Hey you big tin cans, I'm over here!"

Three of the robots sprinted toward the Gecko, rifles at the ready, while two others loaded the crate onto the flatbed. John ran up behind them. It was hard to be subtle while dressed in black armor with a wide cape flowing out behind him, but he did his best. The first robot turned, a controller for the floating crate in its hands. It swung a heavy fist, and John almost dodged it. Its fist hammered into his arm, denting his armor. John snatched at the robot's arm, but it was faster than him and knocked him backwards with a quick kick. John landed on his back, and the second robot trained its rifle on him. John rolled out of the way as it pulled the trigger. A smoking hole in the pavement reminded John this was no game.

John jumped to his feet and put the first robot between him and the second robot so it couldn't get a clear shot at him. He grabbed the first robot's head and yanked it off, and it fell over, smoke rising from the stump of its neck.

The second robot shouted, "You killed Aaron! I'm going to zero you out."

"I killed 'Aaron'? You are the weirdest robots ever." John snatched up the controls to the flying crate. It looked pretty simple, an up and down button and a joystick for direction. He moved the crate between them. A strange hum and slight glow came from the bottom of the crate. "You're not going to shoot the prize though, are you?"

"Sam, be careful," said another voice. It was the missing robot, walking down the steps from the bank. Their voices didn't sound at all like robots, they sounded like ordinary people. "You know what happens if we shoot the crate."

"It doesn't matter, Lindsey, we'll just reassemble back at the factory."

"I'd listen to, uh, Lindsey if I were you, Sam-the-robot." John started guiding the box back toward the egg, keeping it between himself and the two robots.

Sam grunted, a strange sound to come from a robot. Lindsey Robot was between Sam and the crate now. "Use your head. If we make the boss mad he won't let us in on the next mission. Breaking the crate is a zero tolerance failure."

"These jokers already discontinued five of us, Linds. We have to take them out if we're going to make the drop."

The Lindsey robot made shushing noises. "There are easier ways than blasting them," she said. "The boss gave us more than rifles. She reached into her torso and pulled out a round object the size of an orange. It looked like a grenade. John kept moving backward, toward the egg. The crate wouldn't move any faster. No sign of the Gecko, though the nearby shouts and laser fire gave John a rough idea where he was.

"I'll drive this crate into the ground," John said, loudly. "Put down that grenade."

The robots split up as they moved toward him. He couldn't easily keep the crate between him and them. "I wouldn't do that if I were you," the Lindsey robot said. "The box has a stable environment for a class one force field generator. If it's ruptured we could all be trapped in a field. Or if the power core was damaged it could explode."

"Nice try, Lindsey," John said. "I don't believe that for a second." He pushed the altitude button and the box dipped. Both robots flinched.

The Sam robot said, "The engines on this game must be amazing for him to use our names and things like that, don't you think, Linds?"

John cocked his head, uncertain what this meant. He looked back at the egg. Still about thirty yards away. He turned back in time to see the grenade spinning toward his head. It broke in half about two feet from him, and a net with weighted edges came flying out of it. The net hit John so hard he stumbled backward, falling to the ground. A bright blue energy field zipped along the edges of the net, and John couldn't lift his shoulders from the ground. He could move his legs from the knee down, and he could move his hands, but nothing above his wrists and not his torso at all.

Two more robots walked up, dragging the Gecko in an identical net. They tossed him beside John. "Got him," one of the other robots said. "Those net grenades are better than these rifles. We have to tell the boss that the sights are off or something."

The five robots gathered around the two heroes. "What should we do with them?"

"Let's vaporize them. Otherwise they'll show up on our next mission and get in our way."

The Gecko laughed. "Seriously, you're the worst robots. You talk like regular people and you look like guys in armor. Either look like humans or talk like robots. Make up your minds." They pulled both heroes to a sitting position.

"Let's link to the boss and ask him," Lindsey robot said. "Sam, get the field generator onto the truck. Jimmy, get the truck started." She walked back toward the truck, one hand up to her head, as if she was on a phone.

"Only two guards?" the Gecko said. "I'm insulted."

"Please," one of the robots said. "We caught you. Two is plenty to keep you under lock and key."

Sam bent down over John and reached under the net to grab the controller for the crate, the two guard robots watching with rifles raised. John waited until the robot's hands were on the box, then quickly moved his wrists to grab its arms. Sam tried to shake him off, but couldn't. "Pull the net off of him and hold him down," the second robot said.

"That's not going to go well for you," the Gecko said.

The guards yanked the net off John, and John immediately kicked Sam in the chest. Sam let loose a squee and fell to the ground, the lights in his eyes flickering out. The other two robots lifted their rifles, but an explosion came from the truck, and they both turned to see what had happened. The Lindsey robot was on the ground, burning, and the robot in the truck had jumped out to see what had happened.

A woman in skin-tight black came sprinting around the side of the truck, and as she ran sparks flew from her feet. The robot shot at her, but she jumped up at the side of the cab, bounced off it and onto the robot's torso, wrapping her arms and legs around it. Electricity came arcing out of her and sparks shot out of the robot before it fell burning to the ground.

The woman sprinted toward the two remaining robots. In the distance, police sirens were blaring. "Cops," the Gecko said. "Time to run, BV."

John grabbed the net on the Gecko and yanked, hard, until it came loose. "Let's help this lady mop up those robots."

The robots opened fire on her, but she did a forward somersault into a handspring and twisted into the air, both feet trailing blue electricity as they plowed into the robots and sent them, smoldering, to the ground. She landed in front of them, electricity dancing along her limbs. "Hello, boys." Black spandex covered her head to toe. There wasn't an inch of flesh showing, except for around her mouth. "I'm Lightning Cat."

"I'm the Black Vulture and this is the Gecko."

She smiled. "I know who you are. We knew you weren't dead, Vulture. A lot of us have been waiting for your return. And Gecko... I've been cheering you on from the shadows. I wouldn't be out here today without your example." The sirens were louder now. She looked over her shoulder. "You two better get out of here. I'll get the cargo back to the bank." A few dazed bank employees were wandering out onto the street.

"What about you?"

"Don't worry, Vulture, I can blend into the crowd when the time comes." She grinned at the Gecko's ridiculous skin-tight spandex and goggles. "He's not going to blend in with the civilians." She pointed at John's armor, then the egg. "You're going to have trouble hiding how awesome you are, too."

The Gecko nodded. "Let's go, BV. Thanks, Lightning Cat."

She grinned. "My pleasure, heroes. See you soon."

John and the Gecko ran to the egg. John closed the door while the Gecko got himself wedged into a corner, hoping not to repeat the flying embarrassment of the ride in. Commands started to fly across John's viewscreen, but he kept craning his head to the sideways window, trying to catch another look at Lightning Cat. "How old do you think she is?"

The Gecko shrugged. "Sixteen? Seventeen? I don't know. Why?" He sighed. "I thought you were in love with Katherine."

"Katherine?"

"Snap out of it, John. The girl from the Flying Donut."

John nodded. "Yeah. Oh, yeah. Not in love, Gecko, come on, we just met." He pushed his face closer to the window. "Did you see how tight that spandex was?"

The Gecko slapped a hand against his belly, which jiggled and sent waves along his body. "That's what spandex does, John. Now get this crate moving or we'll continue this conversation in jail."

John shook his head. "Right." He had one last glimpse of Lightning Cat, walking the flying crate into the bank as the police cruisers pulled up. Then he focused on the RETURN command and the egg yanked into the sky. The boys gritted their teeth and hung on tight.

"We did good," the Gecko yelled. "Now we just have to catch whoever is planning this doomsday thing!"

John held on tight and shouted, "And clean all the puke out of this thing!"

CHAPTER 7

SUMMER JOB

The manikin helped John out of his armor while the Gecko looked on, laughing and making fun of John along the way. John, sweating and aching from being knocked around in both the egg and his armor, took deep gulps of air once he got out. He stretched his arms and legs.

The Gecko let out an enormous whoop and ran around the room, his fists over his head. "That's living, Johnny boy! We did it! Stopped those robots!" He did a cartwheel and knocked into a stand of rifles, which clattered to the floor. The manikin picked them up with its many arms. Its plastic face looked somehow disapproving.

"What should we call you?" John asked it.

"I am a G class synthetic person, unit 3, serial number 73610372."

The Gecko clapped it on the shoulder. "G3. Good enough for me. You're a robot, I guess."

G3 inclined its head slightly. "The differences are large but difficult to explain. I am not offended by the term." The robot motioned to them, and they followed it into the computer room with all the screens. "While you engaged with the soldiers, I monitored for transmissions and discovered this." A video of the fight came on-screen, a scene of John with the robots. Thin blue lines came out of the sky and into each robot's head.

"The blue line represents a satellite message coming in to the unit. I followed it back to the satellite, and from there to the points of origin. All ten units had signals originating in residential areas." Red dots flashed into life on the next screen, overlaid on a map of the United States.

John scratched his head. "That doesn't make sense. You mean they're controlled at bases all over the country?"

G3 nodded. "Indeed. I also discovered a second signal that originated here and branched out to each of the other locations." His screen blacked out and relit with a satellite image of a large building in a residential area, a parking lot pooled up on the south side of it and a vicious looking chain link fence around the perimeter.

The Gecko leaned close. "Is that razor wire running around the outside?"

"Yes." G3 turned toward them. "This is a retirement home for super villains. Those who were not reformed by Caesar during Rubicon and are too old or infirm to be kept in the Prison Dimension are held here."

John crossed his arms, as if a sudden cold had made its way into the Vulture's Nest. "So it's a prison?"

"Yes. It appears that someone at the Sunnybrook Retirement Home for Villains is building a doomsday device." The robot stared at them with empty eyes for a long time. No one spoke. The only thing John could think about was his grandfather. The maps on his wall were suspicious, sure, but it didn't prove anything. John didn't know of any connections that his grandfather might have to this place, but the fact that he was of retirement age himself made John nervous. Could it be? His grandfather a super villain? Or terrorist? He thought back on his conversation with his dad. He had never denied that he was a super villain. John couldn't imagine how his parents and grandfather could be villains, but he knew that he wouldn't become a part of that, not for love of his parents, not out of family tradition, not for anything.

Finally the Gecko said, "We should go check that retirement home out." He cracked his neck and then his knuckles.

"Hold on," John said. "Let's think this through. We have maps at my grandfather's house."

"Incriminating maps," the Gecko said.

"Let's say suspicious maps. We have a band of remote control robots trying to steal a force field generator, being controlled from around the country, ultimately from this retirement home." He tapped his fingers on a computer console. "Now, why would they want a level one force field?"

G3 held up a thin metal arm. "With a strong enough power source they could cut Capeville off from the mainland completely. They might trap all the capes here and be able to take over the regular human governments."

John rubbed his chin. "But why go to all that trouble? Why try to steal it here, on an island full of capes? Why not fire a missile from the mainland if all they want to do is make sure no capes interfere with them?"

G3 shook its head. "I do not know. Many capes would survive a direct missile strike."

The Gecko grinned. "I have informants I can talk to, see if anyone has heard anything. John, I think you should snoop around the retirement home in person."

"What? Fight my way through the guards and retired super villains until I find the bad guy?"

The Gecko grinned. "I saw you fighting today. That wouldn't work." John punched him in the arm and the Gecko acted like he didn't feel it. "Besides, how would you know which old guy to kick around?"

G3 cocked its head. "I have traced the signal to a room in the lowest level of the building. It appears to be a maximum security location."

John collapsed into a chair in front of the monitor boards. "What about the elevator? The unilink or whatever. Could you use that to send me in?"

G3 hummed to itself. "Not easily. Re-targeting the unilink technology is difficult. None of its current target locations are near the retirement home."

John leaned back, putting his feet on the console. He watched on the large screen as a news crew reported on the mess at the bank. He scanned the crowd for Lightning Cat, but didn't see her anywhere. "It would have made things easier, using a teleporter."

"Unilink technology is not a teleporter. It is not instantaneous. The unilink shunts the chamber through a neighboring dimension and re-enters in the target location. An identical chamber is brought from that dimension for the ten or twelve seconds of transfer. The science is complicated for third level intelligences like yourselves."

"Third level intelligences? Is that good?"

G3 didn't say anything, but turned and stuck one of its arms into a hole in the console in front of it, and pulled out a thick watch, which it put onto John's arm. "This device will lead you to the source of the signal in the Retirement Village. The blue button will allow you to communicate with me on a secure connection."

John studied the watch closely. It looked ordinary enough, but with a few knobs and buttons on the surface. "I need to go back to my grandfather's house first. We should put off entrance to the retirement home until tomorrow. That should give me time to think about how to get in there."

"This seems wise," G3 said.

The Gecko gave John a high five. "Score one for the third level intelligences." He grabbed G3 by the shoulder.

"Does that elevator have a target somewhere close to my house instead of in John's grandpa's house?"

"Of course. Your uncle has used this unilink in the past."

The Gecko tightened his grip on the robot. "How do you know that?"

"He is a previous incarnation of the Gecko. I have access to the Rubicon records, and I have his identity and his current address on file. Yours as well."

"That's not for public consumption. You shouldn't be able to access those records."

"Understood. I will keep your identity private. The unlink is set for your departure."

John held his hand up. "Wait. Did you have me listed in those Rubicon records, too? And my parents and our house on the mainland?"

"Of course."

John told them about Hydra following him and referring to his boss. "Could they have accessed those same files?"

"I would have said it was impossible," the Gecko said, "Until G3 here said he had access. The security must be thinner than I thought."

The three of them walked through the hangar and toward the elevator. The door was standing open, and the Gecko stepped inside.

The Gecko pulled his goggles down over his eyes. "John, I'll get in touch as soon as I have more information. Good luck tomorrow." He held his hand out and they shook. "It's good to have another hero in town." G3 slid the doors shut.

A faint humming sound came from the doors. John crossed his arms. "I guess I just go back to live with my grandpa." He ran his hand through his hair. Earlier this morning a villain had tried to kidnap him, and his parents had sent him to his grandfather for safekeeping. Now he wasn't sure if his grandfather was any safer than Hydra. "Do you think he's likely to hurt me?"

G3 paused. "Your grandfather has plans for you, but it is unlikely he intends you harm." The doors to the uni-link opened. "Contact me tomorrow and we will make plans for infiltrating the retirement home and finding the source of those signals."

John stepped into the elevator. "Sounds good." He put his hand on the door so it couldn't close. "G3? Why did you choose me to be the next Black Vulture?"

"You were born when the previous incarnation died."

"Are you suggesting... reincarnation?"

"No." G3 moved his hand and the door began to close. "Genetics."

John put his hand against the closed door as the uni-link shifted dimensions. It felt even stranger now that he knew what was happening. Everything had happened too fast today. He got out of eighth grade and was attacked by Hydra on the way home. He met a talking dog. His parents went crazy and blew up some police officers. He met Katherine and the Gecko and flew on a weird aircraft, he broke into his grandfather's house and discovered he might be a terrorist or super villain or some other terrible thing. Found out he was supposed to be the next Black Vulture, fought some robots, met Lightning Cat, and found the signal leading, hopefully, to the mastermind of a plot to blow up Capeville. He rested his head against his hand. He was so tired. He wanted to rest. The door opened and he stepped into his grandfather's dark bedroom. He listened carefully, without making a sound. He thought he could hear his grandfather down the hall, in the kitchen. He stepped carefully into the darkness. The maps on the wall were gone. The sheets, too. No evidence they had ever been there. He touched the wall and looked more closely. Nothing. No tape marks, or holes from staples. Just regular walls.

John slid into the hallway and moved toward his room, not turning on the hallway light. There was a slight squeaking. John stopped, his fingers on the wall, and peered into the darkness. Sudden light flared into the hallway, and John squinted in the flood of light to see his grandfather, one gnarled hand on the wheel of his wheelchair, the other on the light switch.

John's heart started pounding, hard. Had Grandpa seen him come out of his bedroom? "Hi, Grandpa."

His grandfather glared at him, a scowl etched in his craggy face. "How did you get in the house?"

"Through the garage door." That much was true, at least.

"I didn't hear the garage door."

John shrugged. "Maybe you were running the garbage disposal."

"Were you in my room just now?"

John thought this through furiously. It seemed likely his grandfather had seen him, or maybe heard him just now. Especially if he had been sitting in the hallway in the dark. "I was using the bathroom."

Grandfather narrowed his eyes. "From now on, you stay out of there. The Master bath is mine. You use the one in the hall. It's closer to your room, and it's for guests."

John looked at his sneakers, letting out a deep sigh of relief. He hoped his grandfather thought it was an apologetic sigh. "Right. Sorry."

Grandfather grunted. "Your parents were concerned you hadn't arrived yet."

"Did they call? Are they alright?"

Grandfather snorted. "Why wouldn't they be? They coddle you too much. A boy should be allowed to have some freedom without his parents checking in every minute to make sure he's okay. A boy should take responsibility for his own safety." He turned his chair back toward the kitchen. "This summer, while you're with me, you'll be allowed to come and go as you please. No curfew. No rules but one."

This sounded pretty good. Too good to be true, really. It didn't match the way his grandpa had acted in the past, and he knew his parents would go crazy if they thought he was running around Capeville without a curfew. "What's the one rule?"

"I called in some favors and got you a job. You will keep that job and do it well."

"So the whole curfew thing and coming and going as I please doesn't mean much because I'll be going to work."

"It's my one condition for the summer."

"Fine. What's the job?"

His grandfather wheeled down the hall and called back to him, "You start in the morning. You'll be working at the Sunnybrook Retirement Village."

John put his hand against the wall, trying not to slump against it. "You have connections at Sunnybrook?"

His grandfather narrowed his eyes. "There are people on this island who are glad that I got all of the dangerous capes isolated here. Yes, I have connections. Don't embarrass me by slacking at work."

So. His grandfather had connections with Sunnybrook, the source of the mysterious signals. It was looking worse and worse. John moved into his room and fell onto his bed, watching the shadows on the ceiling. Anything could be waiting for him at Sunnybrook. A criminal mastermind. Bombs. Robots. His own grandfather. John took a deep breath and tried to sleep. He had to go work with the retired super villains in the morning.

CHAPTER 8

SUNNYBROOK, A RETIREMENT VILLAGE FOR SUPER VILLAINS

Breakfast was cold oatmeal. Cold, because by the time John managed to pry himself out of bed it had been sitting on the table for twenty minutes. His grandfather, true to his word, didn't mention it. John was free to sleep in and eat cold oatmeal if he wanted. His grandfather sat at the table the entire time, his own bowl clean as old bones, the Capeville paper open in front of him. His grandfather slammed the paper down, showing John the front headlines. MASKED TRIO FOILS ARMED ROBBERY. He scanned it quickly. Criminals had attempted to steal a force field generator, which had been safely returned to the bank. Good job, Lightning Cat.

"Capes," Grandpa said. "Never trusted them. Caesar forced them all into Capeville, but he should have taken their powers, too. Now they're wearing masks, running around town, causing trouble."

John squished another cold lumpy mouthful of food into his mouth. "They stopped a robbery. That's good, right?"

Grandpa scowled. "But what are they hiding behind those masks? The Gecko, we've seen him before. He's been popping up around town lately. The young woman, she's new. And then the Black Vulture." He said it like he wanted to spit. He shook his head. "I can't believe someone is wearing that costume. Not after what happened at Kane Bridge." pounded the table and his spoon rattled in the bowl. "Must be kids, too young to know the history. Too young to know that bank robberies aren't their business. Too young to know they shouldn't be leaping around, electrocuting people. They should leave that to the police."

"Electrocuting people is the police's business?"

"You know what I mean."

John pointed his spoon at the paper, a cold lump of oatmeal still in his mouth and said, "Maybe the police couldn't get there fast enough, and those three had a window of opportunity to help."

The old man grunted. "Vigilantes could help by staying home and being model citizens." He set the paper aside. "I want to tell you about Sunnybrook, John."

John stared at his oatmeal. He could feel his heart climbing into his throat, but he didn't want to give away his interest or his fear. "It's just a retirement home, right?"

"Ha." Grandpa rolled backward, took his bowl to the sink, and dropped it in with an enormous crash. He grabbed a knife from a block by the sink and brought it back to the table. He set it between himself and John. He took an apple from a bowl on the table and sliced through it without any effort at all, and when he set the blade down it pointed directly at John. "Not long before you were born there was a man who called himself Chester the Jester."

"Yeah, the guy who blew up Kane Bridge."

"Correct. He was a sociopathic criminal. He started as a small time crook, but he became obsessed with a certain vigilante. A costumed idiot called the Black Vulture." John shifted in his seat and dipped his spoon into his oatmeal again. He tried not to meet his grandfather's eyes. "Chester started murdering people in more and more outrageous ways. He thought it was funny. He turned it into some obscene performance art, but the only audience who really mattered was the vigilante. He would leave him clues, chances to prevent the crimes."

"I've heard that killers like him, some part of them wants to be caught. They mess up on purpose so someone will stop them."

"I thought that once. But the Black Vulture caught Chester over and over, and he always escaped, and he always killed again. The vigilantes, the police, the justice system, they all gave him a pass, they always locked him up. No one had the guts to deal with him once and for all. And do you know why?"

John shook his head. "Because he was insane?"

Grandpa took a slow bite of apple, and turned a sharp stare on John. "Because they *weren't sure* if he was insane. And the line between what he did, dressing as a court jester and parading around the city, and what the so-called heroes did, was a very thin line. And if they locked him up in a regular prison instead of an insane asylum, maybe they would have to lock up the vigilantes, too."

"No way, Grandpa. He was murdering people. The vigilantes weren't doing that."

Grandpa grunted again. "But the murders -- the more spectacular ones, at least -- didn't start until the capes showed up. Capes throw society off balance. The public was never sure how to feel about them. The capes broke the law all the time. But it was like they answered to another law. A higher law. They wore disguises, most of them, but it wouldn't have been hard to unmask them. We never did. We didn't want to know who they were. We wanted them out there, keeping us safe. We wondered if maybe the vigilantes were making the world more dangerous, if they were goading the villains on somehow. Villains and heroes alike, they had so much power. But we always looked to Caesar and felt safe. He was the strongest of them, and he never wore a mask. Any time things got bad, he would swoop in and save the day. He was like sunshine bottled into the shape of a man. We all loved him."

"What does this have to do with the retirement home?"

The old man sighed. "Before you were born, I was an investigative reporter. When Kane Bridge blew up, I was on it."

"You were on Kane Bridge?"

"Yes." He wheeled back from the table. "I was in a coma for weeks. When I woke up, I was paralyzed. They said that I had been trapped under a steel girder for eighteen hours."

"Eighteen hours? Didn't Caesar show up to help?"

John put his bowl in the sink. When he looked back at the knife at the table he realized how distracted he was by his grandfather's story. He had never told John any of this. John reached for the knife, as if he was going to wash it, but his grandfather snatched it, his grip tight on the handle, his hand shaking. "No. Caesar was on another planet. By that time he was splitting his hero time between ten different worlds." He pointed his knife at John. "Two hundred and thirteen souls snuffed out. Six policemen. The Black Vulture died there, too. What happened on that bridge, it was the Vulture's fault, you know. Even though he didn't set the bombs, it was his fault. He did enormous damage." Grandpa pointed at his own shrunken legs. "There was more damage than just the death toll, too."

"You never told me any of this."

The old man shrugged. "I don't like to talk about it. But today it's important. When I woke in the hospital, it was all clear. The capes don't belong in normal society. We needed to unmask and remove them. So I did what I always did. I started asking questions. Figuring out who was behind each mask, and publishing it. I made it impossible for them to be on the street. I forced the police, the courts, to live by their own rules, to stop using a double standard. It took time, but people were furious about the bridge, and afraid. I used that fear."

"There must have been people on the other side, people who thought that the capes did more good than harm."

"Of course there were. But two things happened. One, Chester the Jester came out of hiding and turned himself in."

John grabbed the edge of the table. "That should have argued for the importance of the capes. Because of them the Jester ended up behind bars."

"Not at all. Because the Jester said that he was retiring. Now that the Black Vulture was gone, he had no audience. He hasn't killed anyone since that day. He walked into prison. Pleaded guilty. His lawyers got him life on an insanity plea, but he's still in maximum security. Not a single murder since the Black Vulture's death."

John shrugged. "So, he's still in jail. Because of the Black Vulture."

"No, he's in jail because the Black Vulture doesn't exist. Don't you see? The Black Vulture saved more lives by dying than he ever did by lurking in the shadows around the city. And that's exactly what I wrote in the papers. The public ate it up, because it's true. We started to demand that the capes be removed from society."

"That doesn't seem right," John said. "You shouldn't punish people for doing the right thing. Get rid of the criminals, not the heroes."

The old man shook his head. "You're young. You don't understand. They're all criminals, John." He tapped the table with two fingers. "That was the second thing. When Caesar returned from whatever interstellar adventure he was on, he realized it, too. Humans had grown dependent on capes. He suggested to the President that a new city be formed, here on this island, and that he would build the infrastructure and ensure the removal of any cape who was unwilling to live as a normal person. The Rubicon Protocol. He built a device that let him know when a super power was in use, and in about two months he had relocated nearly every powered human in the English speaking world. He set up similar cities around the world for other cultures. Then he removed himself. He still shows up occasionally... enforces Rubicon, mostly. But he does it anonymously. Quietly. Invisible."

John could barely contain his frustration. He flexed his hands. He knew some of this, but he had never heard it from his grandfather, who seemed so certain it was a great thing. "Why do you even live here, Grandpa?" John tried to say it without sounding bitter, but he didn't quite succeed. "Why live with the capes?"

His grandfather laughed. "To keep watch over them, John. To make sure Caesar and the fail safes he put in place keep the capes in line." He slapped the paper with the back of his hand. "And if they ever cross the line, I'll be here to make sure the world knows."

John couldn't stand this conversation any more. What would Grandpa say if he knew John had been the one out there, in the Black Vulture's costume? "I should get ready for work, I guess," John said, and stood to leave the room.

His grandfather jabbed the knife into the table. "I'm not done talking to you, young man."

John rounded on his grandfather and shouted, "This has nothing to do with me. It's ancient history, from before I was born. I don't care about any of it. If someone wants to stop a bank robbery, what do I care what they're wearing? Cape or no cape, mask or police uniform, I don't care so long as they're doing the right thing."

Grandpa stared at him, his eyes cold. "This has everything to do with you. I've known since you were a child, John. You can't stand to see a bully picking on someone. You hate to see anyone harming someone else. You're not content to stand by and do nothing, to just accept that this is the way of the world."

"Because it's wrong, Grandpa. To stand by and say nothing is the same as being part of it." He threw his hands in the air. "If I see a bully picking on another kid at school, I'm going to step between them. If a rich guy steals from a poor guy, he should go to jail, not get off because he has a better lawyer. Thieves should be stopped. And if for some reason a teacher doesn't step in with a bully, I will. If the courts don't convict the rich, someone else should. If the police can't stop the thieves then the rest of us should help."

"Exactly," grandpa said, laughing. "Exactly. You think we can actually make the world a better place. You're naïve. One day you'll step between a bully and his prey and you'll be a hero. But a week after that you'll take the fight to the bully and you won't be a hero at all. You'll be a bully yourself. You'll be a villain and a lawbreaker. A vigilante, John."

John kicked his chair. "I need to get my sneakers on. I'm going to work, just like you said, but I don't have to listen to your speeches. That's not part of the deal."

His grandfather grabbed his arm. John looked down, surprised by how fast he was. "Chester is there, John. At the retirement home. I want you to see these people, really understand what the vigilantes have unleashed. I want you to know the risks. What do you think will happen when he reads this article? If he sees that someone is out there using the name of the Black Vulture again? We can't allow that to happen. Your parents have some confused ideas on the topic. I want you to hear the other side."

John pulled his hand off. "My parents have never said anything about it."

His grandfather sat back and exhaled hard, as if he had been punched in the gut. "You've never read my book."

"No, they never let me. They said it had dangerous ideas and was full of hate."

"Ha. Full of hate." He waved John off. "Never mind. Never mind. If they haven't let you read it, don't read it now. No reason for you to know."

John shook his head and walked back to his room. He stooped to grab his shoes and pulled them on by the front door. He had on jeans, an Omega Point t-shirt and now, his sneakers. He had found a small backpack in his duffle bag, folded neatly under his clothes. He slung it on his back. He could hear his grandfather in the living room, mumbling to himself. He had to get a ride from him, he assumed, so he started after him when the bookshelf caught his eye. There was a copy of his grandfather's book there. *A Plague of Capes* by Hal Ajax. On the cover was the wreckage of the Kane Bridge. John glanced quickly to make sure his grandfather wasn't in the room, and then slipped it into his bag. "I'm ready to go," he called.

"Someone is picking you up," his grandfather said.

John went into the living room, where his grandfather sat staring out the back window at the pool. He didn't turn to look at John. "Who's picking me up?"

His grandfather didn't turn. "The Thunder family. They're the perfect example of a family who takes the Rubicon Protocol to heart. Their father was Rolling Thunder, a cape who worked together with The Regulars. None of his four sons are vigilantes. They don't use their powers in public. They've settled into a nice, normal life here in Capeville."

"Another lesson disguised as a ride to work?"

"Yes."

John felt his fists clenching again. "What makes you think I would want to be a vigilante, anyway? How would I even start? I don't have any powers."

Now his grandfather turned to face him, his eyes sad. "The heroes didn't all have powers, John." The doorbell rang. "That's your ride."

John turned. "I didn't hear a car."

"You better hurry." His grandfather coughed. "I'll see you after work. Dinner at six, John. But like I said, do what you want so long as you keep that job this summer."

John slung his bag on and pulled the door open. The front porch was empty. He looked back toward his grandfather and the doorbell rang again. John saw someone move out of the corner of his eye, but when he turned the porch was empty again. His grandfather wheeled up next to him.

"It's the boy," he said, and he shouted, "Pronto! You're not allowed to use your powers in public."

A blurred outline of a boy zipped onto the porch and popped into clear view. He was a painfully thin Asian kid, wearing what looked like running shorts and a t-shirt with the Roadrunner on it, and another flannel shirt open over it. He had black hair which hung down over his ears and threatened to cover his eyes, and a giant pair of earphones around his neck. "Sorry, Mr. Ajax."

"It's illegal."

"I know, sir." The kid looked down at his shoes. "It's so slow driving in the car. And we're running late."

"We'll see what your father says about that, young man."

His eyes widened. "Don't tell my dad, Mr. Ajax, please! I'll be grounded forever."

"Don't break the law and you won't get grounded," he said. "This is my grandson, John." He wheeled back toward the kitchen without another word. John watched him go. The old man didn't really set John up for success in new friendships.

As soon as John's grandpa was out of sight the young man stuck his hand out and they shook. "I'm Pronto. And yes, that's my real name. Our family, we're all speedsters." He grinned. "We're the fastest people on the planet."

"That's amazing," John said. They walked out to the sidewalk together. "Sorry my grandpa is such a jerk."

"No problem. I've known Mr. Ajax my whole life, and he's always been a jerk. No offense. My dad will laugh him off anyway. He'll say 'boys will be boys' and your grandpa will say, 'What if the police see him?' and dad will say, 'They'll have to catch him to arrest him' and there's no way they could catch me. I can outrun police cars easy. I'll put your bag in the car." Before John could even shrug the bag off his shoulder, Pronto and the bag were gone in a gust of air. John looked back to make sure his grandfather wasn't watching, and by the time he turned around Pronto was next to him again. "My brother is about three blocks away. He's going to pull up here and we'll jump in. Get ready."

A beat up Crown Victoria puttered around the corner, and as it pulled in front of him, Pronto was already in the back seat, waving at him to get in and leaning across the seat to hold the door open. The car didn't stop when it got to John, just kept rolling past, and he had to run and jump in, pulling the door shut behind him.

"That's my brother," Pronto said. His brother lifted a hand and waved at John. "His name is Thunder Cheeks."

"Thunder Fists," his brother said. "If you call me Thunder Cheeks one more time, I'm going to smack you."

Pronto winked at John and said, "Thunder Cheeks." Then he was gone, his door slamming shut behind him, the car still moving and no Pronto in sight.

Thunder Fists looked in the rearview mirror. "Sorry, John. My brother is a little immature. In our family, we don't get our Thunder name until we can break the sound barrier. That's dad's rule. Pronto is being a brat about it. I'll be right back."

Right back? John grabbed the back of the seat in front of him. Thunder Fists was gone. No one was driving. There was a loud boom. John quickly scanned in front of the car. There was another car about twenty feet ahead of him, and it had just put on the brakes. He didn't have time to jump into the front seat, so he closed his eyes and braced for impact.

"Close one," Thunder Fists said. John opened his eyes. Thunder Fists was in the driver's seat, a smile on his face, and Pronto was next to John, arms folded and a scowl on his face. "Don't worry, John. He'll cheer up in a minute or two."

"No I won't," Pronto said under his breath.

"You guys are amazing," John said. "I didn't even see you leave the car. I thought we were going to hit the car in front of us, but then you were both back in here like nothing had happened."

"I'm the slowest person in the family."

Thunder Fists laughed. "That makes you the fourth fastest person on Earth, Pronto. Besides, you're getting faster."

"You think so?"

"Definitely. I gave you less of a head start than usual and it still took me almost ten seconds to catch you. I'm guessing you were going two hundred MPH or so."

Pronto's eyes sparkled. "Awesome. Do you want me to run ahead and tell them we're going to be late?"

"Nah, it's fine." Thunder Fists put his arm on the back seat and looked back at John. "I've worked at Sunnybrook three summers in a row now. I'm a senior. Dad says it's the closest we can get to being capes these days, keeping an eye on the retired villains. It's not too bad."

"What do we do?" John asked.

"Ahhh, change bed pans, deliver lunches, that sort of thing."

"And watch for evil," Pronto added.

"Change bed pans, deliver lunches, watch for evil," John said.

Pronto grabbed John's shoulder and looked him in the eye. "Not necessarily in that order."

"Jupiter Girl will explain it all during your briefing," Thunder Fists said. "She's in charge of the volunteers."

Pronto sunk down into his seat, his head tossed back and his mouth wide open. "Awww, no. Jupiter Girl is in charge?"

"She's always in charge. She's been doing it forever."

"Argh. Joop is so uptight."

Thunder Fists smiled. "She keeps everyone safe. And she's gorgeous." He winked at John. "Pronto has a little crush on her." John turned to look at Pronto, grinning, but the seat beside him was empty. "Don't worry, he'll be back," Thunder Fists said, laughing. "His moods are faster than he is." He turned the car toward a long chain link fence, topped with razor wire. "There it is. Sunnybrook."

A low, squat building sat behind the fence, surrounded by parking. And guard towers with machine guns. John gulped as Thunder Fists pulled up to a small guard shack with a gate beside it. "Here we go," he said, under his breath. Into the super villain retirement home.

CHAPTER 9

BED PANS... AND EVIL

Jupiter Girl's long red hair fell down her back like a shimmering waterfall, a slight wave dancing through it. The employee shirts were red and white vertical stripes. They looked ridiculous on John and Pronto. But on Jupiter Girl, the stripes hugged her body like the road hugging the side of a mountain, and John wanted his eyes to follow the road as often as possible. The top two buttons of her shirt were undone, and her smooth, clear skin looked like cream beside the white and red stripes. She wore a loose black skirt and knee-high black boots.

Pronto kept bouncing out of the room and coming back in. His hair was parted on the right, then the left, his shirt tucked in then out, then tied in the back and then out and untied again. John grabbed his arm and told him to calm down. "Joop makes me nervous," Pronto said. "I can't stand still."

John whispered, "She's too old for us, anyway. She's a senior, right?"

Pronto covered his mouth and laughed. "Yeah, she's too old, alright." He zipped out of the room and back, his hair slicked back now. "Still, a man has to have dreams."

"Are you two finished?" Jupiter Girl looked at them sternly, her perfect lips turned down in a disapproving scowl. John was almost happy to see her look slightly less attractive. It was a relief.

"We're done," John said. "Just having a little conversation about... uh..."

"About seniors," Pronto said. "Because we're here to help some senior citizens. Am I right?"

Jupiter Girl stared at them for about ten seconds, during which time Pronto's hair style changed at least twice. "Very well. Pay attention because this isn't a normal retirement community. Some of the people here are dangerous." She crossed her arms and studied the boys. "Pronto I know. A speedster like the rest of the family, right?"

"Yes," he said proudly. "I broke three hundred MPH today."

"Impressive. And your name is..." she looked at a clipboard in the crook of her arm. "John Ajax? Any super powers, John?"

"No. I'm just an ordinary human being."

Jupiter Girl's eyebrows shot up. "Are you saying capes aren't human?"

"No, I –"

"Because that's the sort of sentiment we'll leave for your grandfather, Mr. Ajax."

John's face flushed. "I'm not my grandfather. I wish I had powers, but I don't."

Pronto leaned over and said, "Don't worry, John. A lot of us, our powers kick in late."

Jupiter Girl looked pointedly at Pronto and John. "You two will be in our low risk areas. That means you will only be in the top two floors. Under no circumstances are you to enter the basement levels. You are certainly not to go into any locked section or maximum security hallway. Do you understand?"

"Of course," Pronto said, nodding wisely. "How would we do that, anyway?"

Jupiter Girl smiled gently. "I'm sure I don't know, Pronto. But if it happens, you'll be in big trouble." She leaned over him. "Big. Trouble." She handed John a clipboard. "Here are your rooms. Follow the instructions for each room, and when you're done come back here. That is all. See you in a few hours."

She turned to debrief another group. John and Pronto moved toward their cart of food. Breakfast time at the retirement home. Or the prison, whatever this place was. Still, they were going to the low security section, so John and Pronto walked into a hallway that had open doors and people walking in and out, some with walkers or canes, some with robotic legs or tank treads and at least one old lady floated past them on nothing but air. About ten rooms into their rounds, John felt a buzz from his signal watch. He pulled the watch out and pressed the flashing lights. A small round device popped out of the side, about the size of an M and M. John looked closely at it. Tiny letters on the side said, "Put me in your ear."

John slipped it into his ear and immediately heard G3's voice. "Well done, Black Vulture. You have already infiltrated Sunnybrook."

"My grandfather hooked me up with this job," John said.

Pronto looked at him, thinking John was talking to him. "It's not a big deal. My dad got us this job. He used to work with King Jupiter. That's Joop's dad." He looked at his clipboard, and they came up to a room with the name Lance Stewart and in parentheses the name Sea Dragon. "This room looks a little more challenging. Says we have to change some filters or something." So far they had only delivered food, really.

G3's voice sounded in John's ear again. "I've pinpointed the location where the signals originated yesterday. It is on sub level 3."

John tried to think of a way to answer G3 without making it obvious to Pronto. "I wish we could go down to the sublevels."

Pronto grinned at him. "I know. Not much evil to stop in the minimum security wing."

Pronto pushed the door open, and they squeezed into the room. There was only about three feet of room, because the rest of the room was a giant fish tank. An old man sat underwater, wearing green tights and a sour expression on his bearded face. He swam over to them with astonishing speed and knocked against the glass, which rattled in the frame but didn't break. "So that's Sea Dragon," John said. "I thought he was one of the Regulars, one of the good guys. Why is he retired here with the villains?"

The old man pointed at an intercom on the side of the tank, and John went over and pressed the only button on it. Sea Dragon leaned closer to the intercom on his side and said, "I was framed and I can prove it."

Pronto pressed the intercom button again. "Mr. Sea Dragon, we're supposed to slide these fish into your tank. Can you please swim back for a minute?"

He pressed the button again. "I was framed."

John cleared his throat and said (to G3), "Is that true?"

Pronto sighed. "We just deliver the fish, sir."

There was a crackling in John's ear, and G3's voice came through the earpiece, sounding strained. "Technically true, sir, although the Sea Dragon does, indeed, belong in this facility."

"What does that mean?" John mumbled.

Pronto looked at him, one eyebrow raised. "It means we're zookeepers, not lawyers."

John nodded. "Right, I know. I just... I misheard you, I guess."

Pronto looked at their sheet from Jupiter Girl. "Looks like we're supposed to clean out his filter, too. Says here that he often 'fouls the plumbing.' Wonder what that means. First we've got to slip him these fish, though." He hit the button again. "Go to the other side of your tank, please. Thank you, sir." The old man leaned against the glass on the far side of the tank. John pulled open the slot and slipped the tray in, and the Sea Dragon leapt from the side of the tank, shooting toward them like a torpedo. Pronto knocked John out of the way and slammed the slot shut, just as the Sea Dragon's arm came within reach. Sea Dragon floated in front of them, glaring with black eyes that had nothing but hatred in them. He smiled, revealing rows of sharp, white teeth.

"Next time, little minnows," he growled.

John shivered. Pronto laughed and started to zip back and forth in front of the tank. "I'm faster than a minnow, you dirty shark."

"I don't think that's a good idea, Pronto."

Sea Dragon bashed against the glass. It shivered in the frame, and alarms started to go off. Pronto grabbed John's arm, yanked him out of the room at super speed and shut the door. "We better move along," he said. "I'm sure security will want to know what upset him. We don't want to get fired."

"Yeah," John said, and they quickly moved on to the next room, barely looking at their clipboard. Jupiter Girl came around the corner, her red hair flying behind her like a comet's trail, flanked by two security guards. John grabbed a tray from their cart and Pronto pulled the door shut behind them.

A thin curtain on a rounded track separated them from the rest of the room. John put his hand on the curtain, but Pronto grabbed his arm and said, "John. What's a minnow?"

"It's a kind of fish."

"Do you think I'm faster than a minnow?"

"I'm pretty sure you are. Now let's deliver this meal. Some guy named Uther Sanrio." John scratched his head. "That name sounds familiar."

John yanked the curtain back to reveal a room with a hospital bed and one full wall doubling as a television screen. The man in the bed was playing some sort of video game, and a tank rolled across a realistic looking army base while soldiers fired machine guns and threw grenades toward it. A fat old man looked over at them and grinned. The thin wreath of hair around his head tufted up at the ends, and his nose was slightly ovoid, the two things together making him look like a koala bear.

"I'll be right with you, boys, I'm almost to the end of this level."

John watched him manipulate the controller, a large, flat, two-handed device with a joystick and a collection of buttons. The graphics on the game were incredible. The soldiers moved with a smooth, lifelike grace, and the army base was detailed and had a complicated geography. John found himself moving closer and closer to the screen, until he stood beside the old man. John's mouth hung open as he watched the tank trundle through the base. A soldier took a shot at it with a bazooka, but the old man cackled with glee and moved the tank out of the line of fire before mowing the soldier down. "Is this Tread Battalion 3?" John asked.

"Of course," said the old man without looking away from the screen.

"But it's not out yet."

The old man laughed. A chain link fence was all that stood between the tank and the edge of the base now.

He steered the tank toward the fence without stopping, and it scarcely paused before tearing through to the other side. The tank moved down a road, the sound of machine guns fading in the distance. A plane sat in the middle of the road, a cargo ramp open, and the tank steered up onto the ramp. The words OBJECTIVE COMPLETE flashed on the screen and the score bar added up end-of-level bonuses. The old man flopped the controller down and turned to face the boys. "I designed all the Tread Battalion games. The Omega Point games, too."

"Omega Point only has one game," John said automatically.

The old man cackled. "I'm only halfway through developing the sequel." He pointed at the screen, which went dark. "I'm in beta testing for Battalion 3 right now." He rubbed his hands together. "Now what's for breakfast?"

Pronto snatched the tray from John and set it in front of the old man, who gleefully pulled the plastic cover off to reveal a sad assortment of dry toast, watery scrambled eggs and limp bacon. He tucked his napkin into his shirt and started eating. Pronto said, "I thought everyone here was a supervillain. So what's your deal?"

Without stopping to swallow, the old man said, "Oh yes, I was a super villain. The Game Master. After Rubicon I didn't have any money. They don't charge us to live here, of course, but I needed a little pocket cash. Since my only skill was making games I turned my attention to video games and wrote and designed the first Tread Battalion. It's been a fun ride. Of course I miss my petty villainy... mostly bank robberies and elaborate death traps for capes. In fact, I'm working on a new game called Death Trap right now." He smiled at them, a wide, yellow smile.

"We should be moving along, anyway," Pronto said.

"Your games are the best," John said. "I'm glad you're not a villain anymore, because playing Tread Battalion is one of my favorite things."

The old man bowed his head and picked up the Tread Battalion 3 controller. "That means a lot to me, young man. Here." He held out the controller.

"I don't know if we have time," Pronto said. "We've got a lot of rooms still to do."

"Yeah, thanks," John said, eying the controller. "Maybe we can come back when we finish our rounds."

"You misunderstand," said the Game Master. "I want you to take it with you and try it out. You can bring it back next week, or whenever you're done." He pushed it into John's hands. "I need beta testers."

"This makes me nervous," said G3 in John's ear. The sound of his voice startled John, and he put his hand up to his ear.

"We'll bring it back next week," John said.

"Cool," said Pronto. "But how do we play it?"

The old man waved them away while shoveling more food into his mouth. "Just slide the black switch when you're near a computer screen. The controller has all the hardware internalized to do the rest." Game Master tapped the top of the controller. "Don't show it around, though. We haven't even set a release date yet."

Pronto snatched it from John and said, "I'll zip it out to the car, so Joop doesn't see."

John said his goodbyes to the Game Master and moved back into the hallway. He moved their cart to the next room.

G3 said, "I'm picking up those signals again, Black Vulture. You need to get into the sub levels as soon as you can. I'm working on security codes now."

John stuck his finger in his ear and the communications device fell out and onto the ground. He scooped it up and stuck it back in. "I'll need a distraction," he said.

Pronto zipped up, a cloud of papers in his wake. "Joop's looking for us and she is not happy." He crossed his arms. "I think it's time for you to tell me what's going on, and fast."

"I don't know what you mean."

Pronto's hand darted out so fast that John barely felt it when he grabbed the communicator out of his ear. He held it up for John to see. "I know you're talking to someone. Are you here to bust someone out? I can't allow that."

"What? No!" John reached out and Pronto dropped the receiver in his hand.

G3's voice came as soon as he set it in his ear. "I've hacked a loop into the security protocols that will allow me to open a few doors as you approach them. You need to move now, though. I can get you onto the secure floor and into the room where the signals originate."

"Listen," John said. "Someone is planning to blow up Capeville." He pointed at his ear. "I'm talking with this robot who has hacked a way into the maximum security level, where we've traced a signal from the bad guys." He looked down the hallway and saw Jupiter Girl coming, her face set in a scowl, her security guards flanking her. "I'm going to need a distraction. Something that will bring all the guards to this floor."

Pronto hesitated. "I like you, John, but how do I know you're telling the truth?"

"Do I look like the sort of kid who would build a doomsday device? The Gecko can back up my story, if that counts for anything."

"My dad always said to trust my instincts." Pronto turned toward Jupiter Girl. He gave John a thumbs up. "Count to ten and then make a run for it."

Jupiter Girl stormed up in front of them, practically glowing with rage. "You two have a lot of explaining to do. Sea Dragon almost broke his aquarium. What did you do to get him so worked up?"

Pronto grinned and said, "I'll show you." Then he was down the hall and gone, a strong wind flying through the hallway.

"What is he doing?" Jupiter Girl demanded.

John shrugged. "I have no idea." He started counting. One. Two. Three. He heard the sound of crashing glass followed by a tidal wave. Thousands of gallons of water poured into the hallway and Pronto whooped with delight. Sea Dragon started shouting. Seven. Eight.

Jupiter Girl pointed at him. "Do not move." Her feet hovered off the ground and she rocketed back the way she had come, flying straight for Pronto. The guards followed. Nine. Ten.

John ran the opposite way down the corridor. Seniors were crowding into the halls, looking for what was causing all the commotion. G3's voice crackled in his ear. "Take your third left and follow the stairs down two flights."

John took his third left, but there was a heavy door in his way, with a glowing red keypad. "I need the security code, G3."

"Working on it." Numbers spun across the keypad, and then it switched to green. John turned the handle and pushed inside, then ran down the stairs.

Some guards in heavy armor were running up the stairs. "What are you doing in here, kid?" One of the guards looked at John's name tag. "You're not cleared for this area."

"Jupiter Girl gave me the code. She said to hurry and get more people up at Sea Dragon's room. He's broken through his aquarium."

One of the guards growled and another said, "Not again, he should be in the max security section." They hurried up the stairs and said, "Come on, kid." But John had already slipped down to the next level, where the door turned green just as he came up to it. It swung open to a corridor similar to those above, but with heavy metal doors on each room.

"Which room?" John asked, and G3's voice came back as only a crackle. "I'm losing the signal."

"You should see – crackle – room #312 on your – crackle crackle – unlocked for three seconds. Not sure I can unlock again – crackle – so be sure you --." The line went dead. John tapped his ear several times, but there was no response.

At least he had gotten the room number. He counted down the rooms until he found number 312. Written beneath the number was the name SCOTT JENNISON. Underneath that was written: extremely dangerous. Psychopathic tendencies. Do not enter alone and without proper precautions.

Great. A psychopath. Of course that was who was building the doomsday device.

John hesitated before putting his palm on the hand scanner. It scanned him twice, and the second time it glowed green and the door unlocked with a loud clacking sound. John pushed the heavy door open. John wasn't sure if G3 would be able to open the door for him if he was inside. There was a food cart in the hallway. John grabbed a tray off the cart and wedged it between the door and the jamb as he snuck into the room.

The room looked nice enough. An easy chair, a bed, a folding table with a chess set on it. What he didn't see was the occupant of the room. He stepped farther in, looking carefully for a place the prisoner could be hiding. A light laugh came from behind him, and John spun around just in time to see the old man standing beside the door. The old man snatched away the tray that was wedging the door open. The door ground shut, and the lock snapped into place. A red light flickered on, only this time John was seeing it from the inside.

The old man grinned. "You can't get out that way, young man. Believe me, I've tried." He cracked his knuckles. "Let's get to know one another, shall we?"

CHAPTER 10

AN AUDIENCE WITH THE JESTER

The old man was terribly thin, and he wore long slacks, a collared shirt, a cravat and a tightly tailored vest. The small table in front of his high backed chair held a half-played chess game. A delicately woven rug covered the middle section of the floor.

The old man sat down in his chair and gestured with his spidery fingers to a folding chair against the wall. "It is uncommon for Sunnybrook to allow a child into my room." He grinned, revealing long, yellow teeth. "I'm too dangerous, they say."

John said nothing. He kept his back against the door and tapped against it, hoping that Pronto or a guard or someone would hear and open the door. The old man picked up a pawn from his chessboard and turned it in his hand. "I wonder." He held up another piece, a horse's head. "Are you a pawn, young man? Or something else?"

"A horse?"

"Not a horse. A knight. Heh heh heh. 'A horse.' I didn't think you would make me laugh." The old man set the pieces down beside the board and pointed at the folding chair again. "Bring your chair over, boy."

John pulled the chair over and unfolded it, trying to make sure he was out of the tall man's reach. In this small room, that wasn't easy. The light overhead flickered, and the old man's eyes turned up toward the ceiling before coming back to John. "*He* sent you didn't he?"

John watched him carefully. The old man's eyes gleamed, and he was leaning close, waiting for John to answer. "Who?"

"The Black Vulture." He paused, as if waiting for John to say something more. "Is he coming out of retirement? Is it time to begin our games again?"

"The Black Vulture is dead. He died on Kane Bridge, everyone knows that."

The old man slammed his palm on the table and the chess pieces jumped to attention. "No. I don't believe that, I've never believed that. I tried to kill him a hundred times, and he never died."

A white knight had fallen from the side of the table to the floor. John picked it up and turned it over in his hands. He set it on the board. "Everyone dies, you know."

"Ha ha ha. Yes." The old man leaned closer. "Some sooner than others."

A shiver ran down John's back. "Who are you?"

"Who am I?" The old man leaned back and put his hand on his chest. *"Who am I?"* He threw himself from his chair and paced to the door and back to the table, huffing. Words came halfway into his mouth and he choked them down again. His face grew a deeper and deeper shade of red until he shouted, "I'm Chester the Jester, of course! The greatest villain of all time!"

John froze. Chester the Jester was a mandatory topic in school. His destruction of the Kane Bridge and how that brought about the Rubicon Protocol was all that could be discussed in a classroom, but the more frightening stories, the type that were passed around between classes is what ran through John's mind. Chester the Jester seemed to make decisions based on his own warped idea of entertainment. If he thought it would make him laugh, or be to his advantage in some larger scheme he would kill or disfigure someone without a second thought. And he was the man who had crippled his grandfather.

John looked to the door again. It remained locked, of course. There wasn't even a handle on this side. John had hoped to get some information about the doomsday device, but now he just wanted to get out in one piece. He pressed the communicator in his ear, but only static came from it.

Chester wheeled around in the room, gesticulating and raving about how John didn't know him. How could this be? Then Chester became quiet and still, one hand on the back of his chair, the other in the small pocket on the front of his vest. "I have been away entirely too long. It's time for me to make my reappearance in the world."

John cleared his throat. "If you're the greatest villain of all time, you must know about the doomsday device."

"The doomsday device." Chester laughed. "So he did send you after all."

"The Black Vulture is dead," John repeated. "No one sent me. I'm here on my own."

"Yes," Chester said. He stroked his chin. "And if the Black Vulture is back in the saddle -- back on his perch! Ha ha ha! -- then my lengthy retirement is through." He danced around the room, touching the walls, the chessboard, the door. "No more cell! No more prison! No more Capeville!" He paused. "Of course, it also means no more tapioca pudding on Saturday nights, but I'll get used to that, I suppose."

John stood up, trying to stay on the other side of the room from the pacing lunatic. "You don't even know about the doomsday device, do you?"

"Of course I do," Chester said, dismissing John with a wave. "I have bigger fish to filet right now, young man." Chester ran his hand along the seam of his door. He turned and grinned. "Speaking of filleting...." He stalked back to the table and slipped his fingers under the edge, bounced it twice against the floor and, with a grand flourish, removed a thin-bladed knife.

"I don't think you should have that," John said.

"Come closer and I'll give it to you."

"No."

"I need to send a message back to the Black Vulture, to let him know that I understood, that I knew you were from him. I want him to know that we're together again, and I will be waiting for him." He inclined his head twice toward the door. "Waiting out there." He stepped toward John. He whispered. "I want to send him a gift."

John clenched his fists and stepped backward again. "Go ahead and try."

Chester laughed and stepped closer. John took two quick steps forward, right up against Chester, and inside his reach so that he couldn't easily stab. John turned backwards, grabbed Chester's wrist and jabbed his elbow into Chester's stomach. The knife clattered to the floor and John picked it up and turned the blade toward the old man. Chester put his hand against the table, doubled over and breathing heavily. "I'm out of practice, ha ha ha."

John never let the point of the knife waver. "You're going to tell me everything you know about the doomsday device."

Chester sat in his armchair again. "I already have a doomsday device, of course. One little phone call could set it off. It would be a long distance call. Heh heh heh. But I thought it would be entertaining to get another."

"You don't have the force field generator," John said. "Someone stopped your people from stealing it."

Chester waved his hand, unconcerned. "Pish-posh. Someone else will steal it for me, then."

"You don't want the generator?"

"You're not listening. Of course I want it. I'm going to use it to clear the board, to get rid of all the old capes and make space for the next generation."

"Aren't they already out of the way? What do you mean? Are you really trying to kill all the capes? What sort of weapon would allow you to do that?"

Chester laughed harder and pinched the bridge of his nose. "That's the joke, John, that's the joke. You and your friends are my secret weapon. You're going to hand me everything I want."

"Me and my friends?"

The Jester pulled a handkerchief from his pocket and started waving it around. "Yes, yes. Your friends. You do have friends, don't you?" The old man sat down at the table again, picked up the knight and showed it to John. "Your piece is in danger, John. In danger of being captured. Being used. I could have killed you today. But sometimes it's more strategic to leave a piece on the board, to let the game play out." He covered his face with the handkerchief and started to laugh.

Frustrated, John sat down on the folding chair, being careful to keep the blade pointed at the easy chair. "I thought you would be frightening, but you're just a crazy old man."

The Jester stopped laughing and looked at John, slowly lowering his hand from his face. "You take that back."

John shrugged. "Maybe not crazy. But you're not all there, either."

Chester pounded the table. "A court jester is an advisor to the king. His opinions are to be considered carefully."

"The king? King of what? Some old folk's home? You fit in perfectly around here, what with your dementia and everything."

The Jester leaped across the table, knocking into John's chest and sending him flying backward over the chair. The thin man landed on top of him, pinning him to the ground, the knife somehow in his hand and the point of it at John's neck. "Do. Not. Mock. Me." He licked his lips. "Maybe I should carve a message into you after all."

There was a pounding at the door. It was flexing inward. Whatever was wrong with the lock, they must be trying to break in, to get John out. John forced himself to look the Jester in the eyes, tried to ignore the bite of the knife's blade. "Did you hear about the Black Vulture in downtown yesterday?"

The Jester paused. "Trying to distract me from my carving, little turkey?" He looked at the door, then back to John. "I heard about a hatchling, not the great black bird himself. What do you know about him?"

Voices came from outside, and then the heavy thrumming of a machine. "What is your doomsday plan? Who is working with you?"

The Jester narrowed his eyes. "Boring. I explain my sinister plot to you? I don't think so. You'll have to bridge that gap yourself. Hee hee hee. Now you tell me something about this new Vulture."

"With a knife to my throat? No."

The Jester grinned. "I'm not going to hurt you. I'm a man of my word."

"Not going to hurt me ever, or not going to hurt me today?"

The Jester rolled his eyes. "If you want to get all technical. I'm not going to hurt you today. I might kill you tomorrow, I haven't decided."

"Fine. I'll tell you one thing about the new Black Vulture. He's not your enemy."

"He's a villain?"

"No." A creaking sound came from the door and it burst open. Armored guards flooded the room, rifles at the ready and shouting at Jester to drop the knife. John lifted his head and spoke directly into the Jester's ear. "It's just that the new Vulture doesn't think that a washed up criminal in an old folk's home is worth thinking about." The Jester sneered. "You're a cruel boy. I like that about you." He pressed the handle of the knife into John's hand. "Here's something to remember me by. A little souvenir." The guards grabbed him and yanked him off and he laughed maniacally.

A sudden burst of wind blew through the room and then John found himself gasping for air in the lobby of the old folk's home, rubbing his neck where his shirt had choked him. Pronto was shouting, "AreyouokayI'msosorryIcouldn'tgetbackintotheroomandthedoorwaslockedevenfromtheoutsidesomehow –"

"I'm fine, Pronto, I'm fine." A jolt of adrenaline flew through his system, and John shivered. He turned the knife over and showed it to Pronto. "The Jester... he says that me and my friends are a key part of the plot to destroy Capeville. I don't know what that means." John rubbed his neck again while Pronto looked over the knife.

Pronto vibrated his hands at super speed and reduced the knife to a pile of dust. "I hate knives," Pronto said.

"My neck hurts, Pronto. You can't pull me out by the shirt next time."

"Sorry." Pronto zipped away for a second, then popped back into the lobby. "They have Chester locked down again. I don't think he's going to cause any more trouble."

"There's one thing bothering me though, Pronto."

"What?"

John tapped his fingers against his lips. "He called me John. How did Chester know my name?"

CHAPTER 11

THE MONSTER UNLEASHED

Jupiter Girl sat behind a large desk. John and Pronto did their best to stare at their shoes, not looking at her. "Pronto, you shattered the Sea Dragon's aquarium and he got out. Maintenance is still cleaning up the mess. Two guards were bitten. You could have been seriously injured."

"Not likely," Pronto said, without looking up. "I'm a lot faster than him."

"And apparently you two did this as a distraction to allow John to sneak into the maximum security section. For what reason? A friendly chat with the Jester?"

John looked up for a second, and her angry face seemed to have softened to something like puzzlement. "Not exactly," John said. "But pretty close."

She closed her office door. "Boys, this conversation is just between the three of us. No one is listening in. Tell me what is going on." John looked to Pronto, who shrugged.

John said, "Listen, do you know the Gecko? He can vouch for us."

Jupiter Girl frowned. "I do, indeed, know the Gecko. He's a vigilante, he's a law breaker and I'm afraid his good opinion can only reflect poorly on you." She sighed. "You don't leave me any choice. Look at me." They both lifted their faces and met her gaze. "Into my eyes," she said.

John looked at her piercing green eyes and felt like he was moving toward them, like he was falling off a cliff toward a pool of cool water. He felt relaxed and at peace. She was so beautiful. He wanted to get out of his chair and hold her.

"Now," she said. "I have a mind lock on you, and I want you to tell me what you're hiding."

"I think you're so beautiful," Pronto said. "I'm not ready for a relationship but I would like to kiss you. I've been in love with you since I was nine. That's my big secret."

Jupiter Girl sighed. "That's the problem with putting freshmen into mind locks. John, do you have anything to say?"

"I agree with Pronto. Except he says you're too old for me and I don't believe that for a minute."

She sighed again. "I am too old for either of you. You're both hopeless."

Pronto said dreamily, "Oh no, I have lots of hopes. Hopes and dreams. You're the best. The best looking, anyway. Personality wise, you're pretty mean."

John said, "It's true. Lightning Cat is much nicer, and I really like Katherine, too. I should call her."

Pronto started laughing. "John has a crush on three girls."

John tried to think of a comeback but his brain felt like it was wrapped in a blanket. He remembered how they had snuck the Game Master's game out and knew Jupiter Girl would want to know all about it. He didn't think it was a good idea to tell her, so he worked hard to control what exactly he said. He could feel the information making its way to his mouth and he couldn't stop it. "We have a new video game. Tread Battalion 3. We're going to play it later. You should come over." John still appeared relaxed and calm, but deep underneath he panicked that he had mentioned the game.

Jupiter Girl fell back in her seat. "Fine. I give up. You two are free to go. I'll schedule a formal inquiry board to see whether you keep your jobs. I wouldn't count on it. Please think carefully about including me in whatever is going on."

John and Pronto stood to go, and Pronto said sleepily, "We did it, John. We made it through without mentioning the doomsday device. We kept that one from her!"

An explosive pain shot through John's head, as if someone had grabbed the blanket his mind was wrapped in and yanked it away on a cold winter day. He and Pronto both grabbed their heads. Pronto jumped up from his chair and ran in circles around the room. "Joop! That hurt. You can't use mind locks on us, we're the good guys!"

Jupiter Girl frowned at him with her perfect lips. "Don't keep secrets from me, Pronto, and I won't mind lock you. What is this about a doomsday device?"

"We don't know what's going on, and we're not sure who's involved," John said. "We didn't know if we could trust you."

Jupiter Girl laughed. "I've been playing the super hero game since I was twelve, John. You can trust me."

Pronto nodded. "It's true, John. Our parents were in the Regulars together. That was the greatest super hero team of all time. My dad, Rolling Thunder, was one of the founding members. And Joop's dad, King Jupiter, was an early member, too."

Jupiter Girl nodded. "The Black Vulture, Percepta, Rocket Cowboy, The Governor, Chrononaut... over the years there were a lot of members, but they can all be trusted. My dad has much stronger mind reading powers than I do and he gave them all a clean bill of health. They aren't traitors, and they aren't the kind of people to build a doomsday device." She reached across the table and put her hand on Pronto's wrist. His leg started bouncing at super speed. "And their kids are trustworthy, in my opinion. We've grown up together."

"Well, sorta," said Pronto. "You look just the same as when we were kids."

Jupiter Girl blushed and looked away. She pulled her hand back and said, "I need you to tell me everything you know about this doomsday device."

John didn't say anything for a minute. "I don't mean to offend you, but who read your father's mind? Who made sure he wasn't a traitor?"

"That doesn't offend me, John. It's a good question. My father and I have a psychic bond that allows me to know him far better than is typical. I would know if he was planning a surprise party for me, let alone building a bomb."

John thought about that. She knew for sure her parents weren't crazy, but he had no idea if his own parents were super villains or terrorists, and he was increasingly sure that his grandfather was in on the doomsday plot. "Okay," John said. "I've heard rumors about a plot to blow up Capeville. The Gecko – and I know you don't like him – was the first person to tell me."

"People like the Gecko put all of Capeville at risk. Since Rubicon came into being, we capes have been allowed to continue here. But if someone throws off the balance, either Caesar will come and tighten down the rules or human governments will come and destroy us. We can't afford to have some boy running around like a vigilante, especially one with powers."

"Whatever," John said. "The fact is that the Gecko and the Black Vulture and another hero named Lightning Cat stopped some robot crew from stealing a force field generator. Who knows what they were planning to use it for. Something huge, I guess."

Pronto gave John a funny look. "How do you know all this?"

John debated telling them everything for a second: how he was the new Black Vulture, his parents, his grandfather, Hydra chasing him. But he still wasn't sure about Jupiter Girl. "My grandfather is on the short list as one of the masterminds. Chester's in on it, too. The capes... paid me a visit." John reached in his bag and pulled out his grandfather's book, setting it on the desk. "My grandfather hates capes, as you know. And in his room he has a bunch of maps on the wall. Maps that could have to do with the doomsday device. He had Sunnybrook marked on his map, and he got me a job here somehow."

Jupiter Girl picked up the book and turned it over in her hands. "Your grandfather wrote this. I haven't read it in a long time."

"You know him?"

"Everyone knows him. My father and I think that Rubicon was a good thing, but the way it came about wasn't. Your grandfather was a big part of that process. He's not a kind man."

"No, he's a jerk. That's for sure."

Jupiter Girl stood up and looked out the window. "Unmasking so many capes caused enormous damage. I couldn't believe it when he unmasked his own son."

John's stomach fell into his toes. If Grandpa "unmasked" his son -- John's father -- then that meant that his father was either a hero... or a villain. But either way, a cape. John stood up and held out his hand for the book. "Jupiter Girl. Can I see that, please?"

She shrugged and handed him the book. He cracked the spine and it fell open to a series of pictures in the middle. There was the Black Vulture. The original Black Vulture, anyway. Next to his picture was another grey square that said "secret identity unknown." He flipped through the few pages of photos, most of them super heroes or villains he barely knew next to black and white pictures of ordinary people he had never seen. Then his eyes fell on the picture of his father, with the words "secret identity: James Ajax" underneath. John could barely stand the suspense as his eyes moved to the left of his father's picture to see him in a tight brown outfit and a mask with black goggles and the name "The Flying Squirrel" under it.

John fell back into his chair, the book open in his lap. "Was my father a good guy or a bad guy?"

Pronto laughed. "Are you kidding? He's one of the best-loved capes of all time. He was funny, and kind, and he never got caught up in all the politics. He just wanted to keep people safe. He probably didn't even need a secret identity."

John's jaw tightened. "I can't believe he never told me."

Jupiter Girl put her hand on his shoulder, and squeezed. He was angry enough that it didn't even faze him to have Jupiter Girl's hand touching him. "He saved my father more than once," she said. "And your mother has saved people all over space-time. She's one of our greatest heroes."

John flipped through the pages again until he found the picture of his mom, younger and grinning, and then her in what looked like a silver swimsuit, holding a giant laser rifle like the one at their house, her perfect blonde hair bouncing on her shoulders. Underneath it said, "Ms. Universe" and under the other picture it said "Tara Ajax." John shook his head. "This is the worst costume ever. She didn't even wear a mask."

Jupiter Girl squeezed again. "She always said people were too busy looking at her legs to notice her face."

"That's how your grandfather found their secret identities, though. He figured out about your mom and it didn't take much digging from there to figure out your dad."

John stood up. "I can't believe they didn't tell me. They're probably out there looking for the doomsday device, and they sent me here to be safe. I should be out there helping them."

"I'm sure they were trying to protect you," Jupiter Girl said. "And the fact is that, even here, you've been trying to find the doomsday device."

"Parents never tell you everything," Pronto said. "My dad has been up to something, too. He keeps disappearing. Around our house everyone is so fast that you can't always tell but sometimes he goes sort of transparent. He's disappearing for three or four seconds out of every minute. I don't know where he's going or what he's doing."

Jupiter Girl sat back in her chair and folded her hands. "My father has been secretive as well. He told me to be looking out for anything strange. You two fit the bill, but he hasn't mentioned a doomsday device. I don't know why he wouldn't tell me."

She was barely done with her sentence when Pronto blurted out, "So what do we do?"

"We should talk to my father," Jupiter Girl said.

"No," John said. She raised an eyebrow and looked at him. "No. All the adults are hiding things from us. We're not sure who is on which side. We don't know enough to bring more people into the loop. I trust Pronto, and Lightning Cat and Gecko. They've fought alongside me." Jupiter Girl started to object, but John put his hand up. "I trust you, too, Jupiter Girl. But we don't have time to go collect all the adults. We're here now. Downstairs there's someone who knows about the doomsday device. Chester. I say we go down there and you use your mind control thing to ask him some questions. Then we decide whether to start calling in the parents."

Jupiter Girl stood up and smoothed her skirt. "Very well. You're right, we're wasting time. We'll head downstairs and have a quick conversation with the Jester." She fixed each of them in turn with a firm gaze. "If I decide it's time to bring someone else in on the situation, I don't want any pushback from either of you." She pressed a button on her desk. "I need four guards to meet me at the entrance to the maximum security corridor."

A voice crackled back, "Sure thing, boss."

Jupiter Girl frowned. "The guards are getting lax. First you get into the maximum security section, now they're getting sloppy in how they speak to me." She wrote a quick note to herself on a note pad on her desk.

John whispered to Pronto, "Do a quick recon for us. Something's off."

Pronto zipped out of the room. Jupiter Girl called for him to wait, but he was down the hall before she even got out the door of her office. She groaned in disgust and grabbed John's hand. "You're going to stick close, at least."

Her hand was hot. John grinned at the thought of Pronto coming back to see them holding hands. He'd probably faint. Jupiter Girl yanked him down the hall, and Pronto came barreling back, skidding to a stop in front of them. He looked down at their hands. "I see you two became friends while I was gone." John laughed, and Jupiter Girl dropped his hand.

"Don't run off like that," she said.

"You guys are slow. I get bored."

"How did it look up there, Pronto?"

He shrugged. "A couple of guards with their helmets off, waiting at the door. Twins, I guess. They looked a lot alike. Seems like a little overkill, Joop, making them put numbers on their faces."

Jupiter Girl squinted at him. "What are you talking about?"

John's heart started pounding. "Big numbers, written in black magic marker?"

"Yeah."

John grabbed both of them and pulled them to a stop. "It's a guy named Frank Hydra. He tried to grab me back at my parents' house. He's definitely working for someone involved with the doomsday device. He's a replicator, and his powers are pain based, or maybe impact based. Every time you hit him hard enough, he'll split into more copies."

"What does he want?" Pronto asked.

Jupiter Girl shook her head. "Either he wants to snatch John or he's trying to get Chester the Jester out of the facility." She looked at John. "What's the plan?"

John crossed his arms. "He doesn't know we know, so we have surprise on our side." He put his hand on Pronto's shoulder. "We have speed." He looked at Jupiter Girl. "And you know this facility better than him or us."

"And I can change shapes."

"What?"

"I'm a shape shifter. I can turn into a monster and rip his arms off."

John's face flushed. He didn't know why, but something about the ferocity on her face made him embarrassed. "I don't think that will be necessary. Can you make yourself look like a guard? And is there rope somewhere nearby?"

"Turn your head," Jupiter Girl said. They looked away. A horrible sound, like bones grating against each other, came from behind them, and when John turned to look a guard in full uniform stood at attention, looking perfect except for the missing rifle. "Let's move," she said, and her voice sounded deep and rough. "If he speaks first I should be able to rearrange my vocal cords to get closer to his timbre and pitch."

"Great. Pronto, go get the ropes and meet us at the door."

Pronto saluted. "Got it, chief." He sped down the hallway.

"I'll take the lead, try to get a couple words out of him," John said. Jupiter Girl nodded. They came around the corner and found the two men waiting by the maximum security entrance, one of them leaning against the wall with his gun slung over his shoulder, the other standing with his rifle in his hand. Both had their helmets on, so John couldn't see their faces. He walked up close, the disguised Jupiter Girl beside him. He looked around casually. "Jupiter Girl should be here in a minute. I thought she ordered five guards to go with us?"

One of the Hydras shrugged. "Maybe she's picking up the other three."

"Other two," John said, hooking his thumb toward Jupiter Girl.

"Right," said Hydra. "Other two."

"Maybe we should head down," Jupiter Girl said, and her voice matched theirs perfectly. "She can meet us down below."

"Down below?" one of the Hydras said, and both of them moved their hands to their rifles and unclicked their safeties. "We agreed to take care of things here in the hallway if we could get John alone."

"Get me alone? What are you talking about?"

Jupiter Girl grabbed him roughly by the arm. "You're not getting away from us this time."

John spun on her and pushed, trying to make it look realistic, but she grabbed his arm and twisted it behind his back. Pain shot up his arm and his cry must have sounded authentic because one of the Hydras said, "Careful, the boss wants him whole and healthy."

The other said to Jupiter Girl, "What number are you?" She paused. John hadn't explained the numbers thing in detail. Finally she said confidently, "I'm number seven."

The Hydras both laughed, and one of them pulled his helmet off, the other keeping his rifle trained on the two of them. "That's funny. I'm number seven, too." Now both of their rifles were pointed at them. "Who are you?"

Jupiter Girl pushed John to the floor and leapt toward the Hydras. They both fired. As she jumped through the air, her body twisted and grew. Her arms grew long, red and scaly, and another set of arms popped from her sides. Claws burst from her fingers and her face erupted into a long snout with rows of teeth and six black eyes across the bridge of her face. A long tail whipped out behind her, and the Hydras made panicked shots at her. Where the lasers hit her skin, scorch marks appeared, but they only got a few shots off before she was on them. She grabbed one by the chest armor and flung him against the wall. A clawed hand knocked the other's head into the door.

The familiar sucking sound came from the Hydras as they started to multiply. Jupiter Girl dragged them to the center of the hallway and propped they against one another while they were still dazed, and Pronto came barreling past John, a wind blasting with him, and tied the four of them together. John helped tighten the knots.

"You're too late," Hydra snarled. "We're winning."

"Winning?" John laughed. "You've tried to catch me twice and I've tied you up twice."

Hydra spat on the floor of the corridor. "We only need two more artifacts to make the doomsday device work, and then we'll blow all of Capeville to bits. There won't be a cape left. Then we'll remake the world to our liking."

John shook his head. "We're not going to let you do that."

"Besides," Pronto said. "Even if you blew up everybody, Caesar is watching over us. He wouldn't let you get away with it."

Hydra sneered at Pronto. "Caesar is either dead or powerless. You say he'd stop us, but in the same sentence you say 'even if we blew up everyone.' Why wouldn't your precious Caesar come save the day before we blew up Capeville?"

"It doesn't matter," Jupiter Girl said, shifting back to her human form. "I'll use my mind lock on you now and we'll find out everything you know." She crouched down in front of one of the Hydras and caught his eye. He looked at her intensely for a moment, and then his face went slack. "I need to know the next part of your plan."

"The next part of our plan," said the mind-locked Hydra. "Is to knock ourselves unconscious."

"That doesn't make any sense," Jupiter Girl said.

John figured it out, though. He tapped his ear and shouted at G3, "Lock down any transmissions coming or going from Sunnyside!"

G3's response came back in an instant. "It's too late, sir, a message just went out from one of your captives."

Hydra winked at John. "Next time, kid." And then all four of them disappeared with a pop of displaced air, leaving John, Pronto, Jupiter Girl and a pile of ropes.

John kicked the ropes. His friends asked for an explanation, and he told them, "When the original Hydra loses consciousness, all of the copies disappear. He must have kept the original somewhere safe in case he got captured and sent him a transmission." John kicked the wall.

"We can still talk to Chester," Pronto said.

"Right. Jupiter Girl, can you get us in?"

"Of course I can," she said, and quickly entered the door's access code.

As the door slid open, John patted her on the arm and said, "I'm glad you're back to your normal self. That monster was pretty terrifying."

"And ugly!" Pronto said.

She gave them both a strange look. "Follow me." She walked down the hallway and led them to Chester's room. The door still showed evidence of where they had broken it down to get John out. "We moved him from here, but I wanted to take a quick look. We should have him in temporary holding cell A." They followed her further into the maze of prison cells until they came to the temporary holding cells. Cell A was empty. Jupiter Girl pressed an intercom button on the side of the wall. "Control, what cell is Chester the Jester in?"

"Temporary Holding A on the max security floor, miss."

They looked in again. The room was empty. "Confirm location," Jupiter Girl said.

There was a moment of silence on the other side. "Location confirmed. I have a positive visual on the subject through the video feed."

Jupiter Girl opened the door and the three of them walked into the cell. It was empty as an optional math class. Jupiter Girl pressed the intercom button again. "Chester the Jester has escaped. Inform the staff." She rested her head against the wall. "This is not good. We need to do a complete sweep of the facility and make sure he's not hiding out somewhere." She put her hands on the boys' shoulders. "Sorry, guys, I'm going to have you escorted off the property. It's not safe for you here."

Ten minutes later, despite their protests, Pronto and John were in the back seat of Thunder Fist's car. John tapped his fingers against the window. "I'm not sure what we should do next." Something didn't sit right about the information he'd gotten today, but it had all happened so fast.

Pronto grinned and pulled Game Master's controller out from under his seat. "Well, while you're thinking... we should play some video games!"

CHAPTER 12

TREAD BATTALION 3

Thunder Fists dropped them at John's house, but made Pronto promise to text when he needed a ride. "Don't use your powers to run home. Mr. Ajax already called to yell at dad once today."

"Don't worry, Thunder Cheeks. I'll make Mr. Ajax give me a ride just to mess with him."

"Whatever," his brother said, and pulled the car out of the driveway and into the street. John showed Pronto into the house, and they headed for his room. John called for his grandfather a few times, but he didn't answer.

"Come on," John said. "I want to take a quick look and see if my grandpa left his maps and stuff out."

The door to his grandfather's bedroom was unlocked, and John pushed it open. It looked like a hotel room now: a bed, a painting you barely noticed, a nightstand, a bathroom. Nothing to show that anyone lived there, and definitely no evidence of a terrorist or criminal mastermind or even a human personality spending any amount of time in the room.

"Hello, boys," his grandfather said. Somehow, he was right behind them in the hallway.

John and Pronto both jumped, and with his super speed Pronto shot past Grandpa and was about to hit him in the back of the head with a vase when John furiously waved him off.

Grandpa looked over his shoulder. Pronto stood behind him with empty hands, an innocent expression on his face. "I'll thank you not to use your super powers in my house. Living in a city full of capes is enough without them running down the halls in my home."

"Sorry, Mr. Ajax."

"Why are you two poking around in my room?"

"Uh, we were looking for the best screen to use for trying out a new video game."

Grandfather cocked his head to the side. "I suppose the television in your room would be sufficient." He grabbed his wheels and moved himself past John. "Keep your door closed. I hate the sound of video games."

John let him pass and then said, "Maybe you should write a book revealing their secret identities."

John's grandfather didn't turn. His head drooped low. "Ah. So you read the book today."

"More like looked at the pictures," Pronto said. "Busy day at work, not much reading."

The old man turned his chair, and his face looked sunken and tired. "I did it for their own good. Sometimes we do difficult things to protect our loved ones."

"What are you saying? Sometimes you have to hurt people to protect them?"

"Yes." He looked John in the eyes without flinching. "And I will do whatever I must to protect those I care about." He reached out and put his hand on John's. "Whatever you might think of me, that includes your parents. And you."

John pulled his hand away. "What if you hurt someone else in the process? I can't stand back and watch you hurt people, just because you think it's for the best."

John's grandfather shook his head. "Always playing the hero. Like your father. You think protecting strangers is more important than protecting your family. I thought it was best to reveal your father's secret, and I would do it again."

John leaned back against the wall. "Have you heard from my parents? I tried calling them on my way home but no one answered."

"No." He rubbed the armrest of his wheelchair. "I did get a strange call, though. Someone looking for you, calling on the house phone. A girl named Katherine. Did you give someone my number?"

That was weird. Katherine had given John her number, but he hadn't reciprocated. Everything had happened so fast, with her dad showing up and wheeling her away. He couldn't even remember if she had his last name. Maybe the Gecko had given it to her? But how did she get ahold of the Gecko? John didn't even know how to do that. "No, but that's a girl I met on the plane coming out. If she calls again you can give her my cell."

Pronto's foot was tapping against the floor at super speed. Time to get moving. "Let's go, John, I want to try this game."

"Right. Thanks, Grandpa. We'll be in my room." They left quickly, before he could say another word, and John locked his bedroom door. While Pronto took out the controller and studied the buttons, John puzzled over the exchange with his grandfather. It was like they were on the edge of having a fight, but his grandfather had purposely thrown him out of the fight by bringing up Katherine. John snapped the television on.

Pronto bounced on the bed, zipped over to the TV, studied the picture, let out an exasperated sigh, held up the controller, bounced on the bed again, lay down on the floor, jumped up again, leaned against the wall, sat on the bed again and bounced his knees. John put a hand on his arm. "Whoa. Calm down."

"Something's wrong with your grandpa. He's hiding something."

"Yeah, no kidding. He'll probably go out later. I don't imagine him making us dinner. Maybe we can snoop around the house then." John snatched the controller from Pronto. "In the meantime, let's play some Tread Battalion 3." He pressed what appeared to be a power button on the controller, and the screen of his TV flickered, went blank and then brought up the Tread Battalion logo. Some words flashed up, too: "This screen is smaller than recommended. Continue?"

Pronto flopped back on his bed. "Aw, man. I hate playing games when the screen is too small. Does your grandpa have a bigger one we could use?"

"Maybe, but he just said how much he hates video games. Maybe we could go back to the Game Master's room? He might like watching us play."

"Yeah, right. While Joop is searching the place for the Jester. I don't think so. Maybe my brother will come pick us up."

John snapped his fingers. "Or!" He grinned. "Come with me." He stuck his head in the hallway. His grandfather was in the living room, typing on a computer. "Come on." He snuck down the hallway and into his grandfather's room. Pronto snuck in beside him, and John pulled the door shut. They tiptoed to the closet door, and John put his hand on the handle.

Pronto raised an eyebrow. "We could play in the closet?"

"Wait for it," John said, pushing the door open and revealing the elevator car.

Pronto jumped in faster than John could see, then popped back out and grabbed the controller. "Neat! A unilink transporter! Where are we going?"

John stepped in beside him. "You know these things?"

"Sure, my dad was in the Regulars, remember? Greatest super team on Earth. They used one of these things to go to their secret headquarters sometimes, and Dad took us on a tour."

John pressed the green button and the doors slid shut. "I guess our dads probably know each other."

The elevator jolted into action. "Sure. Your dad was never part of the Regulars but he was sort of Black Vulture's sidekick."

"No kidding?" The doors slid open. "Come on, Pronto, you're going to like this place."

G3 met them at the door, his manikin head expressionless as always, his robes flowing behind him as he glided up to them. "Hello, Master John. Pronto."

"You know me?"

G3 inclined his head slightly. "Yes. And I have been monitoring John closely today. You did good work at Sunnybrook, both of you." He looked at the controller in Pronto's hands. "I have some reservations about playing a video game designed by the Game Master."

John waved him off. "Aw, he's retired. Besides I've played all the other Tread Battalion games. They're super fun and nothing bad has ever happened."

G3 led them through the hangar, which Pronto checked out at super speed. G3 had to tell him to stop walking on top of the Vulture plane, and not to touch certain things, which usually happened after Pronto had touched them. "Nevertheless," G3 said. "I will put you on a closed system so that your game cannot access any of the information or capabilities of the Vulture's Nest."

"That's fine. Any chance we could get a couch or something, too?"

"Yes," G3 said. "You can play your game in the lounge." He glided ahead of them to a side hallway. He opened a door that led to a room with fifteen foot ceilings, about twice the size of a garage. A couch sat near the center of the room, and one entire wall flickered to life as they entered, the Tread Battalion logo blazing across the entire wall.

"Awesome," Pronto said. "This will work."

G3 bowed to them. "There are refreshments in the side cabinets. I will be in the control center."

John thanked him and flopped onto the couch. "This is going to be epic. You take first turn, Pronto."

Pronto held the controller up. It took two hands to hold it, and it was shaped like a giant black bean, rounded and fat. A power button and about six other buttons were on the right, and two joysticks stuck out on the left side. "Green means go," Pronto said, and pressed a green button.

The screen went blank, and then said, "Initiating power link. Isolating signals. Removing interference. Hold please." Then the screen came up, that familiar Tread Battalion screen seen from the point of view of the tank. The cannon went out in front of them, and they could just see the treads in the lower corners of the screen. "Two players?"

Pronto looked to John. "Why not, right?" He pressed the green button again, and the controller made a buzzing sound and snapped in half. "Epic." He handed one of the controllers to John, and the screen on one side flickered and then showed a smaller sort of tank with a collection of armed men sitting in it, all in the Tread Battalion uniforms, a bank of machine guns pointed over the top.

The screen asked them which level they wanted to play: New York City, San Francisco, Chicago or Capeville. Pronto didn't even ask, just tapped on Capeville. "The graphics are amazing," Pronto said. "It looks like live video feed."

"They always try to do that in Tread Battalion, but you're right, it looks really authentic. Check out how the soldiers sort of move and talk to each other in the back of my transport tank."

"So cool. Okay, let me get the hang of this." They both moved their tanks around for a minute, John driving a troop transport and Pronto driving a tank, and about the time they both felt comfortable the screen flickered again and said, "Ammunition is now live. Link is live. Mission uploading."

The tanks were on a boat down near the Capeville docks. Pronto led the way and rolled his off the boat. They stood idling near the dock, waiting for their mission instructions. Then the Game Master appeared in the center of their screen, or rather someone who looked exactly like the Game Master but dressed like a five star general, cleanly shaven and with his hair slicked back. Pronto and John both laughed at that. He leaned near the screen and said, "Gentlemen, your mission is to retrieve an item called the MacGuffin from a secure location in Capeville. Green arrows will appear on the screen showing you which way to go. Villainous people have taken control of the Capeville government, so don't be surprised if police officers, military officers or even costumed super villains attempt to stop you." A timer appeared in the upper right corner of the screen, set to twenty minutes. "Within twenty minutes the MacGuffin will be removed from its current location, so you'll need to move fast. Best of luck, gentlemen." The Game Master flickered out, and the screen returned to the view from their tanks. A green arrow pointed the way, and Pronto and John gave each other a fist bump.

"Let's go," Pronto said, and he led the way through the streets of Capeville. The graphics really were amazing, and incredibly detailed. The cars all looked different, and there were pedestrians milling around on the street. Some of them stopped to point at the tanks.

About a minute into the game nothing had happened yet. "Weird," John said. "I'd expect something to come up against us by now. We'll have to tell Game Master to make the first couple minutes more exciting."

"I can fix that," Pronto said, and he steered his tank over a parked car. It crushed beneath the weight of his treads, the car alarm going off, and pedestrians ran away, pulling out cell phones. Within thirty seconds they could hear police sirens.

John grinned. "That's more like it. Let's go!" He pushed his tank into full speed, and as a police cruiser came around the corner he smashed into it, laying down covering fire for Pronto. The green arrows led them to a scientific facility of some sort, with a heavy fence, guard towers and men with machine guns. Pronto took out the nearest guard tower, the guards jumping from it as it crashed to the ground. Pronto's hand eye coordination was so fast that he was the natural to take first shot at anything that came their way. John focused on more distant threats, practicing his aim. But the fact was, there wasn't that much resistance.

The double doors leading into the facility were too small for Pronto's tank, so John popped through them, guiding his troop transport down hallways until his soldiers jumped off the back and ran into a secure room, using explosives to get in, grab a large safe with a floating tray, and load it onto the back of the tank. They pounded the back of the tank and shouted, "Clear! Let's move!"

John burst out of the building, laughing, to find Pronto wrecking police cars, which had formed a perimeter around them. The green arrows pointed them back toward the docks, so they started moving. Pronto's tank was slower, but since John had the MacGuffin, he stayed close. A red proximity alarm started blaring on John's screen. He spun his turret, looking for a target, but didn't see anything. Then the Gecko burst onto the screen, standing on the back of John's tank and fighting his soldiers, who were trying to shoot him without shooting each other. The Gecko fought and kicked, and one of the soldiers went flying off the side. Pronto barely avoided running over John's fallen soldier.

"Awesome!" John said. "The Gecko is one of the bad guys. He'll love this."

"I thought he was a good guy," Pronto said.

"Yeah, but the Game Master made this, so it makes sense that he thinks of the cops and super heroes as bad guys." John spun his turret, but couldn't get a good shot at the Gecko. He steered closer to Pronto, and Pronto turned his turret and knocked it into the Gecko. But the Gecko used his power to stick to things and grabbed hold of Pronto's cannon. John pulled his tank back to protect the MacGuffin. His screen flashed a question: "Order soldiers to switch to anti-cape ammo?" John pressed another button for more information. Anti-cape ammo would temporarily remove a cape's powers. Nice. He pressed yes. His soldiers quickly changed something on their rifles and fired blue bolts of energy at the Gecko, who leapt onto the other side of Pronto's tank.

"Incoming!" Pronto said. Behind them a fleet of police cars gained on them. Ahead of them some sort of electrical discharge arced across the road. John throttled back.

"There's an electrical field up there. Not sure what will happen if we run the tanks through it."

Pronto took a couple shots at the police cruisers, but the Gecko kept smashing the turret with an iron bar he had pulled off the top of the tank. John looked ahead through the electrical storm and saw a shape coming toward him, running and bouncing off the sides of cars, rolling and leaping as she came. "It's Lightning Cat!" John grinned at Pronto.

"Oh yeah, one of your girlfriends, right?"

John blushed. "I wish." His soldiers were taking shots at her and the Gecko now, but she was out of range. "I do feel a little weird having my guys shooting at her."

"Please. She's computer generated. It might be weird if my dad or brothers showed up in the game, though, I guess. Or you! Wouldn't that be cool?" Pronto squinted at the screen. "I think we're only about a half mile from the docks. If you can't get a shot at Lightning Cat to shut down her powers, let's go around that energy field."

"What is the Gecko doing?"

Pronto looked at the screen and spun his turret, trying to knock the Gecko off. "I can't shake the guy. I don't know, looks like he's talking to someone. Keeps touching his ear."

"Weird that we can't hear him. We'll have to tell the Game Master. Another glitch in the game. Hey, pause it and I'll get a pen to write this stuff down."

Pronto clicked various buttons. "No pause button."

"That's weird. Well, do your best to hold them and I'll be right back."

John walked into the hallway. Pronto yelled, "Hurry up, your girlfriend is getting closer. She just electrocuted some of your soldiers!" John trotted down the hall to G3's surveillance room. All the screens were turned off and John didn't see G3. He moved a couple things around, looking for some paper, when he saw G3 in the corner, his arms twitching beneath his robes, his head bowed and unmoving.

"G3, what's wrong?"

G3 slowly turned his head toward John. A crackling sound came from him. Slowly, words started to form. "Virus. Attacking. Sophisticated. All attention must be given to prevent it gaining access." G3 crackled some more. "Turning on exterior communication feed, Black Vulture."

A crackling came over exterior speakers somewhere in the room, and then the Gecko's voice came loud and clear into the room, "Repeat, G3, can you hear me? We need back up. Two tanks and a platoon of soldiers have just stolen the force field generator from TechTonic Labs and – oof – " there was the sound of shots sizzling past. "Just me and Lightning Cat. Tell BV we need his –" The transmission cut out.

John stood still, listening. There was nothing more, and G3 stood nearby, his arms twitching but otherwise immobile. John's mind raced. It couldn't be a coincidence. "Oh, no." John ran down the hallways, skidding on the smooth floor and came barreling into the lounge.

"Hey," Pronto said. "One of your soldiers got a hit on the Gecko. He's lost his powers and I shook him off easily enough after that. We're triangulating on Lightning Cat now."

"No," John said, grabbing his controller. "We've got to turn this off, Pronto."

"We're about to win!"

"Pronto, it's really happening. We're controlling actual tanks. The Game Master is stealing a force field generator and we're the ones doing it for him."

"What?" Pronto frantically pressed the buttons on his controller. "There's no pause, John, and there's no way to stop the game."

John groaned, pressing all the buttons. Both of their tanks spun and shot weapons. "We're more dangerous trying to turn this thing off than when we're actually playing." John threw his controller on the ground as hard as he could and it shattered. Pronto grabbed his and did the same. Both tanks slowed to a stop, and Lightning Cat came bouncing toward the camera, shooting lightning at the guards.

Then the screen flashed the words "Auto Pilot Engaged." The tanks rolled back into life, but now they aimed with deadly accuracy, and Lightning Cat was struggling to stay ahead of the shells from Pronto's tank. John's tank edged around her and poured on speed for the docks.

"We have to get down there. Come on." John ran out into the hallway, but Pronto passed him.

He came skidding back. "Your robot friend is out of commission. How do we get down there?"

"I don't know. All the screens are out. I think the power is down in the Nest. We have to see if there's something we can fly ourselves." Pronto ran out among the various vehicles and John tried to stir G3's attention again. When he couldn't get him even to turn his head, John ran into the trophy room and pulled open one of the Black Vulture costumes. It was an older one, no armor or anything else. He pulled the mask off and tied it on his own head, then wrapped the pointed cape on over his street clothes.

"There's a jet thing here that looks easy enough," Pronto said.

John pushed his hair back with both hands. "An easy to fly jet, Pronto? That seems unlikely."

"What's the other option? Let your friends get killed by our tanks, and the bad guys get away with a force field generator. With that kind of force field... they could hide behind it while they set off their doomsday device. Or they could lock themselves inside with the device while they work on it and no one will be able to stop them."

"Let's take a look." Pronto led him to a two-person jet that looked more like a rocket with long, arced wings on it. A third fin extended into a long groove on the floor, a groove which went straight toward a hangar door. John jumped up on the wing and pulled the cockpit back. There was a clearly marked launch button, a steering wheel and a handle like a joystick to the right of the pilot's seat. A dizzying array of buttons and gauges covered the front of the dash.

Pronto pointed at the steering wheel. "Steering." The launch button. "Launch." The joystick. "Altitude?" The buttons. "Other stuff. Unimportant."

"We'll try it. Either we'll figure it out or we'll be little red stains on Capeville somewhere." John followed the groove to the large hangar doors. "We'll need to open those doors."

"No problem."

"Pronto, you may not have noticed this, but the Nest is way up in the air. It's not like we can go outside and press a doorbell or something."

Pronto laughed. "We're probably a mile up. Gives us plenty of time to get the controls figured out before we crash." He zipped over to the doors. He shot to one side of the hangar and came back with a huge wrench, which he used to bash the latch where the doors came together. He shouted, "Grab the other door and we'll pull them apart." He and John each grabbed a door and pulled. A huge blast of air came as the air in the hangar was sucked out into the upper atmosphere. John held tight to the door, but he lost his footing.

Pronto pulled him back. He ran to the rocket jet and slapped John into the pilot's seat, popping a helmet on him and fastening an air hose to the front of the helmet.

Immediately, cold oxygen filtered into John's mask and then his lungs. He took a deep breath and gave Pronto a thumbs up, and Pronto jumped into the seat behind him and faster than John would have thought possible, pulled down the canopy and tapped him on the head. A tinny voice came in his ear, "All snapped in John, let's go."

"Do you need a disguise, Pronto?"

"No, everyone knows the Thunder family. Putting a mask on doesn't help when you're the only speedsters in the city. I'll blur my face at super speed just in case."

"Fair enough." John's finger hovered over the launch button. "Ready... set..." he pressed the button. "GO!" A loud thunk came from below and the jet flung forward, pressing John flat in his seat. They hadn't gotten the door all the way open, and the wing on the right side hit it on the way out, sending them into a tail spin.

"I don't hear an engine, John!"

"Hold on, hold on." John tried to get a better look at the buttons but they were spinning and bouncing and he could hardly see anything. He pulled the steering wheel to the side, trying to slow their spin, but it didn't work. Pronto was shouting in his ear. He put his hand on the stick and found a button on the side. "Pronto, hold tight," he shouted, and he pushed the button. There was a hollow sound, like a propane tank lighting, and then a burst of power knocked him back against the seat.

John straightened the wheel and pulled the stick back. They were barreling through the sky at enormous speed. Pronto shouted in his ear, giving him directions toward the scene of the battle, but now they could see smoke rising from the town. "Don't go toward the smoke, that's where they've been, not where they're going," Pronto shouted. "Head for the docks." John followed his directions and in moments they were screaming down like jet-fueled hail, headed straight for the docks, where the tanks were about to board a waiting ship.

"Landing gear?" John shouted.

Pronto laughed hysterically. "Probably one of those unimportant buttons."

"Better hope there's not an ejector seat," John said, getting ready to punch some buttons randomly. But then he had another idea. "I'm going to ram the tank." He could see the bigger tank taking aim at Lightning Cat, who was little larger than a ladybug in the distance. John pushed the stick down and steered toward the tank.

"You can't get a date with her if we're dead," Pronto shouted.

"And vice versa."

"You can't die if you get a date with her?"

"No, you idiot, I can't get a date with her if *she's* dead, either!" The jet tilted down and just missed ramming the tank, the fin on the bottom slicing through the turret, metal screaming, sparks flying. The jet hit the ground like a brick wall, the wings snapping off and the jet turning as fire flared up along the wings. Before the jet came to a full stop, Pronto popped the canopy and undid both of their seatbelts. He ran down along the wing, John in his arms, and jumped off, his legs still pumping. He stumbled when they hit the ground, but he recovered and ran just outside the range of the tanks and soldiers.

"How did you do that?" John asked. "It didn't hurt when we hit the ground."

"When I run I make an anti-inertial field. Keeps me from getting killed by hitting a bug at high speed. Or, you know, bullets. Or pavement. It extends to anything I'm carrying, too." He pointed at the jet, which was covered in flame now. "Theoretically I could have jumped off the plane carrying you while we were still in the air. My father could have, anyway. I haven't been allowed to test

that sort of thing, yet, because if it doesn't work you die."
Pronto pushed John to the ground as the jet exploded, a
ball of whitish yellow fire bursting over their heads.

They got to their feet in time to see the smaller tank
loading onto the ship, the soldiers forming a phalanx behind it, guarding its retreat. John did a quick survey of
the surroundings, saw that Lightning Cat was crouched
behind a car, trying to decide her next move. "Pronto, get
me to Lightning Cat."

Pronto grabbed him and in a second of feverish jolting, they ended up next to Lightning Cat behind the car.
She smiled at John, and her almond-shaped eyes blinked
at him slowly. "You look familiar," she said.

"Black Vulture," John said. "We fought some robots together recently."

"I know," she said. "And this is one of the Thunder
family?"

"Pronto," he said, and shook her hand. He rubbed
his arms. "I'm getting worn out from carrying you, John.
What's the plan?"

John peeked over the car. The police were setting up
a perimeter, pistols trained on the soldiers. The soldiers
had the tank mostly buttoned up and looked ready to cast
off. "Can you run fast enough to pop the force field off the
boat without them noticing?"

"Maybe, but it's in a safe. I couldn't lift it."

"The Gecko fell back a few blocks ago," Lightning Cat
said. "Without his powers he was getting in the way, and
I was worried the police would take him in for vigilan-
tism."

"It's just the three of us," John said. "And not much
time." He tapped his fingers against the side of the car.
"Pronto, you go behind the soldiers at super speed and
start picking them off. Cat, you attack them from the
front. If we manage to wipe them out we'll turn the force

field generator over to the cops." He pointed to a manhole cover at the center of the street. "I'll pry that manhole off in case we need a quick escape."

Pronto was gone already, and two soldiers flew off the boat and into the water before Lightning Cat jumped up on a car, electricity crackling from her hands and shooting up the sides of her legs. She ran in front of the soldiers, power arcing over them. Two soldiers went down, with Pronto knocking a third in the back of the head. John ran to the center of the street, and the cops yelled at him to go back behind the car. He put his fingers in the holes of the manhole and leaned back. It wasn't moving. He strained as hard as he could. The ship was pulling its gate up and the soldiers were falling back toward it. John pulled again, but the manhole cover was far too heavy.

The Gecko ran up beside him, still carrying the iron bar he had been using on the tanks earlier. Without a word he put his hands flat on the cover and yanked backward, John pulling as well. The cover moved an inch upward, and John pushed the Gecko's iron bar under it. John used it as a lever and pulled the cover off. He looked up in time to see Pronto get caught by one of the soldier's blue energy shots. His powers turned off immediately, and he flew into the soldiers like a bowling ball, knocking several of them over. One of the remaining soldiers yanked him up, threw his unconscious body over his shoulder and stepped onto the ship. The ship was pulling out now, and the other soldiers piled on, covering themselves with a barrage of fire. Lightning Cat was crouched over a few of the soldiers that she had knocked down, staying low to avoid the enemy fire.

The Gecko grabbed John's arm. "My powers are coming back. They're at about thirty percent. I'm going to sneak onto the boat. I'll contact you via G3." With that he ran full speed at the retreating ship, jumped off the dock and dove into the water, energy beams lighting up the water around him. He surfaced to the left of the boat and put one hand against the hull. As the ship picked up speed, he stuck easily to the side. He gave John a thumbs up with his other hand.

"Put your hands in the air," said a voice behind John.

John put his hands up, and turned to see two police officers, pistols aimed at John's chest. The open manhole was a step to his left. Lightning Cat, hopefully, was still behind him somewhere. "I'm on your side," John said.

"You and your friend are coming downtown with us."

"My friend?"

"The girl in the cat costume."

John nodded. "Is she behind me?"

"Miss, put your hands up," one of the officers yelled, and turned his pistol on her, somewhere to John's right.

"How old are you two? You look like kids."

"I'm thirty-seven," John said, knowing even as he said it that they would never believe him. He heard footsteps behind him as Lightning Cat started running.

"Stop!" Both officers trained their weapons on Lightning Cat now, and John heard the electricity crackling from her as she barreled toward them. She jumped feet first, like she was sliding in baseball, and dropped into the manhole. John took a step sideways and dropped in after her, his hands still over his head. He landed in a puddle of water, and scrambled out of the oval of sunlight. The police were shouting, and far down in the dark he could see Lightning Cat running, her electrical sparks lighting up the tunnel.

John ran after her. The tunnel split, and he followed her light to the left. As he continued to run the light grew brighter, until he found her standing in the tunnel, electricity licking up her legs and coursing down her arms, sparking around her hands. She smiled at him. "The more

I run and jump, the bigger my electrical charge. I need to discharge it or the police will find us down here. But get out of the water first so I don't accidentally electrocute you." John stepped up on the side of the tunnel and put his hands against the ceiling so he could prop himself out of the water.

She turned away from him and crouched down, and a bright ball of lightning shot down the tunnel. She didn't move. "Listen, if I even start walking now I'm going to build a charge quickly. I need you to pick me up and move us down a side tunnel. We'll wait for them to finish searching and then be on our way."

John came up beside her, put one hand on her shoulder blades and she rolled backward, his arms going under her knees. She was surprisingly light. As they moved down the tunnel, she put her head on his shoulder. He noticed that the leather over her knee was torn open, and her leg was torn and bloody. "Are you okay?"

"It will heal," she said. "Turn left here. Watch your head, it's tight." He ducked his head and they made their way another forty yards before she showed him a small chamber on the right. He laid her down against the wall, and then settled in beside her.

"Hi," she said, a tiny smile on her lips.

"Hi." John dropped his head back against the wall. "They got the force field and Pronto. This whole thing was a mess."

"It's not over yet," she said, and put her hand lightly on his chest, leaning close to him. They heard someone tromping through the tunnels and both fell silent for a while. Some lights came close, but no one came down the smaller tunnel. Her lips were close to his. All he had to do was turn his head. He could feel every single place they were touching.

"We have to get back out there," he said.

"Not yet," she said. "We have at least a half an hour before they stop searching for us." Her face was closer, she was rearranging to get into a better position. He started to speak but she put her finger against his lip. "I have to ask, because we have secret identities. Do you have a girlfriend?"

"Um." John thought furiously for a moment. "No, not really."

"The Gecko told me that in your secret identity you have a girl you're interested in. Someone named Katherine?"

John blushed. "He said that? You know, we just met. The Gecko doesn't know much about me."

"Really?" Her fingers dug into his collarbone. "So this girl, Katherine, she's not someone I should be worried about?"

"No, no. She gave me her number but I haven't called her yet. I mean, she's great, she's really nice but she's not... she's not *you*."

She pulled away from him and rested against the wall. "We should be quiet now, in case the police come this way." She turned her head away from him, into the darkness.

"Lightning Cat? Is something wrong?"

She wasn't near him at all now, wasn't touching him. He had no idea what had just happened. He slumped back against the wall and listened to the water plinking into puddles and the distant sound of people sloshing through the tunnels. The terrorists had the force field. They had depowered and kidnapped Pronto. The Gecko was gone, the Vulture's jet plane had been demolished. The police were looking for him and he was hiding out in the sewers with a beautiful but unpredictable woman. Just the ordinary life of a super hero.

Something moved slowly through the tunnel, disturbing the water. He put his hand on Lightning Cat's shoulder and she looked back at him, a question on her face. He put his finger to his lips and pointed into the darkness. He moved, slowly and quietly, to the mouth of the tunnel and was greeted with a fetid, disgusting smell, like sewage mixed with hot garbage. A hulking creature was jammed down into the tunnel, its red eyes glinting like a rat's in the darkness. It spoke, a deep baritone that sent the smell of garbage wafting across them both. "What are you doing in my tunnels?" it said.

John, startled, tried to answer, but before he got a word out it wrapped its gigantic hand around his chest. John struggled to escape, but its grip tightened. "I am the Muck," it said. "And this is my home. You are not welcome here, law breaker." John struggled for a breath, but he couldn't get one. His last thought was regret for his failure... failure to save the city, to save his friends, failure to be a hero.

CHAPTER 13

THE MUCK!

John struggled for breath, the creature called the Muck crushing his chest, when a familiar voice shouted, "Muck! Put him down. He's one of us."

Room to breathe came immediately, and John gulped down several breaths of air that tasted like rotten garbage. The Muck dropped him into the puddle and pulled back out of the smaller tunnel. Jupiter Girl stood in the tunnel, a flashlight in hand, her hair perfect, wearing a pair of knee high boots in the disgusting water, her skirt and blouse looking as if she had freshly pressed them. She helped John up.

"Can you breathe?"

John rubbed his ribs. "Yeah. Thanks. We should probably warn the police officers about that thing."

"I don't harm keepers of the law," the Muck said, offended.

"Just innocent kids," John said.

"Innocent. Then why are the authorities pursuing you?"

"Because of the mask," John said. "It's illegal to be a vigilante in Capeville."

"Then you are not innocent," said the Muck, and he turned and moved down the tunnel. "I released you only because of Jupiter Girl's instructions."

Jupiter Girl's arm was still wrapped around John's waist. She patted him with the other hand on his shoulder. "The Muck sees things in very black and white, very alien terms. My father and I have been training him to have a bit more... flexibility... in his moral determinations."

Lightning Cat emerged from the smaller tunnel, and her eyes dropped disapprovingly to Jupiter Girl's arm around John's waist. "I see you found another friend," Lightning Cat said.

Jupiter Girl laughed. "Don't worry, he's too young for me. I'm not competition."

"You can say that again," Lightning Cat said.

Jupiter Girl frowned. "Put your claws away, little kitty. I already told you I'm not in the market for a fourteen year old boyfriend." She stepped away from John. "I assume that's who I think it is under the mask?"

He sighed. "Man, I am not good at this secret identity thing." He pulled his mask off. "I'm the new Black Vulture." He hadn't introduced himself by name to Lightning Cat, only by his superhero identity, so he held his hand out and said, "John Ajax."

"Nice to meet you," she said, but she didn't take her mask off.

Jupiter Girl said, "It's probably best to put your mask away for now, John, because the Muck has a hard time remembering not to punish law breakers. It will help him if you're not reminding him you're a vigilante." She looked Lightning Cat up and down. "I take it you're not ready to part with your secret identity."

Lightning Cat shook her head.

"Fine. Let's go. I found you two because the news is going crazy about the four young vigilantes who attacked the tanks. It's a good thing I came down, because the Muck was very distressed. He has something going on down here that he's not sure what to do about, and he wanted my advice." She started walking down the tunnel after the Muck. When they didn't immediately follow, she stopped and motioned impatiently for them to catch up.

The Muck turned his red eyes on Lightning Cat and moved toward her, but Jupiter Girl put her hands up and said, "She's not breaking the law, she's on her way to a high school Halloween party. You know, the kind where girls dress up in ridiculous skintight costumes trying to impress someone."

The Muck nodded. "This way," he said.

Lightning Cat grabbed John's hand and squeezed it, leaning close to say, "I have to wear this outfit because it helps me control the electricity. It has special circuitry built into it."

John didn't know what to say, so he awkwardly kept holding her hand as they followed through the tunnel. It made it a little harder to keep up, and occasionally a spark of electricity would shoot up John's arm. Finally, Jupiter Girl said, "When you two are done playing Ring Around the Rosie, we need to pick up the speed."

John let go of Lightning Cat's hand and let her go ahead. He heard a small spark of electricity in front of him, and a yelp from Jupiter Girl. Nothing more came of it, though, because the Muck told them to be quiet. "We're near. Follow carefully. A misstep will lead you to places you would rather not go."

The Muck moved down a branching tunnel to a place where it met a much larger tunnel, at least twenty feet high. The water moved through here much faster, like a river, and further down there was a giant wrought iron grate. The water coursed through the grate, and pieces of trash caught on it. As the Muck passed, the garbage came upstream through the water and attached itself to him. He pointed out a place where the grate was broken and a person could fit through. "If you went through that hole, you would fall down a waterfall and then travel an underwater tunnel for some distance. Perhaps a mile or so before coming out into open water."

The water moved fast, but it didn't come up above their knees. They followed the Muck across the river, and he took them through another tunnel, this one tilted upward, away from the river. Eventually the water trickled away and they were, for the first time in over an hour, in a dry tunnel.

"These tunnels are very strange," Lightning Cat said. "They don't make sense as sewage tunnels. They're too large in places, too accessible, and this tunnel, for instance, doesn't appear to be good for anything other than walking in."

The Muck grunted. "They were built in strange times by strange peoples. There are stranger things to see." He took them into a wide room, almost like a balcony. A waist high wall ran across the room, and flashes of blue light came from the room beyond. John moved to the edge and put his hands on the cement. A gigantic cavern stretched out below them. Blue flashes of light filled the closer dark, but could not penetrate the darkness beyond. A busy crew of men and women moved in a vast network of scaffolding which had been built around what appeared to be a gigantic robot, at least twenty stories tall. The chin of the robot stood at the level of their balcony, and the head and crown stretched above them.

"What is this place?" John whispered.

"You see my conundrum," the Muck said quietly. "This cavern is a natural one and predates Capeville by many centuries. It is not, technically, within the city limits and thus is outside of Capeville law. There is no need for building permits and such things. And yet, I cannot avoid the suspicion that to do such work in the dark argues that the work is meant for evil and destruction."

Jupiter Girl let out a long breath. "You did well to show us this, Muck. I will tell my father immediately."

"This is the doomsday device, isn't it?" John moved along the balcony, trying to get a clearer view. "The giant robot, the crown on its head. It's so ridiculous, which the Jester just loves. And the gaming aspect of it... the Game Master must think this is the greatest thing ever."

"The Game Master?" Jupiter Girl crossed her arms. "What makes you think that old man has anything to do with this?"

John quickly told her about the video game and what had happened while they tried it out. She agreed that it did not look good for the Game Master, but was furious that Pronto and John had taken something from him and fallen for his trick. John said, "There's no use fighting over it now. We had no idea it was something dangerous."

Jupiter Girl put her hands on her hips and laughed. "It never occurred to you that the 'Game Master' -- a retired super villain -- might be playing a game with you?"

"I thought he was retired. I didn't know he was still in the evil scientist game." He looked at the giant robot again. "That's weird, actually. There are never giant robots in Game Master's video games."

Jupiter Girl stopped, her mouth open and finger ready to wag, then put her hand down and walked past John. Lightning Cat was curled up in a ball, quietly sobbing. Jupiter Girl went to her, kneeled down beside her and stroked her head. "It's okay," she said. "We're going to stop this thing."

Lightning Cat sat up, a fierce expression on her face. "Oh, we're going to stop it, that's for sure." Her face softened again, and then she started to cry. "I recognize some of those components. My father makes them. I think he's involved in this somehow. He's been telling me we'd be leaving town soon. Going somewhere safer." She wiped at her eyes. "I kept wondering where could be safer than Capeville? Now I know. My dad is helping blow it up."

John slid down beside her and put his hand on her arm. "I think my grandfather is in on it, too. He had all these maps on his wall, with a bunch of places circled."

"My dad's difficult," Lightning Cat said. "But I never thought he'd be a criminal."

Jupiter Girl grabbed each of them by the chin and pulled their faces toward hers. "We are not defined by our parents. Or our grandparents. They shape us. They direct us. But in the end, we make our own choices. We are heroes or villains because of our own decisions, our own actions." She let go of their faces. "We will stop this thing."

Something she said stopped John cold. We're not defined by our grandparents. We're not who they are, but... something bothered John about this. His grandfather, working with Chester the Jester. The same person who had blown up Kane Bridge, and crippled him. That didn't make any sense. The pieces didn't fit together right. He turned and looked at the robot. He didn't know what it was, but it didn't make sense for the Game Master to build a giant robot. It wasn't his style. And the force field generator. What could that possibly be for?

Jupiter Girl's voice broke him from his thoughts. "Muck, can you take us to my home, please?"

The Muck bowed his head. "Of course. But what should I do about this thing being built in my cavern?"

"Do nothing, Muck. My father will bring reinforcements and we will deal with it together. For now, keep an eye on the workers and the robot, and let me know at once if something changes."

"Yes," the Muck said. "Now I will show you the way to your home." He led them away from the balcony and found a narrow passageway that had a chalk moon drawn over it. He lifted one garbage-laden hand to the moon and left a smudge over it, and when he bent to enter the passage an icy wind touched John's face. "Come quickly," the Muck said, "Or the shadow wolves will smell your living souls as we pass through their land."

"Maybe we shouldn't go through their land, then?" John raised his eyebrows at the Muck.

"These tunnels are terrible mazes," Jupiter Girl said, "And we can't risk going above ground with all the authorities after you. This will be faster, and it's safe if we don't linger. Besides, the Muck has dealt with them before."

The Muck bent down into the tunnel. "I received my share of wounds as a result. I am now permitted to bring the occasional guest through their land. If the aroma of living flesh does not overpower their volition. Come quickly."

John followed. The tunnel was cold, and it opened almost immediately into a wide, starlit plane. A low, pale crescent moon stood out above mountains with tops like broken fingers. "What is this place?"

The Murk stopped and looked around, as if he had never done so before, and the blue moon glinted off the lumpy refuse on his skin. His red eyes turned to John. "As I said, the tunnels were made by strange folk. They struck a series of agreements. Some wise, some foolish. This tunnel was made to pass through our own lands more quickly. I do not know the bargain they made with the wolves, but it was almost certainly foolish." He walked a few more steps, and paused again. "Perhaps it was meant only for emergencies."

Lightning Cat put her hand in John's again, and he didn't think for a minute about dropping it. He squeezed her hand, hoping it was reassuring. Jupiter Girl walked ahead of them, and then she took John's hand, too, and with her other hand took hold of one of the Muck's giant fingers. "It is wise for us to keep together," she said, and she smiled at Lightning Cat with genuine affection.

The Muck, increasingly concerned about their speed, moved the entire group to a trot. The only problem was that the increased physical movement was building up an electrical charge for Lightning Cat. Sparks flared, lighting up her legs and down her arms. A cold, merciless howl rolled down from the mountains, filling the plain and echoing across it.

The Muck grunted. "Your light is drawing them, little one. Are you able to extinguish it?"

"The sparks? No. Whenever I move, the electricity builds up. I could fire it all off, but it would be an even bigger light. And every step I take, I start to recharge."

Another howl came. This time, a second answered, but it was much closer. "Can we exit here?" Jupiter Girl asked.

The Muck shook his head. "I did not consider the little one's light. This is my own mistake. Still, we have not transgressed the law, and if the wolves think to make a meal of my guests they will have a sorry time of it."

Jupiter Girl took Lightning Cat's hands. "Let all your power loose. I will carry you the rest of the way so you won't build up more."

"That will leave her defenseless," John asked.

At least three creatures were howling now. A short bark and several yips followed. The Muck growled. "They have our scent. The light does not matter. We must move quickly." He began to run, and with his great, long legs he was nearly out of sight before John and Lightning Cat started after him. Arcs of electricity curled around Lightning Cat as she ran, shooting bright blue and white light into the darkness. Jupiter Girl was flying alongside them, and did not appear to be going her top speed. She was protecting them, John realized.

"How many powers do you have?" John asked.

"I'm a Class 1 metahuman, John. Flight, super strength, speed, shape shifting, limited telepathy." She smiled at him. "And I haven't turned eighteen yet. Most of those powers should only increase."

An inky shape lunged out of the dark and snatched Jupiter Girl from the air. She rolled to the ground, her hands moving in and out, woven into the shadows.

The Muck immediately fell back and spread his arms across John and Lightning Cat.

Jupiter Girl lifted back into the air, her hands tight around the thick neck of a black wolf the size of a kitchen table.

John could only see its shape where its form blocked out the stars, and when it opened its mouth, he could see white teeth and a blood red tongue.

It snapped at Jupiter Girl, and her arms thickened and lengthened, keeping it at bay. The howling increased, and Lightning Cat's sparks shot out into the darkness, growing in intensity until she glowed like the filament of a light bulb. Everywhere her light touched, eyes shone back at them.

The Muck pulled himself up, filling the space around him, and he was nearly nine feet tall. John kept Lightning Cat's hand firmly in his, but he could feel her body tensing, getting ready for a fight.

The Muck said, "Wolves of the shadow, you transgress our covenants. You break your own laws. I have the right to bring guests through this narrow bit of your land, so long as we do not tarry. And yet you have attacked my guest."

One of the wolves, bigger than the others, sat on its haunches with its tongue hung out. "Servant of Entropy and Spirit of Law. The Shadow Wolves do not break agreements. You know this. Any transgressor is eaten by the pack."

The Muck pointed to Jupiter Girl, floating, the shadow wolf still in her grip. "And yet you attack my guests."

The wolf laughed. "Cubs at play." It cocked its head to the side. "She is an alpha among your kind?"

"Yes," the Muck said. "Yes, and she is still a cub. You see clearly."

The wolf stood and stepped closer, head lowered. "I do see clearly. I am the alpha among my kind. You know this. And our prophecies tell us about this one." It flicked its eyes toward Lightning Cat. As it moved farther into the light, John could see the individual hairs in its fur, each one made of shadow and quivering in the flickering glow. "They tell us that she will come, and that she will rule us. Unless we devour her."

"You are mistaken. She, too, is a cub, and holds you no ill will. Let us pass."

The alpha growled. "You dare insult me before my pack? Now I must tear your rotten throat from your body."

The Muck breathed in. "Shadows cannot harm me, not with any lasting wound. Let these children pass and you and I shall have words. Perhaps you are not mistaken. But I know you are no devourer of cubs."

All of the wolves growled at this. Jupiter Girl tensed, and Lightning Cat's light intensified. The wolves moved back a few steps. "I am no devourer of cubs. Not of my own kind. But of my enemies? Male or female, cub or elderly, I will rend them piece from piece!" It leapt, snarling, toward Lightning Cat.

Lightning Cat shoved John to the side and burst into brilliant light, electricity arcing out from her in a thousand stormy fingers, piercing the wolf in mid air. It glowed, and darkness tore from the wolf, ragged shreds of shadow flying off it like black ash escaping a fire. It struck the ground and Lightning Cat jumped on its back, her hands on either side of its head, just behind its eyes. She looked out to the shadows and shouted. "I am not your enemy! Or I wasn't before today." Her eyes, hard as sunlight, glared out at the wolves. "You threaten me? You threaten my friends? When I return here it will not be to rule. It will be to destroy!" She grabbed hold of the alpha wolf's ear and released a torrent of electricity through her hands, and the wolf howled in pain.

Jupiter Girl spun in the air and threw the wolf she held far out toward the mountains. She dropped through the air, snatching Lightning Cat from the back of the wolf and she scooped John up from the ground, one tucked under each arm. She flew, and the cold wind pushed against them like a wall. The alpha shouted for the pack to kill them, and they ran alongside faster than John would have thought possible, the ground passing in an astounding blur. Several of the wolves managed to keep pace. John looked back to see the Muck at his full height, shadow wolves tearing at him, surrounding him, leaping up at his chest. He had one in his left hand and delivered another a blow to the head in midair.

Jupiter Girl dropped toward the ground suddenly and shoved them through a small, wooden door as the wolves pounced. They were in the tunnels again, all three panting. Jupiter Girl slammed the door and leaned up against it with her back. On the tunnel wall above her was a small chalk moon.

Lightning Cat, panting, fell to her side and pulled her legs up to her chest. "I'm no better than my father," she said.

Jupiter Girl took her hand. "You've done no harm, Lightning Cat."

John helped her to her feet. "We still have a doomsday device to stop."

Lightning Cat held both their hands and pulled them close. "I don't have many friends," she said. "My father has kept me locked away much of my life. Are you my friends?"

John didn't hesitate. "Yes. Of course."

Jupiter Girl considered this carefully. "Where I come from, such things are not promised lightly. I hope we will be friends in time."

Lightning Cat laughed, her head toward the ground, and a tear fell from her mask. "Close enough." Her grip on their hands tightened. "You must never let me kill those creatures. Do you understand?"

"Yes," John said.

"Promise me."

"I promise."

"Jupiter Girl?"

"Yes, I can promise you that."

Lightning Cat relaxed, and she almost fell. John caught her, and scooped her up in his arms. Jupiter Girl offered to carry her, but John refused. Lightning Cat put her head on his shoulder. He didn't know from her soft breathing if she was asleep or just exhausted.

"I know the way from here," Jupiter Girl said.

"What about the Muck?"

"He can hold his own." John followed Jupiter Girl down the tunnel, her feet floating above the water. It wasn't too far, but by the time Jupiter Girl turned up another branching tunnel and said they were beneath her home, John's arms were burning.

The walls of this tunnel were different. Smooth and metal, with no evidence of seams or bolts, the walls glowed with a soft green light. The end of the tunnel was blocked by a large orb, as if a globe the size of a house had been rolled up against a pipe. Strange markings decorated the surface of the orb, each of them unique and none of them like anything John had seen before. They almost looked like Chinese characters, but more rounded and complex. "I need you to look the other way while I unlock the door, John. For security's sake."

"Oh. Sure." John turned around, but when he heard the strange sounds behind him -- like bones cracking mixed with high pitched musical tones -- he snuck a glance over his shoulder. Jupiter Girl stood there, shaped like a giant lizard with four arms, dusty red, scaled, heavily muscled, and with eyes across her snout. She reached her arms up, her clawed hands picking out a series of characters with startling speed. He turned away, worried she had seen him, but a minute later she told him he could follow, and she looked like her regular self: seventeen, red-haired and beautiful.

"Quickly, John." He followed her into a chamber the size of his family's kitchen. She pressed a button and the door irised shut. "I'll show you where you can clean up." They passed a series of corridors, all of them identical except for the strange marks on the walls. The only different passageway they saw was one on the left with bright lasers crisscrossing the center. "Don't go in there," Jupiter Girl said lightly.

"What's in there?"

She smiled. "Oh, just your basic terraforming equipment."

John slowed, studying the lasers. "Terraforming? You mean like the kind of stuff we could use to make Mars a planet habitable for people from Earth?"

"Exactly. Or make Earth habitable for Jovians." Her feet lifted off the ground and she floated backwards, not bothering to look where she was headed as she led him deeper into her home. "You and Lightning Cat should stay where I leave you. We've retrofitted certain parts of our home to be suitable for Earthers, but there are areas that could be dangerous or even fatal for your kind."

"My kind? Are you, um, don't take this the wrong way, but are you an alien?"

Jupiter Girl laughed so hard she couldn't keep herself in the air. She landed and put her hand against the wall, trying to hold herself up. "What gave it away? The name 'Jupiter Girl'?" She patted him on the back. "Right this way, John." They walked into a room that looked a lot like a formal bedroom from the 1800s. There was a high bed, gigantic pieces of furniture against the walls and a high-backed chair with an ottoman. A painting of men on horses chasing a fox was on one wall. "You can lay her there."

John set Lightning Cat down on the bed, which seemed to sigh as it received her. John jumped back, surprised. The blankets pulled themselves down and covered her, and she sunk deep into the bed. A curtain pulled shut around the sides. "What is going on?"

"Sorry, this room is a little old fashioned. It doesn't think a young man should be in a lady's bedroom. And it certainly doesn't think you should be watching her while she's sleeping."

"Watching her? I was carrying her and --."

"You don't need to explain yourself, John, this room never listens." She tugged him by the arm and they crossed the hallway to a second room. It had the look of a 1950s hotel room. Two beds, an old television set and an ashtray, with accompanying burn marks on the side table. "Just set your clothes on the bed when you shower. I've given the room instructions on what to do with them."

As she walked out the door, John grabbed her arm and said, "Listen, Jupiter Girl. I didn't assume you were from outer space because... you know, my name is Black Vulture but that doesn't mean I'm a bird."

"I understand, John." She crossed her arms across her stomach, watching him carefully.

"And I... well, I hope I didn't say anything that was offensive to, um, Jovians earlier."

"You mean, things like saying my Jovian form is terrifying and ugly?"

He blushed and looked away from her. "Thanks for the place to clean up. And for saving us from the Muck and the wolves and, well, everything."

She put her hand on his face and turned him back toward her, until his eyes met hers. "Among my people I am called Byon'g ana K'reth, from the second pairing." She kissed him on the cheek. Her lips were warm, soft and decidedly human-feeling. "And now you know my secret identity."

"Byong," he said, softly.

She giggled, shaking her head, her hair falling over her face. "Byon'g, not Byong. And that's my family name. The name I share with my family. My familiar name, like your John, is K'reth."

"K'reth," he said experimentally.

She stepped back into the hallway. "Or you may call me Joop, as many who are close to me do."

"No. I'll learn to say it correctly. Byon'g ana K'reth, from the second pairing."

She smiled, but this time her lips did not turn as high as in times past, and tears pushed into her eyes. "It has been a long time since anyone other than my father said my name. Thank you, John Ajax." She wiped at her eyes with the heel of her hand. "Take a shower, you smell like the Muck." She shut the door.

John tentatively touched the bed, but the blankets stayed put. He kicked his shoes and socks off, and threw his mask on the bed. He stripped out of his cape, his jeans and his shirt and tossed them on top of the mask.

The bathroom did not look like something from the 1950s. It was a large, round, seamless room. "How am I supposed to shower?" John asked, and suddenly a show-erhead the size of a street lamp protruded from the wall, hot water shooting from it. A pedestal came out of the floor with soap on it, and John stood for a long time in the steam and water. When he was finished, the water turned off without a word from him, and hot air came from the walls, blowing him dry. John felt awkward without a tow-el, and peeked around the corner into his room. There was no one there, so he stepped up to the bed, looking for his clothes.

What he found amazed him. His cape looked large-ly the same. The mask was like a helmet or visor that curved down over his face like a bird's beak. There were grey pants, definitely not his jeans, and when he pulled them on they fit perfectly. He pulled on a grey shirt with the blood red logo of the Black Vulture, and it somehow connected to the pants as if there were magnets in them. It looked like one piece of cloth. He pulled on black gloves that went to the middle of his forearm. He could feel per-fectly with his fingertips still, it didn't feel like he had on gloves at all. A pair of boots with metal greaves on the top fit his feet and rose to just below his knees. He swung his cape on, and it hung heavy and low, like ragged wings behind him.

There was a knock at his door, probably Jupiter Girl come to see how he liked his new costume. Before he touched the doorknob, the door swung open. On the other side was a girl in a towel, her hair wet and slicked back from her face.

"Joop," she said, "I need a costume that –"

John didn't know what to say. He cleared his throat.

The girl looked up and shrieked. "Eeek! You're not Joop!"

"Katherine?"

"Ohmygosh," she shouted and ran across the hall, sparks flying out of her dark hair. The door opened like arms for an embrace and slammed shut behind her. They didn't open when John knocked.

"I can't believe this," he said. "Jupiter Girl is an actual alien. From Jupiter. And Lightning Cat is Katherine. Who gave me an electric shock every time I touched her on the Flying Donut." He smacked his hand against his forehead. "Katherine. 'Kat.' I am the biggest idiot." Then he thought of the tunnel earlier, and how he had told Lightning Cat that Katherine wasn't someone she needed to worry about that. That she was nice and everything but he hadn't even bothered to call her when he got her number.

He fell onto the bed and covered his face with his hands. "Oh please, let me get captured by a super villain or arrest my grandpa or fight a giant robot. I can't take this anymore." He punched the pillow. "Idiot."

When he finally got the guts to go back into the hallway, Katherine wasn't answering her door. John didn't want to hang out in his hotel room anymore. The embarrassment of insulting Lightning Cat/Katherine burned in his cheeks. He wanted to think about something else, anything else.

For instance, his new friend Pronto, kidnapped by the Game Master's soldiers. Gecko was with him, though hopefully not in a cell or captured. It was time to get Jupiter Girl and head back to the retirement home, to see if they could shake some information out of the old man. He knocked one more time on Lightning Cat's door. The careful silence on the other side told John all he needed to know.

He trotted down the hallway, unsure where to look for Jupiter Girl. From what she had said there were sections of her house he didn't want to wander into. He hoped they all had lasers barring the way, like the terraforming area. As he moved farther along, the hallways started to change. At one intersection there was a hallway that looked identical to the one he was in except for the fact that it was thirty times larger. Branching tunnels barely big enough for a mouse went in other directions and at least once there was a hallway that went straight up with no handholds or obvious way to access it. Jupiter Girl could fly, of course, so that made sense.

Voices came from down the hall. John trotted toward them and came to a wide, terraced stairway. He walked up, not trying particularly hard to be quiet, but as he got closer to the voices he realized they were both male. Not wanting to surprise whoever else might call this place home, John slowed until he heard one of the voices say with surprising clarity, "doomsday device." John crouched down and moved carefully into hearing range. A large screen faced him, easily two stories tall. A silhouette of a man's head filled the entire screen. In front of the screen, his back toward John, was a gigantic version of the creature that Jupiter Girl had shape shifted into: dusty red, six heavily muscled limbs, a reptilian slab of a head on a long neck, and a tail as thick as John's chest twitching lazily on the floor behind it. He wasn't sure exactly how tall it was, because it was sitting on a long, white bench, but he suspected it would have to crouch to walk into his parents' house.

The man on the screen said, "—regardless, they have the force field generator now. You know what kind of power that is in the wrong hands."

The lizard thing nodded. "Of course. It's our technology. With a little creativity it could be used to destroy any number of things."

"And our enemy has never lacked for creativity. Worse, the truce is in tatters. We won't be able to rebuild it after this."

The lizard's tongue licked the air. "No. But the spirit of the agreement was broken long before today. We should be grateful it lasted this long. Hatchlings could grow to maturity in the space of time we've provided."

"And they have. Or mostly so. I fear the children will fail. Or, that they will succeed by praying too great a price."

"Is there too great a price? Would you have hesitated to pay when you were young?"

The shadow sighed. "We both know the answer to that, old friend. I did not hesitate. But that does not mean I am without regrets. I would save these children from that pain. Perhaps we should intervene."

The lizard lifted a hand with thick, sharp claws. "But if they cannot defeat this enemy, what of the ones to come? You know the Golden Dragon is preparing something. I can feel it in my bones."

"Perhaps Caesar could be convinced to intervene, when the time comes."

"Such is not his way, not any more. You know this better than most."

"He is still intervening for us, King Jupiter."

The creature bowed its head. "So you have said. And I, for one, trust your insights on this matter." He paused, and his tongue flickered out again. "Do you smell that?"

A cool hand covered John's mouth and yanked him backward. Jupiter Girl whispered in his ear, "His hearing is not good in this form, and his eyesight is terrible. Come with me, quickly." She removed her hand and John fell in step beside her. "You shouldn't be wandering in my house. It's dangerous." Her feet lifted from the ground, and her clothing changed as she moved along next to him, morphing from her retirement home uniform into a white, tight fitting top and a white skirt, with a rotating image of Jupiter on her chest. A white cape with red lining fluttered behind her, and the red of her hair glittered and seemed to compliment the Jovian planet on her uniform. John couldn't take his eyes off the rotating planet. He had never seen something like that, like a moving cartoon on someone's clothing. Jupiter Girl noticed, and the planet disappeared, replaced by a complex golden symbol.

When John looked up at her again she said, "Besides, he might try to stop us if he heard what we're doing next."

John hurried to keep up with her as she glided down the hallway. "What are we doing next?"

She smiled at him. "Your new costume looks dashing."

"Thanks. Yours looks amazing, too. Thank you for making mine."

"It was your room who did it, you should thank her."

"I, uh, I don't know what to say to that. What is it we're doing next that your father would want to stop us?"

"We're going to burn Sunnybrook to the ground unless Game Master tells us where Pronto is. And then we're going to destroy that doomsday device."

"Right." John punched his fist into his palm. "Let's do this. Just the two of us?"

Lightning Cat slipped out into the hall in front of them. Her new costume was black, but a thin, almost unnoticeable trace of blue lightning patterns ran through the fabric. Blue lightning patterns were on her legs and forearms. She smiled, and her even, white teeth made flashed at John. "Trying to ditch me, Vulture?" Her lips went into a pout. "You could at least call me to let me know you're about to save the world, couldn't you? I mean, you do have my number, right?"

"I wish I was the one kidnapped by the soldiers," he said miserably.

Lightning Cat put her arm through his. "So you'd rather be with villains than with us, John, is that what you're saying?"

Jupiter Girl put her arm through his other arm. "This should be fun."

CHAPTER 14

AN EXPLOSIVE ENCOUNTER

Jupiter Girl had security clearance and it didn't take her long to get John and Lightning Cat onto the grounds of the Sunnydale Retirement home, even in costume. The security detail wasn't pleased about letting masked kids onto the lot, but then again they were with the boss's daughter, so who were they to say no? Jupiter Girl moved so fast down the hallways that John and Lightning Cat had to trot to keep up. Lightning Cat's electricity was building up, but her new costume retained it better.

The door to Game Master's room was open, and on the screen was a game John knew well: Omega Point. The old man sat up in his bed, a controller on his lap, and he was smiling as the plucky little space hero of Omega Point piloted his ship toward the enemies. He turned his head slowly as they entered, keeping his eyes partially on the game. "Hello, John," he said.

"Where's Pronto?" John asked.

The old man leaned back against his bed. "I have to keep playing the game, John. I always keep playing the game. You know Omega Point?"

"Where's Pronto?"

"It's a wonderful game, really. The enemy -- who is never named -- is trying to collapse his solar system. He wants to use the computational power of the entire universe to create an island in time. This island -- called the Omega Point -- gives him access to all the energy of creation, and the power to do whatever he wishes. Resurrect the dead! Control time lines! Snuff out life with a gesture!"

"I know the game, Game Master. You don't have to explain it to me. I want to know where my friend is, and I want to know about the doomsday device. Jupiter Girl, can you use your telepathic whammy on him?"

Game Master stared at his screen. "It's a funny game, Omega Point, because the villain is trying to make himself God. The hero, he's trying to prevent the enemy from gaining these god-like powers. But they both the miss the fact that the villain can only be successful if the omega point already exists... without the cosmology of the omega point the villain cannot be successful. And if the omega point is pre-existent, then God (or something very like God) already exists. Which means either that the villain has already succeeded (and become God) or that he has already lost (for God already exists). It's a philosophical conundrum."

Jupiter Girl moved between him and the screen and caught his eye. She stared deep into his eyes, concentrating hard. Game Master looked right through her, still playing his game. "My mind lock isn't working." She rubbed her temples. "He must be shielded somehow."

Game Master snickered. "Your problem, John, is that you think this so-called 'doomsday device' is the end game when it's just the opening moves. You're worried about Capeville instead of the planet, or the solar system, or the universe." He pointed two fingers in the general direction of John's face and jabbed them at him. "I hope you make it, John. I really do."

Lightning Cat squeezed past John and said, "If he says one more word about this game I'm going to electrocute him."

"Wait," John said. "Game Master, you must have thought it was pretty funny when you gave me and Pronto Tread Battalion 3, knowing that we were going to steal for you, right?"

"You think you're playing Tread Battalion but you're in a game of Omega Point."

"That's it," Lightning Cat said, and sparks came off her fingers.

"No!" John said. "Something isn't right." He got down on his hands and knees, scanning the floor. There were several strange things on the floor... some of the Game Master's medications, a few paper cups, a pair of handcuffs that must have belonged to one of the guards, but not what he was looking for. He found it near the entrance to the room... a small electronic eye, like the one on a garage door. He waved his hand in front of it. The Game Master leaned back in his bed.

"Hello, John," he said. "I have to keep playing the game, John. I always keep playing the game."

John waved his hand in front of the electronic eye again, and Game Master said, "Hello, John. I have to keep playing the –" Jupiter Girl grabbed Game Master by the head and yanked. It came off in her hands, a shower of sparks and wires following its neck. "Another robot."

"We should have known he wouldn't wait around once we were on to him."

"He'd have to be crazy to do that," said another voice, this one coming from the hallway. They spun around, and Chester the Jester stepped in, dressed in a tailored tuxedo with a ruffled shirt, tiny spectacles perched on his nose, and spinning a walking cane in one hand. "Nice duds," he said, and picked a bit of lint off of John's shoulder. John flinched when he felt the maniac's hand on him.

Jupiter Girl appeared behind Chester, moving so fast John barely saw it. Chester was trapped in the room with them. "Where is Pronto?"

"Safe," he said, and then started to giggle. "Wouldn't that be funny if I had actually stuffed him into a safe? Oh well, next time. I need to plan these things ahead." He frowned. "Do you get the joke? I would put him in a safe, and then say that he was 'safe' when you asked."

"It's not funny," John said. "Tell us where our friend is or we're going to make you."

Chester looked at him over his spectacles. "Oh, my little hatchling. One day you'll grow up to be a nice big vulture but today you're still a wee little chick." Chester spun around. "So where is he? The big bird himself?" He raised his hand in the air and wiggled his fingers. "Oh, Black Vuuuultuure, over here."

Lightning Cat stepped up behind him and electricity arced out of her hands and into his body. Chester convulsed and fell to the ground, twitching. John shoved the Game Master robot off the bed, and it fell to the ground with a heavy thump. They lifted Chester onto the bed. His eyelids flickered and he said, "I felt a spark between us, darling."

Jupiter Girl pushed Chester back and tried to connect with his mind. "It's there," she said, "But the pathways are intertwined, I can't follow them to the right information."

Chester flopped his chin toward Jupiter Girl. "Do you think you could use your fancy brain-reading powers and find something that's gone missing in my mind? I'm trying to remember what you call a baby vulture. A goose is a gosling, a chicken is a chick, a duck is a duckling. What's a baby vulture? A vultling? I can't remember."

John pushed him back against the bed. "Where's Pronto?"

Chester smiled, and his lips stretched farther than John would have thought possible, revealing yellow teeth that were sharper than they should be. His eyes were small and black, but they twinkled with merriment. "I remember."

"Where Pronto is?"

"No. I remember what you call a baby vulture." He threw his head back and laughed, hitting his hand against his thigh. He stopped and leaned toward John and whispered, "A baby vulture is called John Ajax."

John flexed his hand in his glove, debating what to do. Chester had known his name earlier, and now he knew his secret identity. He could deny it, of course, but something told him the time for such deceptions had long since passed. He stood up straight and looked down on the thin stick of a man. "I'm the Black Vulture. That's all you need to know, Chester."

Chester laughed, covering his eyes with one hand and trying to wave John away with the other, tears falling down his cheeks. "It's too cute, it's too funny, watching you try to fill his boots. Precious little hatchling." He grinned. "But beggars can't be choosers. We'll pick up where we left off."

"That's it," Lightning Cat said, and she grabbed Chester, lightning flashing off her arms. Chester laughed hysterically and grabbed Lightning Cat's forearms. Electricity arced backwards, shooting back into Lightning Cat. She screamed and collapsed to the ground, then flickered and went dark. John jumped to her side and felt her throat. Her pulse tapped weakly under her smooth skin.

"Amateurs," Chester said disdainfully. He tossed a small device onto the bed. It landed between his knees. "Have you seen one of these before?"

Jupiter Girl picked it up and turned it over in her hands. "It's a neutralizer, but the safety circuit has been removed."

"Yes, yes, very good." He rolled his eyes. "You always have to be head of the class. A+." He twirled his finger in the air. "Yawn."

John took the neutralizer. A black scorch mark scarred the lower half of the device. "What does that mean?"

Jupiter Girl said, "It's something Dr. Dynamo invented ten years ago. At close range it can turn off a cape's powers. He wanted to use it to reintroduce capes to the rest of society. Caesar bought the patents and destroyed the devices."

Chester stood up from the bed and nudged Lightning Cat with his toe. John pushed his foot away, and Chester smiled indulgently. "Violating those patents has been keeping me up at night, wracked with guilt. And you can imagine my disappointment when I discovered that removing the safety mechanism causes a cape's powers to backfire. It burns the neutralizer out, of course. And the cape." He pulled another one out of his pocket. "I have a pocketful of these, Jupiter Girl, so your powers won't work on me." He closed his eyes and steepled his fingers in front of his lips. "And now we can discuss why we're all here."

Lightning Cat moaned and opened her eyes. John stroked her forehead through her mask, and she looked up at him and put her hand on his before sitting up.

Chester tilted his head to Lightning Cat, as if he was politely acknowledging her on the street.

"What do you want?" John asked.

"Let's review," Chester said, smiling. "I have your friend locked away somewhere safe, though not in a safe (sadly). I know your not-so-secret identity. The Game Master has played you precisely as we planned.

Our doomsday device is poised to destroy Capeville, the force field generator all set to do what it's set to do." He leaned back in the bed. "Who's to say I want anything but to gloat?" John pulled his fist up, but Chester pulled out a small black transmitter with a red button. "Ah-ah, my little egg. If I press this button something will blow up."

Jupiter Girl snatched it from his hand so fast that John barely saw it. Chester looked at her with genuine surprise. Chester pulled out a neutralizer and pointed it at her, pressing the button on it. She grinned at him, and as her smile stretched out to the corners of her mouth, her mouth widened and turned a dusty red. Her teeth stretched larger and extra arms sprouted out of her side while a long tail with spikes on it grew and spooled itself out on the floor. "Dr. Dynamo's neutralizers have never worked particularly well on me."

"Good to know," Chester said, and he dropped the neutralizer and put his wrists out. John picked up the handcuffs from the floor and slapped them on him. Jupiter Girl leered at him with her gigantic alien mouth. "My what big teeth you have, grandmother," Chester said, and snickered to himself.

"I guess we'll call your dad to come pick him up?"

Jupiter Girl nodded. "Dad's a better telepath than I am, maybe he can make sense of all the strange connections in there." She morphed back to her human form and helped Lightning Cat off the floor. John grabbed her other arm. "Are you okay?"

Lightning Cat rubbed the back of her head. "I think so. I hope Pronto is okay."

Chester stifled a laugh and dropped his head to his chest. "My feelings are hurt, honestly, John. It's like the original Black Vulture didn't tell you anything about me."

"He's dead," John said. "He died when I was a baby."

"Yes, yes, in an explosion on the Kane Bridge. I know the whole story. I was there, you know. I had packed bombs all along the bottom of the bridge." Chester paused and smiled at them. "Much like I did in this facility."

As soon as Chester said "in this facility," Jupiter Girl moved into the hallway and began barking orders into an intercom.

John narrowed his eyes. "But we took away the detonator."

Chester shrugged. "What if I put them on a timer?"

John grabbed him by the shirt. "Did you?"

Jupiter Girl sped in. "Lightning Cat, I need your help with evacuation. Black Vulture, can you get that maniac outside?"

"Of course."

Lightning Cat and Jupiter Girl ran out of the room, and John listened to their footsteps down the hall. Alarms were going off, and red lights flashing. Chester looked relaxed. He put his handcuffed hands behind his head. He sighed. "It's not a very restful place anymore. These alerts are going off all the time."

John yanked him to his feet. "Guess what?" He pushed him forward, into the hall. "You better get used to it, because those sirens might be the last thing you ever hear."

"Ha ha ha. Your tough guy talk needs some work, but I appreciate the effort."

"Come on," John said. The emergency evacuation flowed around them like a burst of water from a dam. John pushed them against the current and toward the maximum security section. The doors stood wide open. The maximum security area looked like it had been evacuated earlier in the day, probably during the search for Chester.

Chester laughed nervously. "Where are we going, my featherless friend?"

"To your old room, Chester. I'm sure that's where you set the explosives."

"Oh, very good, little man. Clever of you. I do like the little touches." Chester grinned back at him. "Aren't you supposed to take me outside?"

John grunted. "Parts of you will make it outside without any help from me."

Chester laughed at that one. "Is it something about that costume? You're just like him. The original. A baby version, of course, that goes without saying."

They turned the corner and John kicked the door until it opened. The room was stacked to the ceiling with explosives. There was scarcely room to walk inside, but John shoved Chester in anyway. To see that many explosives packed into the retirement home was amazing. John stood for a moment in awe, wondering how Chester had managed to pull this off. The chairs, the table, everything was covered in explosives. John wouldn't have known there was a chair in the room if he hadn't been in there earlier. Sitting on one pile of C4 the size of a crate was a laptop computer, with wires running out of it and into the explosives. John snapped out of it and said, "As soon as you tell me where Pronto is, I'll take you outside."

"Fair enough," Chester said. "In fact, I'll even give him back to you... for a price."

"I don't make deals with kidnappers, criminals or insane people."

"Hee hee. Well, if you change your mind later, here's what I need. There's a stone called the Broadcaster. It's about half the size of a football. You get me the Broadcaster, I get you your friends."

John noticed that he said "friends" instead of "friend." So they had caught the Gecko, too. He ignored it, just in case Chester was bluffing, trying to get him to reveal something.

"What does it do, this Broadcaster?"

"It increases super powers. Doubles them. Triples them. Makes fast capes faster, makes strong capes stronger. And it's being held in the secret headquarters of the Regulars, the original super team. I need you to steal it and bring it to me." The Jester was doing his best not to burst out laughing. "The look on your face... priceless!"

"Pronto would rather die than let you kill innocent people. I'm not giving you anything."

Chester rolled his eyes. "It's not like my entire plan hinges on a fourteen year old. I do have a spy, you know. An associate who works for the Regulars. A teammate. I can always have my spy steal the Broadcaster if you refuse. Hee hee hee."

The computer on the stack of explosives flickered and the screen turned white. John grabbed Chester by the arm. "What's happening?"

"I don't know, that wasn't part of the plan." He laughed nervously. "It should be on a timer, but it doesn't look like it was wired up the way I instructed."

"Good help is hard to find," John said.

The screen flashed, went dark and then a live stream of the Gecko and Pronto flashed on. They were both chained into chairs. The Gecko's mask was still on, but he looked furious. Pronto looked weak and maybe nauseous, but he perked up. "Gecko, the light just came on the camera!"

"Guys, can you see me? It's the Black Vulture."

The Gecko immediately started talking, "We're about sixty miles southwest from the retirement home we discussed. Get G3 on the horn and tell him to send reinforcements. They have a whole army here, BV."

John leaned in close, "G3 is out of commission. I haven't heard from him since the force field was stolen." He didn't add that he and Pronto had infected G3 with the Tread Battalion virus.

The camera twisted and the smiling face of the Game Master filled the screen. "Hello, John. Would you like to play a gaaaaame?"

Chester spat at the computer. "You fool! I told you, no games. You're messing with the plan."

Game Master cracked his knuckles. "Sometimes the rules aren't interesting, Chester. You have to change them, try something different to see if you can make it more fun."

"No, no, no, this is my game, you play it my way!"

Game Master's face filled the whole screen. "You're handcuffed to a fourteen year old boy. I'm calling the shots for now."

Chester frowned. "I'm not handcuffed *to* him, Game Master. I was handcuffed *by* him."

Game Master straightened and walked between his two captives. "Nevertheless. Here's the new game, Black Vulture. I didn't set a timer on those explosives stacked all around you. Not yet, anyway. However, when you press the Control button on the computer in front of you, it will release Pronto, the speedster. His chains will fall off. But, the control button also starts the timer for the explosives. Three minutes."

Chester choked. "Three minutes? We'll barely be up the stairwell in that amount of time. You're killing us."

John scowled at the Game Master. "What if I don't press the button and I come over there and take my friends away from you instead?"

"That's all part of the game, isn't it? I can choose when to explode that retirement home, you can choose whether to control the timing or not. Pronto will have three minutes to make the sixty mile jog to you." Game Master snickered. "Oh, and I forgot. This chamber your friends are in? It will be filling with water." He walked toward the door. "They should survive if you press the button early enough."

"Don't press the button," Pronto said, " I can't get to you in three minutes."

"Don't forget all the people at Sunnybrook," the Gecko said. "They're criminals, but some of them have served their time. They don't deserve to die."

John smiled at Gecko's constant concern for others. "Don't worry, Gecko, Lightning Cat and Jupiter Girl are evacuating the building."

A crackling came from the intercom. Jupiter Girl's voice came to him, tinny but clear, "This building should be completely evacuated. All patients have been removed to a safe distance. Black Vulture, if you're in there, let us know. You're not out here at the rendezvous point."

John put his hand on the computer screen. "Pronto, listen to me. I'm going to press the button. When I do, haul Gecko somewhere safe, and then run here as fast as you can to get me out."

"And me," said Chester. "I've always loved the Thunder family. I've never killed any of them."

"I can't run that fast, Vulture. I'd have to break the sound barrier and I've never done that. I haven't even done my stretches."

The Gecko said, "Hey, Chester is sneaking out the door behind you."

John twirled to see a sour-faced Chester. "You dirty Gecko! I hate lizards. Or amphibians. Whatever you are!"

John jumped across the room, but Chester had already passed the doorway. He shook his wrists and the handcuffs fell to the ground and clattered into the room. The door slammed shut, followed by the sound of heavy locks snapping into place. John slammed against the door.

Chester's muffled voice came to him from outside. "Enjoy my hospitality, John. I'm sure you'll have a blast! Ha ha ha!"

John slammed his shoulder into the door again and again, but it didn't move. Pronto shouted to him from the computer. On the screen, John could see the water up to their chests. The Gecko thrashed in the water, trying to break his chains. "Hold on, I'll press the button!"

Both of the prisoners shouted at him not to do it. "We'll find another way," the Gecko said.

Pronto said, "Joop must be looking for you by now, let's wait and see if she gets to you first."

"Guys, listen. Chester is getting away. This isn't about me or you, it's about the doomsday device. If we don't stop him, he's going to destroy the whole town, including all three of us." He looked back at the thick metal door. "If I press it now, the explosion should catch him, too."

"No," Pronto said. "No, that's not the way this is supposed to play out, John. You can't sacrifice yourself for Capeville, not like that."

"I have to, Pronto. I don't know how my grandfather is all wrapped up in this, but he is. I'm responsible. I have to do what I can to protect the rest of the city. It's what my parents would do."

Pronto and the Gecko exchanged glances. The Gecko nodded solemnly. "You're right. It's what we have to do. I would trade places with you if I could, John."

John touched the screen. "I know that. Thanks, man." He cleared his throat.

Pronto shook his head. "I'll make it, John. Somehow I'll do it. Sixty miles, three minutes. I've never run that fast. I'll have to break the sound barrier but I'm going to do it, John, I promise."

The water lapped at their necks now. "Don't worry, Pronto, I'm sure Jupiter Girl will burst in here any second." They all sat silently. John could tell they were watching the door behind him, willing it to burst open. John put his finger on the Control button.

"John, if things don't work out... do you want us to tell your parents anything?"

John frowned. "Yeah. Tell them I can't believe they never told me they were super heroes. Tell them I can't believe they hid all this from me."

Pronto said, "John, you don't want to --"

He pressed the button. "Pronto, go!"

"John...."

"Two minutes and fifty-eight seconds!"

A water spout swirled up, there was a blur and all that was left on the video was troubled water, spinning helplessly in the chamber. John tried the door again, but it stood as strong as before. A quick look around the room showed nothing on the other side of the explosives. No window, of course, not in a room that was meant as a prison. Two minutes and twenty seconds. He kicked open an empty closet. It wouldn't be much protection. He flung open the bathroom door. No explosives, but not much help either. He pushed the closet door halfway open and popped the pins out. One minute, thirty seconds. He lifted the door, took it in the bathroom and laid it across the top of the bathtub. It didn't fit perfectly, but again, better than nothing. Should he wait for Pronto? Stand at the front door? No. Even if Pronto got this close, John hoped he wouldn't try to come down here. There's no way they'd make it out together. Forty-five seconds. He waited by the door and counted the seconds. He closed the bathroom door, standing outside it. There was still a chance. "G3, if you can hear me, this would be a great time to teleport me out of here." John counted to ten. Twenty seconds to go. He crawled into the bathtub. It took him a second, but he got the closet door arranged over him.

Eight seconds.

Seven.

Six.

He heard a booming sound somewhere above him. Another set of explosives? Pronto breaking the sound barrier? He didn't know.

Four.

Three.

John said a quick prayer.

Two.

One.

A blinding white light filled the room before there was even a bit of heat and he didn't hear an explosion at all, just saw the closet door flip away and a burning white light reaching for him, a light that looked almost like a man. John squeezed his eyes shut and waited for the end.

CAPEVILLE: THE DEATH OF THE BLACK VULTURE

CHAPTER 15

THE END

John never heard an explosion. His chest hurt, like all the air had been crushed out of him. He pushed on his eyes with his fingers, rubbed them and opened them, slowly. He was on a white leather couch, with a blue, red and green handmade blanket laid over him. His mask and cape sat draped on a white plastic chair, and his boots slouched on the polished marble floor.

John paced to the end of the room, about the size of a football field. A long bank of rounded windows, thin and tall like in a cathedral, lined the far end. Outside, streaks of whitish blue stabbed toward the windows, and a faint blue light tinted a black void. The icy cold glass sang like a tuning fork when he touched it.

A voice behind him said, "That's the blue shift." A tall man with a wide chest and shoulders and a full head of dark hair stepped up beside him. He wore round glasses, slacks and a loosely buttoned dress shirt, the sleeves rolled to his forearms. His hair kept slipping down into his eyes. He had a square jaw and sparking blue eyes. "It's the universe running toward this place."

John didn't ask him if he meant heaven. He knew he wasn't dead. He figured his eyes and chest wouldn't hurt if he was dead. "I thought the universe was expanding. Moving away from us."

"Away from Earth, yes. But it has to move toward something, doesn't it?"

"I... I don't think so. I never heard that."

The man laughed. "I call this place the *Theatrum Pompeium*. It's a little private joke."

"I don't get it."

"I wouldn't expect you to. Maybe after sophomore English class."

John put his hand on the glass again. "You're Caesar, aren't you?"

He had perfect white teeth. "Of course. And you're John Ajax."

"Yeah. I'm the worst with my secret identity. Everyone knows it."

"Some of us only have one identity, John. I'm one of those people. Maybe you are, too."

"I guess. I might not have a choice. I'll probably be getting mail for the Black Vulture at my grandfather's house."

"We only have about thirteen milliseconds, John, at least in objective time, so I'm going to walk you through things pretty quickly." He walked toward a corner of the room and beckoned John to join him. He pointed out a white ladder, almost invisible against the wall. "When you get to the top of the ladder, you'll be back in action again."

"What is this place?"

"I already told you what I call it."

"So, you burst into Sunnybrook and snatched me out before the explosion."

"That's close enough to the truth. I move at speeds fast enough that causal language gets a little confused."

John put a hand on a rung of the ladder. "What do you mean?"

Caesar put his hands in his pockets and floated up alongside the ladder. "Oh, I haven't saved you yet, that's all. It's related to that omega point cosmology stuff that Game Master was explaining, though he doesn't have the firmest grasp of it. We're at the tail end of the universe now, time wise, and there's enormous energy available if you know how to use it. In a few milliseconds I'll step out of the Theatrum and yank you in here. I'm talking to your mind now, getting you ready for the journey."

John looked down, about ten feet from the floor now. "So how long has this conversation taken?"

"Oh, it's instantaneous, John, and it happened a while ago. Maybe six milliseconds ago. Your mind is still processing the burst. You won't remember it all, but I'm trying to make sure the highlights stick."

John didn't get it, and he figured talking about it over and over wouldn't help, so he asked another question. "Why don't you just use your weird powers and stop the doomsday device? You're the greatest hero ever, why don't you step in and save us? Why are you letting Chester do whatever he wants?"

Caesar crossed his arms and stroked his smooth chin with one hand. "There are a lot of answers to your question, John, but I'll give you two. One, you don't need me."

"Yes we do! I'd be dead if you didn't snatch me out of the retirement home."

"Well, sure, this situation got a little out of your control, and losing you this early in the game isn't acceptable. So I did step in this once. But I won't next time, John. When you try to keep Chester from destroying Capeville, that will be on you and your friends. No super Caesar zipping in to save you."

"But why?"

Caesar held his palms up. "This might not make sense to you, but I have enough power here to do *anything*. I could stop every natural disaster. I could keep anyone from ever harming a child. I could keep all the super villains in check. Exercising that power would be as easy as yanking you out of the explosion. But how would you ever become a hero?"

"What?"

"If I do everything: stop every crime, right every wrong, fight every battle. If I do that, how will you learn to become like me?"

"You're saying that if you turned the world into paradise I would never be a super hero?"

Caesar laughed. "It's like parenting. If your children are old enough to take care of themselves but you keep doing it, you're preventing them from growing up."

John couldn't see the bottom of the ladder anymore. The ceiling was ahead. It looked like it was open to the void. A small black square dappled with blue shift was framed in the ceiling ahead of him. "What's the second reason?"

Caesar's eyes lost their sparkle, and his lips drooped at the edges. "The human race has to decide what you're going to allow each other to do. And you have to decide how to keep one another from crossing the lines you draw."

"I don't understand."

"Take Chester. He's killed a lot of people. But for some reason, your predecessor never killed him. The Black Vulture tried to stop him. Tried to protect people from him. Tried to keep him in jail, or an insane asylum. Once he marooned him in the prison dimension. But he never killed him. Why is that?"

John realized he had left his boots, mask and cape back on the ground. "Aw, man!"

"Don't worry about those. Keep climbing."

John went up another rung. The blue shift worried him. "I don't know why he never killed him. I guess the

Black Vulture had a moral code against killing or something."

"That could be. But why?"

"Because human life is precious?"

"It is, certainly. I think all people believe that, John. Even Chester believes that. He kills because he knows taking a life is the most precious theft he can accomplish. Chester deserves to die. He should be put down like a rabid dog. He should have been killed a long time ago."

John stopped on the ladder. "Then why didn't Black Vulture kill him? Why didn't you?"

Caesar floated closer to John. "There are two competing values here. One is justice. Justice demands Chester's death. Cries out for it. The man has countless deaths on his hands."

John looked at the blue shift in the void outside the ceiling. He shivered. "You're saying I should kill him? I... I'm not sure I could do that."

"If you knew everything he's done, John, and you had a gun to his head, I think it would be easy to pull the trigger. He is not a good man. He's a mass murderer, and he deserves a violent death." Caesar's brow furrowed. He looked troubled. "If his final words were *Ista quidem vis est* I would not lose a moment's sleep over it."

The square above them loomed, maybe ten feet from John's head. A strong wind howled across the top and John felt his breath being pulled from his body. He could smell smoke, acrid and thick. "What's happening?"

"Almost time to go, John. But here's the problem. The second value, the value competing with justice, is forgiveness. Forgiveness *requires* transgression. What I mean is, you have to hurt someone -- on purpose or accidentally -- to receive forgiveness. Another word is mercy. Sometimes, instead of justice, we choose to give someone mercy. We forgive their wrongdoing. Mercy means to give someone leniency, to not give them their full punishment or maybe no punishment at all."

The wind pummeled them from above. John yelled over the roaring sound, "You're saying the Black Vulture *forgave* Chester the Jester?"

"Yes."

"Why would he do that?"

"Your parents."

"What?"

"Your parents. They lied to you."

John tucked his chin to his chest. "Yes."

"And your grandfather... he's not the man I knew once. He's changed. He has not treated you with love, has he John?"

John snorted. "Love? No, I don't think I'd use that word."

"Sometimes, John, mercy is more powerful than justice. It's a decision the human race needs to make. Do you embrace justice or mercy? If you choose mercy, how long before you cry out for justice? And if you choose justice, how long until her sword turns on you and you beg for mercy?"

"I don't understand!"

"You can do this, John. The whole city depends on you." Caesar snatched John off the ladder and flew straight into the blue shift. All the air dropped out of John's lungs, and the Theatrum disappeared in a blink. The blue in the void shifted red and John found himself skidding along the ground, coughing and spinning through the dirt, coming to rest partway up a grassy hill. Smoke laced with fire roiled in the distance.

John sat up. The smell of smoke hung on him. He got to his feet and took a breath. He sat back down in the grass, head spinning, disoriented. Nothing but grass around him, and a little way from the bottom of the hill, a line of trees. A dark bundle burst out of the trees and rolled up the slope, coming to a stop beside him. He pulled it open. It was his boots and mask, wrapped in his cape. He pulled his boots on first, then his mask, and as he walked he threw his cape on, tied it in the front.

The walk back to what remained of Sunnybrook took about ten minutes. John tried to clear his head. The stars, where they weren't blocked out by smoke, shone like specks of sand in bright sunlight. By the time he got to the road there were emergency vehicles speeding down it, sirens blaring and lights painting the darkness blue and red. Prisoner transport buses were filled with residents from the retirement home, helicopters hovered overhead, spotlights picking out details in the woods. There was a half-hearted attempt at a security perimeter on the road, but John slipped into the shadows and around the barricade.

Lightning Cat sat on the edge of an ambulance, head bowed. John sat down beside her, bone weary. "Hi, Cat."

Her head popped up and her eyes flew wide and she jumped on him so fast he couldn't have stopped her if he tried. She squeezed him, hard, and sparks flew off her shoulders and into the night. A crab-like thing the size of a manhole scurried out of the darkness, taking on Jupiter Girl's shape as she came closer and also hugged John tight. "Where were you? Where's Chester?"

"I don't know how to answer that, exactly. Caesar pulled me out just before the explosion. I don't know about Chester. He locked me in the room. He might have had time to escape."

Jupiter Girl raised an eyebrow. "You saw Caesar?"

"Sure. Tall guy, square chin, glasses?"

"Hmmm. Sometimes." Jupiter Girl looked at him strangely. "There's more to you than I thought, John Ajax."

A tremendous commotion came from the perimeter, guards shouting and things flying through the air as Pronto burst past them. He stumbled to the ground and Jupiter Girl caught him. His eyes flew from Joop to Cat to John and he collapsed into Joop's arms, completely exhausted. "Joop. You got him out." He let out a deep breath and relaxed completely. "Good work, team."

John punched him in the arm. "Good run, Pronto."

"Was that three minutes?"

"More like thirteen. Not bad. Where's the Gecko?"

Pronto rolled his eyes. "Where do you think? Off doing something heroic. He's tailing Game Master and his people." He leaned his head on Jupiter Girl's shoulder, and looked up into her eyes. "You know how he likes to stick to things. He's plastered all over the bottom of some airplane or something right now I bet."

Jupiter Girl shook her shoulder, trying to get Pronto off of her. "Good run, Pronto. Time for you to stand up now."

A silly smile spread on his face. "I almost died today, and it made me think that I shouldn't put things off any more. Will you go on a date with me?"

She dropped him, and he almost hit the ground. "I'm too old for you, Pronto."

"What's a couple of years?" He stared at her carefully. "Do you have a boyfriend or something?"

"A fiancé," she said. "Or maybe a husband."

"Oh, har dee har har," Pronto said. "Just say no if you don't want to go out with me."

She sighed. "I did."

"Come on, you two," John said. "We have work to do."

"Oh yeah?" Lightning Cat said. "Sounds like you have a plan."

John cracked his knuckles. "I do. Chester let slip the last thing he needs for his doomsday device. So the four of us are going to head to the Vulture's Nest and try to get ahold of the Gecko, and then we're going to do something crazy."

Jupiter Girl put her hands on her hips. "What kind of crazy?"

John grinned. "We're going to break into the headquarters of the Regulars."

Pronto's jaw dropped open so far it almost hit him in the knees. Jupiter Girl's eyebrows furiously expressed her displeasure and Lightning Cat laughed, sparks shooting from her hands while she clapped. "The greatest super hero team in the world? We're going to sneak into their headquarters?"

"Well, they are disbanded," John said reasonably. "And we're just going to, uh, borrow something."

"Wait!" Pronto said. "The Regulars and all the other super teams disbanded, right? Back when Rubicon went into effect?"

"Yeah."

"You know what that means?" He jumped into the air and did three laps around them. "It means *we're* the greatest super team in the world!"

"We are *not* a team," Jupiter Girl said.

"We just need a name now," Pronto said, ignoring her completely.

"Let's get moving," John said.

"Something like... PRONTO AND THE SLOW POKES!"

"I'm going to poke you in the eyes if you don't shut up," Jupiter Girl said.

"Pronto, the Slow Pokes and the Cranky Jovian," Pronto said. He was twenty feet away before she could take a swing at him.

John said, "Jupiter Girl. We need a car. We need to drive to my grandfather's house."

She glared at Pronto. "Of course."

Within five minutes, Jupiter Girl was driving a dark sedan down the road, Lightning Cat in the front seat beside her, John stretched out in the back, trying to rest. Pronto ran along outside. He came up next to the driver's side window. "How about 'The Roadrunners'?"

Jupiter Girl gritted her teeth. "I will hurt you, Pronto."

He shot off ahead of them and shouted "Meep meep!" over his shoulder. John grinned and closed his eyes and didn't open them again until they arrived at his grandfather's house.

CHAPTER 16

THE REGULARS

"You have to take your mask off," John said, staring Lightning Cat down. She glared at him, her face fierce and decidedly masked. "My grandfather hates capes. He'll freak if he thinks I'm bringing three heroes into the house." He looked down at his own smoke-infused costume. He tucked his mask and gloves into a pocket inside his cape.

"No. If he knows my dad and recognizes me it's going to be a huge mess. I'm not supposed to be out walking around. I'm supposed to stick in my wheelchair and not move."

"It could cause problems if he recognizes us," Jupiter Girl said. "In fact, your grandfather wrote about me and my dad in his book. I should probably change my face, too." Her hair turned black and her features and coloring changed to take on a more Asian appearance. Her costume quickly shifted into school clothes.

Pronto clapped his hands and jumped in place. "You're amazing. Now I could take you home and introduce you to my dad."

"I already know your dad, Pronto." She frowned at him. "And are you saying you couldn't date me unless I was Asian?"

"You're not even human," Pronto pointed out, amiably. "But I still want to be with you."

"Fine," John said. "Cat, stick in the car until I send you the signal, and then creep up to that window over there and I'll let you in to my room. You two, come with me." The walk up to his grandfather's house had never seemed so long, up the cement, through the perfect lawn and onto the porch. He tucked his helmet/mask under his arm. "He's not even home a lot of times." He used his key to open the door and they went inside. "Grandpa?"

"What is it, John?" He rolled in from the kitchen and stopped as soon as he saw them, a stony scowl on his face. "What are you wearing?"

"It's for work," John said quickly.

"And why would your work require you to dress like a law-breaking vigilante?"

Jupiter Girl jumped in. "Aversion therapy. We're trying to get the inmates and other guests not to fear the capes who fought them in their youth."

Grandpa's frown deepened and he squinted at Jupiter Girl. "He's dressed like the Black Vulture. So, you're saying my grandson was allowed into the maximum security wing and spoke to Chester the Jester? A fourteen year old boy with no powers?"

"No, Grandpa. The Black Vulture didn't just cause trouble for people in maximum security. He caused trouble for everyone. Purse thieves, people like that. Everyone is afraid of him."

Grandpa humphed. "And your name, girl?"

Jupiter Girl opened her mouth to speak, but Pronto quickly shouted, "She doesn't have one." Grandpa looked at him skeptically, "Uh, what I mean is, she doesn't have an English name and I don't think you could pronounce her Chinese name."

"Is that so? And what is her Chinese name, Pronto?"

"I can speak for myself," Jupiter Girl said.

"I'm asking Pronto," Grandfather said.

"It's, uh, Zhu Pi Ta," Pronto said, his eyebrows high, his shoulders hunched and his hands clasped in front of him, as if he was begging grandpa to believe him.

"Zhu Pi Ta, eh? A strange name." He inclined his head toward Jupiter Girl. "A pleasure to meet you, Miss Zhu." He pointed at John with a crooked, wrinkly finger. "You don't come into my house wearing a cape. Change into your street clothes or come home naked, I don't care, but I won't have the Black Vulture coming in and out through my front door."

"Right. Sorry, Grandpa." This was a new rule, but John figured he would keep his mouth shut. He had, after all, just come from the burnt out wreckage of his workplace. He wasn't sure if that counted as losing his job.

Grandpa wheeled backward toward the kitchen. "I won't be home tonight, John. Make yourself and your friends some dinner, and stay away from the Capeville Bridge. No matter what you see or hear on the news, stay close to home."

Pronto laughed. "Watch the news? What are we, seventy years old?"

John shot Pronto a dirty look. He gave his grandfather a contrite look. "Of course, Grandpa, whatever you say." Grandpa gave him a skeptical look, then wheeled away back into the kitchen. "Come on," John said, and led the other two to his bedroom.

"What's the secret message for Lightning Cat to let her know the coast is clear?" Pronto asked, looking out through the blinds.

John picked up his cell phone and set his thumbs to work. "I thought I'd send her a text." A moment later he pushed his window open and popped out the screen and with some pulling and grunting he and Pronto managed to yank her up into the room, where they all collapsed into a heap on the floor.

"Now what?"

"Now we go to the Vulture's Nest!" John said, and stuck his head around the corner. "Come on." John walked quickly through the house to make sure his grandfather was gone. Then he led his friends into his grandfather's room and popped open the closet door. Everyone gathered around to see an empty, regular looking closet.

"It seems a little low tech," Lightning Cat said.

John closed the door and opened it again, and again they all four stared at an empty closet. "It must be some sort of inter-dimensional disguise or something to keep my grandpa from seeing the elevator." He scratched his head. "Or it might be broken. My robot was dealing with a little virus."

Jupiter Girl narrowed her eyes. "You have a robot?"

"Sure."

"What kind of robot? What class and model?"

"I don't remember. G3 something."

Jupiter Girl grabbed John by the top of his cape. Her fingers were sharp and dug into his skin through the shirt. "You have a G class synthetic person in your secret hideout?"

"I -- uh -- yeah, I think I do."

"What's the problem?" Lightning Cat asked.

Jupiter Girl stood and stared out the window, not saying anything. "The G class was... discontinued. After the Martian War. Their operating systems were defective, and they had been re-programmed as planet killers. They wiped out more than one civilization and would have annihilated the people of Mars if not for Caesar and the Governor." She shivered. "If you have a G class synthetic person installed here on Earth, that's a greater threat than any doomsday device."

John shut the closet door and opened it again. The unilink elevator finally appeared. "Aha. Well, here's our ride. Joop, I don't think my robot is a planet killer or whatever, but you can meet him and I promise I'll listen to what you have to say."

Jupiter Girl put her head into the elevator. "You have a unilink teleporter? Your planet is not rated for this level of technology. This is illegal, John."

"So don't tell anyone, K'reth. It's not like I installed this, it was already here." He stepped in and Pronto zipped in after him.

"This thing is so cool," Pronto said. "I love it. My dad would never allow me to have my own elevator."

"It's more than an elevator. It's a inter-dimensional teleporter or something."

"We used to have one at our house but it doesn't work any more. I'm gonna put it on my Christmas list."

Lightning Cat squeezed in, pushing up against John. "Not much room in here."

Jupiter Girl squeezed in also. Pronto looked deliriously happy. She sighed and pulled the door shut. John pressed the button, there was a moment of jolting and a sensation of motion and the door opened at the Nest. Lightning Cat stepped out, followed by John and Pronto. Jupiter Girl stood on the unilink, her hands pressed against the empty air as if against a wall. "What are you doing?" John asked.

G3 rolled up, six slender arms extended, each glowing with a white-hot light. "Yikes!" Pronto shouted. "Should I bust him to pieces, Vulture?"

"No," John said. "G3, put those weapons away. I'm John Ajax. Do an identity scan or whatever."

"Apologies, Black Vulture. But should I grant access to the others?"

"Oh, yeah, sorry. This is Pronto from the Thunder family, and he's allowed to have access. You met him already, remember? We played video games. And this is Lightning Cat." He jerked his thumb toward the elevator. "That's Jupiter Girl."

G3's arms didn't retract. "I cannot allow a Jovian into this facility without certain promises."

John stepped between the robot and the Jovian. "What do you mean? She's my friend. Her dad used to be one of the Regulars. She's a hero. She and her dad are heroes."

"No doubt that is true among the humans. But among my kind the Jovians are regarded as butchers and race murderers."

Jupiter Girl snarled at that. "The G class transhumans killed more sentients than the Jovians have in their entire race history."

G3 rotated toward her, its gun arms all facing her. "If you are to enter the Vulture's Nest, it must be under the terms of the Sol Accords."

She slammed her fist into the invisible wall keeping her from exiting the unilink. "Those accords are not binding on the planet Earth! Their race doesn't meet the necessary requirements to enter into an agreement of equals with the other races in this solar system."

"Nevertheless, I will not allow you to exit the unilink --"

"A technology that cannot legally be used on this planet!"

"The unilink's core components are dimensionally shifted and in orbit around another planetoid. The setup is legal."

"Barely. It's a violation of the law's spirit if not the letter."

"Barely legal is still, by definition, legal, Jovian. Do you wish to enter the Nest or be returned to your place of origin?"

Jupiter Girl pushed her hands up against the invisible wall and glared at the robot. G3 said, "I am shielded against psionic attacks, Jovian."

"I'll enter," she said, her fists clenched at her side. "Under the terms of the Sol Accord. I solemnly swear it as a sentient citizen of Jupiter." She stumbled forward, the invisible barrier between her and the Nest suddenly gone.

"Welcome," said G3, and it put its gun arms away and glided deeper into the Nest.

Jupiter Girl put her mouth beside John's ear and said, "That thing needs to be destroyed. I'm under oath to do it no harm now, so the three of you will have to do it."

"I don't know what's going on," John said. "But G3 has done nothing but help me try to destroy the doomsday device. It does everything I request of it, and I'm not going to destroy it. I'm not even sure that I could."

"You're right," Jupiter Girl mumbled. "It would probably kill us all."

G3 led them into the main information center. All the screens were black. "The program you introduced to the system was primitive but virulent. I have isolated all systems until I can go through them with careful attention. I am deeply troubled that it jumped from a closed system into the greater operating systems."

John took a chair in front of one of the screens. "Can you bring anything up?"

"Only the files in my personal database."

"What do you know about something called the Broadcaster?"

G3 paused for a tenth of a second and Jupiter Girl hissed, "He's altering the data."

"Relax," Lightning Cat said. "You need to chill out, Jupiter Girl. Also... where's Pronto?"

"He is in the weapons hangar," G3 said calmly. "The Broadcaster is a level seven artifact from an advanced human civilization, brought back through time by the Chrononaut and his Time Skippers." An image appeared on the screen of a jolly man in what looked to be an ancient sailor's uniform, surrounded by a strange collection of cowboys, Roman soldiers, Victorian women and aliens. A series of rapid images fired across the screen, showing the Chrononaut in ridiculous costumes with a variety of time-lost traveling companions.

"Wait," John said. "Go back one."

"Very well," G3 said reluctantly, and put the image back up. The Chrononaut stood at the center wearing a Roman toga and a Yankees baseball hat, a laser pistol in his hand, and next to him stood a woman in tall 1960's boots and a short skirt, her perfectly coifed blond hair framing her determined face, a short sword in her hand.

"Is that... my mom?"

G3 hesitated. "That is Ms. Universe. She is displaced in time and had many adventures with the Chrononaut before settling in one era. She was present with the Chrononaut when he discovered this." A new image showed the Chrononaut with a stone in his hand, about half the size of a football and a similar oblong shape. It was yellow and translucent, like amber lit from inside. "According to the Chrononaut, the Broadcaster was invented by a despotic future ruler of the Pangaeic Coalition of the Western World from Earth 372-A6. The Chrononaut deemed the device too dangerous to leave within the Coalition's grasp, so he brought it into the past and entrusted it to Caesar, asking him to take it to the Theatrum. Caesar refused, instead giving the device to his colleagues in the Regulars."

"What does it do?" Lightning Cat asked.

"It vastly increases the powers of super-normal humans, allowing whomever controls the device to supercharge powers to their upper range. The Coalition had used this device to create an unbeatable army." G3 paused. "Correction. Unbeatable by forces within its own world. The Time Skippers dismantled them and removed the Broadcaster."

John steepled his fingers, his brow furrowed. "What does Chester want with it? He doesn't have any powers. Neither does the Game Master."

"Perhaps he has an army of capes," G3 suggested.

"Hmm," John said. "Maybe. He does have Hydra working for him." John tapped his fingers against a computer screen. "It's a little straightforward for Chester. He'd want some irony of some sort. A joke."

Lightning Cat said, "Maybe he's going to use those devices he used on me, the power dampeners. With the overrides turned off, it could send everyone's powers out of control."

John's eyes widened. "That makes sense. He could super-charge the entire city and then, when they're full of energy, cause their powers to go out of control. The capes would destroy the entire city. That has to be it."

Pronto appeared among them, a gigantic energy rifle he could barely lift in one hand, a helmet loosely on his head and reams of ammo hanging around his chest, another pistol holstered to his leg. "Chester has an army. Gecko and I saw them on our way into their HQ. But by the time we got out of that chamber, Game Master had either moved them along somewhere or hidden them. Mostly, anyway. Gecko managed to follow the last of them."

"Chester's gone," Jupiter Girl said. "No one survived that explosion."

"I did," John reminded her, spinning in his chair. "He had the whole thing planned down to the last moment. He planted those handcuffs, for instance. And taking over the world with an army of super villains isn't his style. He wants a joke. An irony. He wants the Broadcaster to destroy the capes. Although it wouldn't surprise me if there's still a bomb involved."

Lightning Cat said, "Does it matter? If he knows where the Broadcaster is, let's make a decoy and remove the original. When Chester steals it, we can track the fake."

"G3, can you make a convincing fake?"

"My fabricators in the hangar are making one now in response to this conversation. It will be little more than a 3D printing with similar-looking materials. It will not be able to amplify powers."

Jupiter Girl hovered to the long windows overlooking Capeville, peeking through the clouds. "It won't matter. Breaking into the Regulars' headquarters and switching them out is impossible."

Pronto pointed his rifle at the glass, down at the town. "Nah, we're the greatest super hero team in the world. We could totally do it."

John snatched the rifle from Pronto. "Give me that. Are you crazy? What if that had gone off?" He tossed it to Lightning Cat, who caught it and set it on the bank of computers in front of G3. "Besides, wasn't your dad in the Regulars, Joop? And yours too, Pronto? I thought you said you'd been in their HQ before."

"Yeah," Pronto said, "But the entrance has all sorts of high tech stuff to keep intruders out. Genetic scanning and voice prints and all that good stuff."

Lightning Cat kicked Pronto gently. "You'd have similar genetics, at least."

Jupiter Girl put her face in her hands. "Oh no."

"What's wrong?"

"I just thought of how I could get us in. My dad will kill me if he finds out, but it should work." She glared at G3. "Can your illegal unilink get us into the airlock?"

"Of course. The Black Vulture was a member in full standing."

"Airlock?"

"Yeah," Pronto said. "The Regulars HQ is a spaceship in cloaked orbit around the Earth. That's where they parked it when they closed up shop."

Jupiter Girl stretched and grew, her face thickening, and her clothes taking on the appearance of the dusty red skin of her father. She looked exactly like the creature John had seen in her home, talking on the view screen with the shadowy figure. "Hey kids, meet my Dad. King Jupiter." Her voice was rough and deep. "This may not work. I don't have enough mass to correctly make a shape of this size."

"Looks pretty convincing," John said.

"To you, yes, but it might not to the ship. The ship is designed to keep enemy Jovians out. The only chance we have is that I'm family, and the programming is weighted toward allowing family entrance if there's a question."

"So that's as big a critter as you can make?" Pronto asked.

"No, I can make larger things, like Jovian wind climbers. They look like gigantic airborne manta rays. About the size of a whale, but they have hollow bones and gas sacs to help them fly. Like blimps, sort of. But they don't have much more mass than my native form."

"The facsimile is ready and the unilink coordinates are set." G3 held out a hand and a small cart came rolling into the room, a rock that looked like the Broadcaster sitting on top. G3 picked it up and held it out to John, who tucked it into the crook of his arm. G3 handed him a small pack. John dropped the fake Broadcaster inside and slung it over his shoulder.

"G3, keep an ear out for the Gecko and fill him in on what's going on. Can you outfit us all with listening devices?"

"No," Pronto said. "The HQ would see that. Sketchy. We have to go in without it."

Lightning Cat tapped the computer bank, a small spark rising up between her fingers with each tap. "Couldn't we just go to the Regulars and explain the situation? Tell them to be on high alert or something?"

"No," John said. "Chester has a spy in the Regulars. We can't trust any of them, not until we know who it is."

"That's impossible," Jupiter Girl said, her strange, rough voice making her sound extremely frightening. "Chester is lying."

"We can't take that chance." John looked at Pronto. "What are the chances we're going to run into them at their HQ?"

"They're retired," Pronto said. "I don't think they even go up there any more."

"My dad does," Jupiter Girl said. "Maybe once a week, but mostly just to make sure everything is secure."

John stood up. "So if your fake dad costume works, we might be able to walk in, get the Broadcaster and walk out."

The giant Jovian nodded her head. "If it works."

"Let's go."

They moved to the unilink. John, Lightning Cat and Pronto got in first, and then Jupiter Girl wedged herself in. She decided she needed to stay in her father's form, just in case the HQ noticed her shifting as they stepped out. The HQ scanners were specifically calibrated to look for trickery from other Jovians. They were wedged up against each other like people playing Twister in a box. Pronto looked a little less happy to have his cheek wedged up against the chitonous shell of Jupiter Girl's armored form.

Thirteen uncomfortable seconds later, the unilink opened in a non-descript space about the size of a mini van. "The airlock," Jupiter Girl growled. She motioned for them to stay near the unilink and stomped over to a large door on the front end of the airlock. Her six arms moved quickly over the various symbols on the outside and a voice asked her to identify herself. "Byon'g Kaver'n Rezlin," she said, her voice deep and rough. Lights began to play over her red skin, and she leaned her face against a retinal scanner.

A laser dropped down from the ceiling and pointed at her head. Another dropped down and pointed at John and the others. "Mass and genetic sampling are not exact matches," a voice said. "Additional passkeys are required. What is the current Regular password?"

She looked back at John. He didn't know what to do. He whispered to Pronto, "Get ready. If that laser fires, you need to knock both of the guns out."

"It will totally fry you and Cat before I can get them both."

"Also, you need to switch the Broadcaster and keep it safe." John slipped the fake from his shoulder and set it on the ground. Pronto eyed it, and in a blink it was strapped across his back.

Still looking at John, Jupiter Girl said, "Black Vulture...."

"Access Granted." The lasers retracted into the ceiling.

"What?" John looked up at the ceiling. "Why would my name be the password?"

"I don't know. Something strange is going on." Jupiter Girl put an arm into the rapidly opening door. "Three guests for immediate entrance."

"Confirmed."

Pronto laughed. "It's because the Regulars are all old people. They're terrible with passwords. It probably just rotates through their names."

Jupiter Girl hurried John, Pronto and Cat into the ship. "The trophy hall is this way. The Broadcaster should be there, as well."

The trophy room was enormous and filled with bizarre artifacts from the Regular's adventures. Giant gloves, rifles, a city in a bottle, a spaceship that looked like a beetle, a series of crystal knives, costumes, masks, a glowing blue fire and more. It took them nearly five minutes to find the Broadcaster. Or rather, the place where the Broadcaster should be. An empty pedestal with a bronze plate declaring it the resting place of the Broadcaster was all they found. "Someone already took it," Lightning Cat said. "Pronto, take a quick look around, maybe they're still here."

He gave her a mock salute and ran out of the room.

"What do we do if it's not here?" Lightning Cat asked.

John shrugged. "If it's not here, Chester must have it. I guess we should try to gather all the retired heroes and confront Chester's army head to head."

Pronto appeared again in a burst of wind. "Trouble. This place is crawling with Regulars."

"What?" Jupiter Girl shook her giant red head. "They shouldn't be here."

"They're having some sort of reunion, then. And Chester was right about having a spy, I found –"

Pronto stopped speaking, because a couple of capes walked in. They were easily John's grandfather's age, maybe older. Neither of them wore masks. The man was dressed in long brown robes, like a monk. The woman wore an outfit that looked like a Halloween Cleopatra costume. She spoke first. "King Jupiter. You arrived here much more quickly than expected."

To her credit, Jupiter Girl didn't hesitate to answer to her father's name. "Yes," she said. "And I brought some young heroes with me. You know Pronto, from the Thunder family. Lightning Cat, a new addition. And the newest incarnation of the Black Vulture."

Percepta nodded toward them, her face minutely twitching. Her smile looked nearly genuine. "A pleasure to meet you, children." Then, to Joop, "I thought we had agreed to keep the children out of this."

"Ah... yes. We did. But what place is safer than here?"

The brown-cloaked man nodded. "Percepta, let them be."

She paused, her eyes flickering between the children. "Something is not right here, Wise Owl, but I cannot put my finger on it."

His hooded head nodded slowly. "But what harm can come of them being led into the presence of the others?"

Jupiter Girl said, "I was hasty to bring them here. I will return them to their homes. No need for them to come into our, uh, solemn assembly."

Percepta smiled. "Oh, King Jupiter. You know that time is of the essence. If our assembly is to be effective it must begin now. Bring the children with you."

Jupiter Girl sighed. "Very well. Children, follow us." She glared at Pronto, her tiny six eyes glinting in the light. "Quietly."

Lightning Cat grabbed the boys by the arms and yanked them close. Percepta and Wise Owl walked ahead of them, with Jupiter Girl between them. "What do we do?"

Pronto shook his head and held a finger to his lips and shouted, "Hey, Percepta, can you still hear a whisper from a mile away?"

"Of course, my dear Pronto. I can hear your every word. I can hear the folds of your clothing when you walk, and the blinking of your eyelids."

Pronto made a face and mouthed the word, "Busy-body." He pushed his head close to theirs, but he still whispered when he said, "You know that little 'present' we brought on board for my dad? The surprise birthday gift? The one I carried on board?"

"Yeah," John said.

"We brought a gift to the party that someone else bought already. A duplicate. You know?"

Lightning Cat choked. "Who, um, brought it?"

"I saw it in, like, a suitcase thing. Not sure whose it is, or if anyone else saw it." He grinned. "But if we need it, I know how to get ahold of it."

Percepta stopped and put her hands on her hips. "Children, your code is primitive enough to be insulting."

Jupiter Girl loomed over them and growled, "I believe I told you to come quietly." She stared at them with her creepy rows of eyes until they all looked away. "Come along," she said, and when they looked back at her she winked. With three eyes.

They followed the older capes into a conference room with a long, oval table and a variety of strange chairs floating around it. Jupiter Girl settled into a specially de-signed chair with stirrups for her giant feet and a hole for her tail. Percepta and the Wise Owl stood at the foot of the table.

Pronto pointed out a wide man with a scarred face. He was dressed in a rumpled cowboy outfit, but with a ray gun in the holster on his belt. "Rocket Cowboy," he said. Then he pointed to a woman in an orange cloak called Network, who sat beside a massively muscled man in lit-tle more than a loincloth called The Fist. A skinny guy completely covered in green and red spandex jumped from across the room, landed on the table and asked who they were. "That's the Mighty Flea," Pronto said. He elbowed John and pointed out a silver case leaning against the wall. The Broadcaster.

Percepta said, "They are guests of King Jupiter. All newer members of our fraternity."

Pronto threw his hand up lazily. "Hey guys."

A man in a blue and white wetsuit jumped to his feet, his long blond hair and beard almost bristling in anger. "Does your father know you're here?"

"I don't know," Pronto said. "Does your dad know you're in outer space instead of patrolling the oceans?"

"How dare you speak to me in this way! I am The Pacific, and I will be treated with respect!"

Pronto laughed so hard he doubled over and grabbed his stomach. "Relax, Pacific, I was just busting your chops! Dad keeps a pretty close watch on us, I'm sure he knows where I am."

A deep voice came from behind them. "I certainly do now."

"Uh oh. Hi, Dad." He hadn't even finished saying hi when an older man in spandex appeared in front of them, a crash helmet and goggles on his head, and a gray beard close-cropped on his face.

"What are you doing, son?"

The Pacific threw out his chest. "He is insulting the Pacific, one of the seven sons of The Deep, and I demand restitution."

Pronto stuck out his tongue. Pronto's dad reached out at supersonic speed. John covered his ears and turned away, and when he looked back Pronto's dad had grabbed hold of Pronto's tongue. "OW! Daaaaaa!"

"Show some respect to the Pacific, son."

Pronto bowed low. "Apologies, O Master of the Salty Waves."

The Pacific looked at him skeptically, not sure if Pronto was being sarcastic. He nodded reluctantly, and Pronto tried not to smile.

Percepta spoke again. "Something is amiss. It's time for you children to tell us what exactly is going on."

John cleared his throat. "Maybe you should tell *us* what's going on. The Regulars disbanded years ago. What is this, a reunion?"

"We don't have time for this," The Mighty Flea said. "We need to spring into action."

Rocket Cowboy's face burned bright red. "We have no idea where to attack, or what the enemy's plan is."

"We know what they want," Lightning Cat said. "It's the Broadcaster."

"Cat," John said. "Don't tell them anything."

"The Broadcaster?" Pronto's dad shimmered and solidified again. He had gone so fast John hadn't even clearly seen his absence. "It's gone. And someone used the Regular's release code to remove it. Which means one of us -- one of the Regulars -- took it."

The Wise Owl made a humming sound into his hands. "The Jester must be empowering a cape army. Has Caesar made contact?"

Heads shook around the table. No one had heard from him. "He spoke to me," John said. "He said he won't be helping with this one."

The Pacific shouted, "These children should not be here!"

"And," John said. "There's a traitor among the Regulars."

"That's a serious claim," Network said. Her face fell and she looked pale. "But the Regular Headquarters has given me disturbing news. It claims that King Jupiter has just docked in his personal spacecraft."

All eyes turned to Jupiter Girl. She stood, quickly. "I will take the Broadcaster and keep it safe."

"Take the Broadcaster?" Percepta said. "Is that what the children were murmuring about earlier? Rolling Thunder, quickly, the case there!"

Several of the capes jumped for the case, but Thunder had it in his hands already. He cracked it open, and held the Broadcaster up. "Who removed this from the trophy room?" No one said anything. "Network? Percepta? King Jupiter? Can any of you discern who took this? To put it in that carrying case is surely evidence that they intended to deliver it to the enemy."

Jupiter Girl held out her hand. "I believe it would be safest with me." She shrank back. "Oh, no." Standing in the doorway was the real King Jupiter, a look of fury on his face.

"Daughter, it is the greatest shame imaginable to steal the form of one's father." His four arms grabbed hold of the doorway around him and he shouted in rage, the doorway straining under the assault.

Jupiter Girl crumpled into her human form, a look of pure dejection on her face. "Father...."

"Silence. There is no time for this nonsense. I have spoken with the Shadow Director." King Jupiter looked around the room, everyone waiting on his words. "His newest intelligence has provided us with the location of the Jester's army. He is gathering them at Capeville Bridge. It appears that he intends to march his army into ordinary society. The Shadow Director is putting out word into the cape community, that every able-bodied hero meet him there for one last confrontation with the Jester and his army. I suggest that we take the Broadcaster and use it to amplify the powers of the Regulars and any other heroes who may join us."

The capes began to stand around the table. John looked at the toes of his boots for a minute. These people had been saving the world since long before he was born. There was no reason they should listen to him, and he wasn't sure if he should tell them anything with a spy standing there among them. But he had to try. "I think that's exactly what the Jester wants you to do. To bring the Broadcaster into his reach."

"Please," Rocket Cowboy said. "That old coot could never take something from us unless we let him."

"That's the problem, isn't it?" John reached out and squeezed Lightning Cat's hand, hoping she would know he was sending her a message, hoping she would know what he was about to do. "One of you, maybe more, thinks the Jester has a pretty good idea. Maybe you never liked the idea of Rubicon in the first place and you think this is a good chance to set things right. Maybe over the years you realized you never liked the Regulars. I don't know why, but one of you is a traitor. Look at that empty brief-case. That alone should tell you the truth."

"Is this the boy?" King Jupiter asked.

Pronto laughed. "Your English is terrible. I think you mean, 'who is this boy?'" Pronto's father wacked him in the back of the head and repeated the instruction to show some respect.

John watched Lightning Cat out of the corner of his eye. She had managed to get about twenty feet away. Lightning Cat was on the other side of the room. Pronto was right next to him. "The best thing we can do," John said, "Is to hide the Broadcaster. We don't know why he wants it, so let's keep it out of his reach. Give it to us. The kids. We'll hide somewhere until this is all over. He doesn't know us like he knows you. He won't be able to find us."

"*I* don't know you at all," Pacific said. He glowered at Pronto. "Those I do know I have precious little patience for. Give it me. I'll hide it in the depths of the ocean. No one will be able to retrieve it."

"Including most of us," Wise Owl said. "If you should be the traitor."

Pronto's father, Rolling Thunder, said, "Young man, I'm faster than anyone in here. I see your friends triangulating for a position. If you think you can get the Broadcaster out of my hands and get out of here in one piece, you're sadly mistaken."

"What if we already have it?" Pronto asked.

"But you don't," Thunder said. "And I'm still twice as fast as you, son. *More* than twice as fast."

Pronto grinned. "What if I found it earlier? What if I found it and its been supercharging me the last ten minutes or so?" He opened the bag slung over his back and pulled out the Broadcaster, glowing a bright yellow. "What if I already switched out our fake for the real thing?"

"Now," John said, barely more than a whisper. Lightning Cat lit up like a firecracker, rivers of electricity shooting out of her hands and through several of the Regulars. Jupiter Girl snatched up the Regulars closest to her. King Jupiter made a dive for John, and both Pronto and Rolling Thunder disappeared completely, running at unbelievable speeds. There was a boom as they exited the room and an enormous wave of air knocked everyone backward. King Jupiter was slammed against a wall, giving John a moment's reprieve. "Let's go!" John jumped to his feet and ran for the unilink, Lightning Cat close behind.

The Mighty Flea bounced past them, blocking the hallway. Cat ran and bounced off the side of the wall, building up more energy, but the Flea was a better jumper by far. He snagged her from mid air and swung her down to the ground. "Kids," he said. "I'm with you. Whoever's the thief, and it's not me, we gotta stop him. You make a run for it and I'll hold your escape route."

They ran past him, and John shouted his thanks. As they moved further down the hallway he heard the Flea shouting that they had run the other way. John opened the airlock door, and Lightning Cat got the unilink door open. Jupiter Girl came flying toward them, "Guys! Wait for me!"

"Hold the door," John said.

"John, we don't know if it's Joop or her dad."

"Hold the door, we can't leave her."

"How will we know?"

"We'll ask her a question."

Lightning Cat bristled with static, and the hairs on John's arms stood up. If she released all her power in this enclosed space, John knew it would hurt. He wondered what it would do to the unilink. "Joop, we can't let you in unless you answer a question for us."

"That seems reasonable," she said.

Lightning Cat frowned. "Too nice. Definitely not her."

Joop's face twisted into a sour frown. "Shut up, you dumb alley cat."

"Okay, maybe it is her."

John shushed them both. "Joop, if that's you... who asked you out on a date today? Me or Pronto?"

Joop laughed, and as she laughed new arms sprung from her sides and blocked the unilink from closing. "Oh, you're both much too young for her." She grew, and John knew it was King Jupiter by the intense viciousness in his voice. "Much too young for my daughter."

Joop swooped up behind him and yanked him out. She shouted for them to close the door. She and her father shifted shapes so quickly that John could barely see as she turned into some sort of snake and he into some sort of bear and then both of them into lizards, then she a bird and he a carnivorous looking plant. Lightning Cat hit the button to close the door over and over, but John stood at the space between the doors, hands out, chanting to himself, "Come on, come on, come on." Just when the doors were seven inches apart a massive explosion of air knocked him and Lightning Cat against the wall and the doors sealed, the unilink bouncing through its normal trans-dimensional journey back to the Nest. John and Lightning Cat collapsed against each other. John looked down, and nestled in his arms was the Broadcaster. "Good job, Pronto."

"He must have been going fast!"

"Yeah. He broke the sound barrier, that's for sure." He looked around the unilink, as if Pronto could somehow be hiding in the small space. "I guess he just threw it in as the doors closed."

"Now we just have to hide this thing and wait for it all to be over." The doors to the unilink slid open.

Frank Hydra was sprawled in a chair pulled up outside, the soles of his boots facing them, his dirty jeans ragged and his scalp gleaming with sweat. He had a gun pointed directly at John's chest. "Hullo there, John. Welcome home." He held out his hand. "I think you have something that belongs to my boss."

CHAPTER 17

CHESTER'S PLAN IN MOTION

John cradled the Broadcaster in his arms. Lightning Cat stood near him, her fists at the ready. In fact, it looked like she was angling to get between John and Hydra. As for Hydra, he leaned forward in his chair, the pistol in his hand still leveled at John's chest.

"Who is this guy?" Lightning Cat asked.

Hydra's eyes flickered to her for the briefest instant. "I'm Frank Hydra. One of the bad guys. Isn't that right, John?"

"Yeah." John noticed the bite marks along Hydra's throat from where Dogface had bitten him. "Last time I saw you, a dog beat you up and knocked you unconscious."

Hydra sneered at him and stood up. He was a good foot taller than either of them. "Actually, last time you saw me I was getting knocked off an aircraft by your Gecko friend." He flicked a switch on the pistol. "Or maybe, thinking about it, your Jovian girlfriend was beating me up. I don't have lots of good feelings stored up toward you."

"You're not my first choice for prom, either," John said.

Lightning Cat smiled demurely at John. She looked so sweet and innocent that John had a confusing moment where he wanted to reach out and kiss her right there, just ignore Hydra and the doomsday device and enjoy how great she was. Lightning Cat slid her arm into John's. "Hydra asked you out the prom?" She bared her teeth at Hydra. "He's mine, pal."

Hydra laughed. "Listen, kids, this is fun and all, but I need to collect that little rock and be on my way." He looked over his shoulder. "If you're waiting for that robot, we had another computer virus set on a time delay. It piggybacked on the Tread Battalion one. He'll be busy for hours. Made it pretty easy to get up here, actually, with one of the boss's hovercraft." He pointed at the Broadcaster with the barrel of his gun. "Hand it over."

"I don't think so," John said.

Hydra laughed. "It's not like I'm afraid of a couple of teenage wannabe capes."

"You will be," Lightning Cat said. "You've been beat up by a dog and a gecko and the kitty cats are feeling left out." She shoved John, hard, into the back of the unilink car, and reached around and pressed the button to activate it.

Hydra lifted his gun to fire, and she threw a ball of lightning into the barrel. It exploded in his hand and he immediately tripled. John put his hand out, trying to stop the door from closing, but Lightning Cat kicked him in the chest, her leg barely slicing through the opening and sending him into the back wall of the elevator car. The doors shut, the unilink bumped along and opened in his grandfather's house.

Should he go back for Cat? He could hide the Broadcaster first, then head back. It's what he wanted to do. But keeping the Broadcaster safe was more important than Cat, or him, or Gecko or any of them. It was more important than his friend. Or girlfriend. Could he call her his girlfriend after that prom comment? He wasn't sure. He did know he needed to keep the Broadcaster safe.

John ran to his room and stuffed the Broadcaster into his backpack. He needed to figure out where to take it. The house wasn't safe. If Hydra figured out how to use the unilink it could bring him right here. For that matter, his own grandfather couldn't be trusted. He needed to figure out where he could go, and how to get there. He ran through the house. He could use his cell to call a cab, but that would take forever. He ran through the kitchen, through the sunken living room and burst into the garage. His grandfather's old car was there. There wasn't even a bicycle. The keys dangled in the ignition.

He threw the garage door open and tossed his bag on the passenger side of the bench seat. Starting the car came easily enough. He couldn't figure out how to move the gear shifter, though. He kept pounding on the gas and it would rev up. He sat there, staring at the steering wheel. If only this whole thing had happened two years from now, when he would have his driver's license. He had flown the Vulture jet, for crying out loud. If this whole thing went south because he couldn't drive a sedan, he would be furious. On the other hand, he had completely wrecked the jet.

Then he remembered Captain Anytime. He had said to call, well, any time. John fumbled through his backpack until he found the stub for his ticket. There was a phone number on the edge, and he called it.

The good captain himself answered. "Fighting Fifty-Five Airlines! This is Captain Anytime speaking!"

"Captain, it's John Ajax."

"Mister Ajax! Keeping our good Mr. Gecko out of trouble?"

"I'm afraid not, sir. In fact, I'm in a bit of trouble myself."

There was a long silence on the other line. Finally, Anytime said, "Are we talking about my-parents-are-going-to-kill-me kind of trouble, lad, or full out, put-the-ma-chine-guns-on-the-flying-donut kind of trouble?"

"Oh, it's definitely machine gun donut stuff, sir."

"Ha ha! Excellent! Well, son, I'll outfit the Donut and pick you up. At the airfield?"

"Yes, sir. I'm on my way there now. I'll… call a cab or something."

A blast of wind knocked the phone out of John's hand, and Pronto leaned into the car. "Hiya, Vulture."

"Pronto! What happened?"

"You missed an awful lot of parental lecturing, I'll tell you that much. Once you and Cat got away they tried to reverse engineer the coordinates but Joop did something to the computer. Her dad is furious. If we save the city she's going to be grounded forever. I think she's hoping the city blows up. My dad put me under house arrest while he and the Regulars head to Capeville Bridge for the big fight. My brothers were supposed to babysit me, but they couldn't stand not going to the fight themselves. The Regulars are sending out emergency signals to every cape in the city. So they left me unattended, and I started running around town trying to find you."

"Won't your brothers be in trouble, too, then, for leaving you alone?"

Pronto shrugged. "Poor impulse control. Runs in the family."

"Listen, I just talked to a guy we can trust, and he's going to meet us at the Capeville airfield. Can you drive this car or should I call a cab?"

"Neither! I'll run you there. It will be way faster. And how do you know you can trust this guy?"

"Because he has no idea what's going on. How are you going to run me there?"

Pronto scratched his chin. "Hold on." He disappeared down the street and returned a minute later carrying a bike. He bounced it on its wheels, jumped on the seat and motioned to some pegs on the back. "Hop aboard."

John pulled his backpack on slowly. "Are you sure this is a good idea?"

"It's the best idea. Come on."

"What about poor impulse control?"

"Man, I totally thought this one through. Come on!"

"I don't know. Are you going to break the sound barrier on a bicycle? What if we fall off?"

Pronto snapped his fingers at John. "We are wasting time. I told you, I have an inertial field. So long as you're in physical contact with me we're practically invulnerable."

A motorcycle came around the corner, flames painted on the sides. Riding on the back was Hydra in a black leather jacket, sunglasses propped on his nose, his scalp shining in the sun, the number 27 in black across his face. Hydra saw John and grinned, then gunned the engine. John jumped on the pegs and slapped Pronto on the back. "Let's go, let's go, let's go!"

Pronto gulped and pedaled hard. The motorcycle was more than halfway to them, and Hydra was laughing at the top of his lungs, though the sound of the engine drowned it out. Pronto grunted. Getting up to speed was taking too long. Hydra reached over his shoulder and grabbed a shotgun from behind his back. He laid it across the handlebars and took aim at John, grinning. "He's got a shotgun aimed at us!"

Pronto looked over his shoulder, panicked. "At our backs? But the inertial field only works on things coming from the front!"

"What?"

"Yeah, like if I run into something. Not if it comes from behind!"

Hydra drew a bead on them. Pronto's frantic legs were starting to blur and they were speeding up, but there was no way they were about to outrun Hydra's motorcycle, let alone his bullets. "I wish I'd brought a helmet," John said.

Pronto yelled for him to hold on and he spun the bike into traffic, weaving between cars on the little residential street. "We're headed for the highway."

"No! Are you crazy?"

A blast came from the shotgun, and a tiny bolt of wind lifted John's hair. "See?" Pronto shouted. "That would totally kill you, coming from behind like that."

"That is not encouraging news, Pronto. Pedal faster!"

A second motorcycle moved through traffic and settled in beside them. Pronto pushed his legs faster, panting. "There's two of them now!"

"We need to use the Broadcaster," Pronto said. "Pull it out of the bag. I'll leave them behind like so much --"

A third motorcycle was coming toward them now and Pronto actually laughed. "One in front of us now! At last. Don't let go, John, whatever you do." Hydra number three pulled the trigger. John heard the boom, and then the air just in front of Pronto flashed as flecks of metal disintegrated or fell away. Pronto put his head down, poured on the speed and headed straight for Hydra. John's fingers clenched into Pronto's shoulders and he gritted his teeth. Hydra tried to get out of the way but Pronto steered the bike straight into him and wham! Hydra flew to the side, skidding along the ground, his motorcycle torn to bits and burning as the maniac teen on the bike rocketed past.

Pronto merged onto the highway, and he had no problem getting on. They were going at least seventy miles an hour now, and the pedals were spinning so fast that it didn't look like the gears could turn faster even if Pronto pedaled faster. "You've done this before, right?"

"It's on my bucket list," Pronto said. He steered to the left of a semi and flew around it. The remaining two Hydras split up, one going left and the other right, but both close behind. "I just had a thought, though. Not sure the brakes on this thing are sufficient to slow us down. When the time comes."

"He's about to fire again!"

Pronto leaned hard to the left and almost bumped the car next to them. The car swerved, a little girl in the car seat in the back waving at them. "Hang on," Pronto said.

"I'm hanging on! If there's one thing you don't need to keep telling me, it's to hang on!"

Pronto pulled into an open lane. The Hydras pulled up on either side of them. They both had their shotguns on their laps, facing toward John. One of them shouted, "Give us the Broadcaster and we'll leave you alone!"

John pointed to his ear and shrugged. *Can't hear you guys, sorry.* Pronto suddenly leaned his bike to the right. Hydra #2 had to yank his bike hard to keep from getting hit, and he almost rammed a red hatchback in the next lane. He lost control of the bike and slammed into the wall on the side of the shoulder. Hydra #1 peeled off and dropped back. He started reloading his shotgun.

Pronto leaned back and turned his head. "Think you can balance this thing if I jump off?"

"What? No!"

"It's easier at high speeds. It's just like riding a bike."

"No!"

"We're too slow, I can take care of this if I hop off. I'm much faster if I run."

"No! Are you crazy? If I fall I won't have any inertial dampening or whatever. I'll be street pizza."

Pronto grinned. "Everyone loves pizza." He pulled his legs up, sat side-saddle and rolled off the bike. He hit the ground spinning, caught his feet and ran off ahead of

John. John was on the pegs still, but leaning over to hold the handles. His hands were sweating, his jaw hurt from gritting his teeth. Then Pronto rocketed past him like some sort of comet, ran up to Hydra's bike, set his foot on the front tire of the motorcycle and ran up it, snatched the rifle from Hydra's hands, did a flip over him, planted his foot on the back of the bike and jumped to the ground. Hydra screamed at him, but Pronto turned and came up behind him, running alongside and then slightly in front of Hydra.

"Kid, give me that shotgun or I swear I'll --"

Pronto flashed him an innocent smile and then said, "Here ya go. Meep meep!" He stuck the shotgun through the spokes of Hydra's front tire. Hydra's face went white and his mouth went wide before the back wheel of his bike flew up, and he smashed face-first into the pavement. Pronto jumped back onto the bike and gave the pedals a couple of pushes. "Almost to the airport. It's on the cliffside, near the ocean." He took the next off ramp.

"We should probably slow down now," John said.

"I'm trying!" Pronto had both hands clamped tight on the brakes. Smoke billowed up from the tires.

John screamed. "We're gonna die!" There was a line of cars waiting at a red light at the bottom of the off ramp. A sharp sting hit John's forehead. He reached up and pulled off a dead bug. "I just got hit by a bug! What happened to the inertial whatever?"

"It's a little spotty when I'm slowing down!"

"Gah! Speed up! Speed up!"

Pronto pedaled harder and tried to dodge the cars in front of them, but they winged one on their way past. The bike wobbled, losing momentum. They hit the curb and went flying through the air, both screaming. John wrapped his arms around Pronto's neck, hanging on with everything he had, and Pronto's feet kicked through the air, touching the ground once, twice and then they went through the bushes on the side of the road and crashed into a chain link fence. Pronto slid to the ground, John crumpled next to him and they both lay there for a minute, staring at the sky. "That. Was. Awesome." Pronto jumped up and brought the bicycle over to John. Or what remained of it. It was bent and the tires were worn through where the brakes met the rubber. "Okay, man. Next time we try this, I think when it comes time to slow down it would be better if I was running instead of on the bike. So I'll jump off, and then you stand on the bike and jump into my arms."

"Are you nuts? What we just did was insane enough."

"No, seriously, just jump and then I'll snatch you out of the air and the inertia field will bring you up to speed with me and I'll carry you."

"I don't know if that would work."

"I'm just saying, next time we could try it. Instead of wrecking the bike. Which I totally borrowed from one of your neighbors. You're going to have to pay for that, John, because I don't have any money. I mean, nothing."

"Hey, kid. Think fast." Another Hydra stood ten feet away from them. He tossed something through the air and Pronto, a look of complete disdain on his face, plucked it out of the sky.

"Please, buddy," Pronto said. "You're going to have to throw it a lot harder if you want to make it a challenge for me to catch something."

"I didn't say catch. I said think fast."

In Pronto's hand was a power dampener, just like the one the Jester had used on Lightning Cat. "Drop it!" John shouted, but Pronto was already shuddering as an electrical pulse went through the device.

He dropped the thing to the ground, the case scorched. "I feel weird. But I'm still going to wipe the ground with you, pal." He moved toward Hydra, but at regular speed. In fact, he was slower than John, and awkward. Hydra grabbed him by the wrist, twisted him around and dropped him to the ground on his chest. He pulled some zip ties out of his pocket and zipped them tight around Pronto's wrists.

John ran toward them. Hydra looked up to check on him, but by then John was close enough to kick Hydra, hard, in the chin. Three Hydras popped into being next to him. "You know what, John? I know you have the Broadcaster with you, because my powers are changing. That didn't hurt at all. I don't feel confused. In fact, I think you're about to have an entire platoon of trouble." Each of his doubles turned and punched each other and now there were twelve of him. John backed away, but they circled him easily. Two of them grabbed John, and a third ripped his backpack from him and pulled the Broadcaster out. Hydra tossed the Broadcaster, underhanded, to the first Hydra. "There it is. The last piece that Chester needs for his big plan." He chuckled to himself, and an eerie echo of chuckles started among his doubles. "You boys enjoy what comes next while I deliver this to the man."

"What comes next?" John asked.

One of the Hydras twisted John's arms behind his back and he felt the zip ties tighten into place. They shoved him forward, and a cargo van with no windows screamed up the curb. They tossed John inside.

"Well, Johnny Boy, the boss doesn't need the speedster kid, so him we're going to kill. And you, for some reason, the boss wants you to watch what he does over at the bridge, but he doesn't want you too close to the action. So we're going to take you up to the bluffs overlooking the ocean, where you can see Caesar's bridge, and we're going to let you watch."

"And when it's all over?"

Hydra shrugged. "I guess we'll kill you. Directions were unclear on that point."

John shuddered. "Listen, there's no reason to kill the other kid. He's causing trouble because of me. He's a complete idiot. If you let him go he'll probably just go home and play video games. I'm serious."

"Kid. I don't want you to have any illusions, so we're going to let you watch."

"Watch what?"

Hydra grabbed John by the hands and steered him to the passenger seat of the car and pressed his face against the window. He could see the off ramp from the highway, and two Hydras holding Pronto up between them. A third Hydra stood twenty feet away, a pistol fully extended in his hand. Hydra rolled the window down a little way. "You might want to hear it, too."

Horns were honking from people at the off ramp. Maybe someone would get out, try to stop it. No. They all drove away as soon as the light turned green. The two Hydras let Pronto go and he yelled at the top of his lungs and ran toward the man with the gun. There was an echoing crack and a flash of light and Pronto fell forward, skidded on the ground and stopped at the gunman's feet. Hydra kicked at Pronto with his booted toe, but he didn't move.

"No!" John beat his head against the window and lashed out at the Hydras with his feet. One of them shoved him down against the seat, and another pinned his legs. They pulled the van onto the street and dragged John into the back. One of them kept a boot on his back, but none of them spoke. John couldn't believe it. He knew this wasn't a game, but now... there was no way he could allow this to go on. He bit his tongue, trying not to make any sound, not to let them know he was on the verge of tears. The thought of Pronto's family finding out about this made a dull, empty place in John's chest.

The van bounced along, obviously on a dirt road or possibly no road at all. When it pulled to a stop, John felt battered. They slammed the side door open and pushed John onto his feet. He blinked in the sunlight and felt the salt spray of ocean nearby. He did a quick head count. Six Hydras. Three of them in a loose semicircle behind him. In front of him was a jagged cliff, and beyond that the ocean. One of the Hydras stayed in the van, and two more acted as loose sentries. Dust rose from the direction they had driven in.

In the distance, John could see the Capeville Bridge. Insanely long and dark against the water and sky, he could see people and vehicles moving into place on the bridge. "Get ready for the fireworks," Hydra said. "On the left are Chester's people. There are a lot of them."

"Quantity, not quality," John said, and got a punch in the face for his trouble. In the distance, battle lines seemed to be drawn. Capes were lifting into the air on either side, and the occasional outburst of flame or colored lights or electricity came from both sides. Storm clouds roiled in the distance, headed for the bridge. "Where's the giant robot?"

"What are you talking about?"

John squinted at him, trying to see if he was lying, but it appeared Hydra wasn't aware of the robot. He stared mournfully at the distant assembly of capes. "I should be there."

"You're fourteen years old and you don't have any powers. What good could you possibly do? Or what harm for that matter?" An explosion of light came from the bridge. The battle had begun. People flying, running, jumping. Flashes of light, and low, rumbling sounds like thunder. Hydra gestured toward the bridge. "You're completely meaningless in the scheme of things."

John frowned. "Before this thing is over, Hydra, you're going to rethink that. And you're going to pay for killing Pronto."

Hydra snorted. "Was that his name? Hilarious."

Another Hydra said, "Hey, what's that?" A funnel of dust was rising from back the way the van had come. "Must be a car." The Hydras all pulled their pistols and clicked the safeties off.

They had their backs to John. He stepped to the side, putting a few steps between him and them. How would anyone even know he was here? It must be another Hydra, or some of Chester's other men. But... then again. John squinted at the cloud in the distance. It was moving fast and looked to be gaining speed. In fact, John doubted a car could make that sort of time over the rough terrain. It almost looked like someone... running.

A goofy grin broke out on John's face. At the speed the dust cloud was approaching, John knew it was only a few seconds away. An idea hit him and he immediately acted. It was an all or nothing moment. He sprinted, hands still tied behind his back, for the edge of the cliff. Two of the Hydras saw him and grabbed for him, but he had just enough distance that he slipped through their grasp. He ran toward the edge of the cliff, forcing himself not to slow down, not to break pace. He could see the waves beating the jagged rocks below. When his toes hit the edge he crouched and jumped, pushing up as high and as far out as he could. No going back now.

A half second later something hit him like a whooping jet plane, boosting him faster and farther. His stomach dropped into his toes as they flew upward like a rocket. "I think I broke the sound barrier!" Pronto crowed. "Without the Broadcaster, too!"

Pronto had his arms wrapped around John's chest. They were still headed up, but of course their speed was failing. John shouted, "Do you think your inertial field will keep us from dying when we hit the water?"

Pronto laughed triumphantly. "We're not going to hit the water!"

At the apex of their leap a gigantic creature glided up beneath them. It looked like a manta ray, but it was half the size of a city block. It soared up under them so perfectly that when they hit its back it felt like John had jumped down a few stairs instead of leaping off a cliff. The skin was rubbery and cool beneath his hand. "Pronto, what is this?"

"It's a Jovian wind walker, of course!" He turned and looked back at the cliff, where the Hydras were taking long shots at them with their pistols and he laughed and shook his fist at them. "In your face, pal!" He put his arm over John's shoulder and they laughed together.

"In his faces," John said. "Plural."

"Right!" Pronto did a frenetic dance, prancing and spinning around at high speeds. "Joop! Take us to the Capeville Bridge!" She banked that direction, and a low, mournful sound echoed out over the water. In the distance, capes fought capes on the bridge. "Woohoo! Our first big fight! The greatest super team in the world!"

"How did you do that? I saw them shoot you!"

"They shouldn't have let me run toward them. My inertial field kicked in and stopped the bullets and then, after they thought I was down for the count, I gave them a thrashing to remember." He chuckled to himself.

"But the dampener took your powers. How did you get them back?"

"I have a fast metabolism," Pronto said. "The effect didn't last very long."

John turned his back toward Pronto. "Any chance you can help me get these zip ties off my wrists before we get there?"

"I'll give it a shot," Pronto said. He put his hand in the middle of the zip ties and vibrated his hand at super speed. The plastic fell off John's wrists, hit Joop's back and slid off into the ocean below. "This is going to be amazing."

Joop dropped suddenly in the choppy air caused by the coming storm. The temperature was dropping rapidly. John steadied himself by lowering himself to his knees. Time was running out, and he had to stop that doomsday device. And now that all the capes were gathered on the bridge... could Chester be planning to destroy the bridge with all of them on it? Of course. Exactly how he killed the Black Vulture. He'd short circuit everyone's powers and kill them all in an explosion.

Joop swooped near the bridge. Pronto picked John up and ran full speed, leaping across from Joop's wing to the edge of the bridge. He dropped John, windmilled his arms for a second, and then they were both safely on solid ground. Jupiter Girl took her human form and landed gently beside them. A strange tingling sensation went over them as they entered the bridge.

"Someone set up a force field," Jupiter Girl said. I felt it about ten feet out. We're trapped on this bridge."

The battle raged in front of them. People slugging each other, slicing with energy blades, lasers and bullets and fists flying. "Whoever's in charge is going to be on the other side of this chaos," John said. "I say we skip everything else, stick together and make our way as fast as possible to find Chester."

Jupiter Girl nodded. "I'm practically invulnerable, so I'll take point."

Pronto said, "I'll bring up the rear, so if there's trouble I can power John to safety."

They stood in a circle and all put their hands in the center. "We have an advantage," John said. "No one is expecting us. Hopefully people won't know which side we're on and we can make easy progress to the other side."

The darkness from the storm had become significant now, and a cold wind blew across the bridge. A gigantic image filled the sky. Chester the Jester, complete in his jester outfit. He looked thin, unhealthy and old, his spindly legs bent, his papery white skin standing out against the yellow and red cloth against his face. The bells on his hat jingled brightly when he threw his head back and forth.

"Hello, everyone!" Chester's voice boomed out across the bridge. "I'm so glad you all could make it. And we have a wonderful honor tonight! My dear friend, my confidant, my nemesis, my reason for the season, the Black Vulture is with us!" The gigantic image flickered, showing John and his friends crouched on the bridge.

"So much for no one knowing we're here," Pronto said.

Chester's face reappeared. "I feel conflicted, Black Vulture. Like when my ex-girlfriend comes to visit. We used to have something special, but all these years later, she never wrote, she never called. And now she wants to see me. I'd like to see you, but on the other hand I don't. At least, not until my business here is done." He held up the glowing yellow Broadcaster and gestured behind him to the force field generator. "I assume you've figured it all out by now. The fireworks start soon, my dear carrion bird. You had best hurry to find me! Ha ha ha!" He paused. "Oh yes. You might like to see this, too." The camera panned to show four people bound in metal stocks. The camera zoomed in. Lightning Cat was the first. John clenched his fists. The second was the Gecko. And the last two... were his parents. Chester poked John's dad in the cheek. "I remember this one from when he was your age. The Flying Squirrel! Ha ha ha ha!" Chester pinched the brow of his nose. "Oh, the memories."

John started running through the battle, which had fallen into disarray from all the people stopping to watch the giant video playing out in the sky. Lightning from the storm lashed out at the bridge and hit a rod. Thunder rolled immediately. "One more thing," Chester said. "No fun if the Black Vulture just walks over to me. So, for all my allies out there: kill him." He waved a hand toward the camera. "Not that I think any of you imbeciles is able to kill the Black Vulture, but do your best. Maim him if you prefer. Kill the speedy kid too -- it's creepy how fast his little legs go -- and the girl from Jupiter.

"I'll be waiting for you," he said to John. He popped his head back and forth, and the ethereal jingling worked its way through the crowd. "With bells on! Ha ha ha ha!" John forced his way into the melee, not stopping to notice whether Jupiter Girl or Pronto were near him, focused only on finding Chester and making him pay.

CAPEVILLE: THE DEATH OF THE BLACK VULTURE

CHAPTER 18

THE DEATH OF THE BLACK VULTURE

Halfway down the bridge, the fighting grew more intense. Nearly half of the enemy seemed to be made up of Hydra and his doubles, and hitting him only made more. Since a lot of the capes didn't know this, there was an increasing number of enemies.

Jupiter Girl took the heaviest hits in the front, doing her best to shield John as they moved forward, and more than once Pronto grabbed him and ran him out of harm's way. Once a ten-foot tall man, half covered in steam-powered implants, shouldered his way past Jupiter Girl and nearly smashed John, but John had stepped inside his (very long) reach and started pulling out as many hoses as he could until the man simply stopped moving, the battle raging on around them. Still, it was slow going, and Chester could kill them in a moment if he blew up the bridge.

They could see the Regulars now, toward the front of the battle lines, the heroes of Capeville, making a hole in enemy lines. "This is going to take forever," John said. "K'reth, do you think we could fly around? Maybe go under the bridge, come in from behind?"

Joop punched a talking glob of gelatin in the face and tossed it aside. "You're forgetting that force field. Even if the barrier is far enough out, we're going to be sitting ducks for anyone with a rifle or a bow."

"I could stop an arrow," Pronto said proudly.

Jupiter Girl grunted. "With your chest."

John kicked a Hydra in the knee and rolled him to the side. They kept moving forward as fast as they were able. The rain had started in now, and everyone was drenched. A heavily muscled man stepped in their path, his blonde hair cropped short, his neck bulging with veins. "I am Mass Culture," he said. "And you're not going another step."

Pronto ran at him, but Mass Culture held out his palm and Pronto skidded through a puddle and fell to the ground, pinned to the pavement. "Gravity powers," Pronto shouted. "Stay clear of him!"

Jupiter Girl stepped between Mass Culture and John. "You're going to have to go through me to get to him."

"No problem. Here come my teammates now. Kitsch! Fundamentalist! Capture that boy in the black mask!"

Jupiter Girl grabbed John's hand and dragged him away as fast as she could move. She quickly took on John's shape and shouted, "Split up! I'll try to lead them somewhere we can get help!" John froze for a second, watching Jupiter Girl as she ran into the crowd, looking just like him.

A cold hand fell on his shoulder. A girl in a white 1920's dress and entirely too much makeup stood beside him. She was young, with short black hair and a melancholy look. And, strangely enough, she was transparent. John could see the bridge and the ocean faintly through her, and she wasn't wet from the rain. She said, "Don't worry, Vulture. We'll help you get through the mess."

"Who are you?"

Pronto appeared next to him. "I think Joop must have distracted that Mass Culture guy enough that his powers wore off of me." He stopped when he saw the girl. Three other capes arrived, flanking her. "Cool!" Pronto shouted. "It's the Avant Guard." He bounced excitedly from foot to foot. "Check it out! It's the Situationist!" He pointed to the short, thin man beside the transparent girl. He looked like he had come from a black and white photo. Color didn't stick to him. He wore a conservative gray suit and his black hair was slicked into small curls, parted in the middle. He had round-rimmed glasses on.

"I don't know if we have time for introductions," John said. "But if you can get us to the other side, that would be amazing."

"That's Readymaid," Pronto said, grinning. Readymaid had on sensible work clothes, heavy boots and a blue handkerchief tied over her platinum blonde hair. "And the lady you were talking to, that's Avant Ghost." He cocked his head at the last guy, who wore a tuxedo and bowler hat and had painted his face an apple green. "I don't know that last guy."

He tipped his bowler hat toward them. "The great lament of my obscurity. I am Captain Dada."

Avant Ghost smiled. "Situationist, can you clear us a path?"

The Situationist pulled out a tiny notebook and scratched in it with a pencil. "Yes. Readymaid, make a funnel please."

Readymaid punched the pavement and pulled up a chunk the size of a coffee table. Somehow, it curved and flattened in her hands. "Ready!"

"Captain Dada, distract the crowds."

"Christmas trees are naughty!" he yelled, and a swarm of colored lights that looked like butterflies flew out of a small door in his hat and fanned out in the immediate area, attaching themselves to the shoulders and heads, faces and thighs of unsuspecting people. He threw his hands up and shouted, "The incomparable beauty of bad-gers eating fire in a field of giant purple. He who has ears, let him wear earmuffs!" Anyone who had been touched with a butterfly jolted, as if they had seen something shocking, shook their heads and closed their eyes, com-pletely unable to connect with the world around them.

A streetlamp hurtled past John and the others, and they all ducked. The Situationist said, "Hurry. Use the funnel, Jupiter Girl, to corral the Hydras."

"But what will I do with them? They'll just keep mul-tiplying."

The corner of the Situationist's lip twitched up. "Avant Ghost... ghost out the bridge floor under the funnel." She bent down and put her hands to the pavement and it turned transparent, like her. Rain water poured down through the transparent parts of the bridge.

As Jupiter Girl pushed Hydras into the funnel, they dropped through the transparent bridge and, about fif-teen feet below, they landed on the smooth inner sur-face of the force field. Pronto started throwing Hydras in, too, and in a matter of minutes the hundred square feet around them was empty of Hydras. Pronto snuck up be-hind Mass Culture and dragged him into the funnel, which brought particular praise from Captain Dada, who start-ed prancing around the funnel and shouting, "Donkey in the hayloft!" and "Chicken Pot Pie! Chicken Pot Pie!"

A shimmering blue wave ran along the force field that surrounded the bridge. Jupiter Girl turned her chin up, watching the wave of color.

"What's happening to the force field?" John asked.

"He's turning it off," Joop said, and just at that moment all the Hydras who had been thrown to the force field be-low shouted as they continued their fall. One by one they winked out before they hit the churning gray water.

Some sort of ruckus was happening over near the Regulars now. They were attacking something with concentrated force. Something that was moving toward John and his friends. "Brace yourselves," John said. A car flew up from the crowd between them, and King Jupiter deflected it before it could harm anyone. King Jupiter saw Jupiter Girl, John and Pronto and roared for them to get out of the way, to go somewhere safe.

In the center of the maelstrom was Chester the Jester. He had traded in his jester outfit for a top hat and tails. He carried a walking stick with a jewel on the end and a cravat twined perfectly around his neck and tucked into his vest. An opera cape slithered from his shoulders and a pair of pince-nez crouched on his nose. Walking directly behind him was one of the robot soldiers John had fought with Lightning Cat and the Gecko, at the bank. The robot was carrying a tray with a variety of things on it, one of which was the Broadcaster. The Regulars were trying to reach Chester, but apparently he had turned off the giant force field so he could provide a smaller, portable one for himself. They couldn't touch him.

"Bored," Chester said. "Boring. I thought it would be fun to involve some other people, Black Vulture, I did. I blame myself. I told them to kill you. But now I'm tired of it. This has never been about those other people. It's always been about you and me. The Vulture and the Jester."

The Avant Guard were trying to break through the force field, but they couldn't. Even Avant Ghost couldn't go through. Chester nodded at them. "Yes, my force field makes an excellent umbrella. I'm terribly sorry you're all in the rain."

Captain Dada stepped up to the force field and ran his hands over it like a proud parent rubbing a pregnant woman's belly. "Even permanent air knows about Rule Zero." A glowing purple cat leaped out of Captain Dada's hat and stepped through the force field. It rubbed itself on Chester's legs and then jumped at his face, disappearing into his eyes.

"He should be overwhelmed by the surrealist vision in about thirteen seconds," Avant Ghost said. But thirteen seconds came and went and then again.

Chester smiled at them, taking his formal gloves out and slowly pulling them onto his long, white fingers. "Ooooooh, so scary. Are you tapping into the collective unconscious, my dear? How do you do that?"

Captain Dada just stared at him with a mopey look on his face. "But... but... you're too old to be Jung."

"And you're too idiotic to be schizophrenic." He lifted the Broadcaster in one hand, holding it like an egg. "Now it's time to set my plan in motion. Come closer, Black Vulture. I want you, especially, to see this."

John moved right up against the force field and hit it with his fists. It didn't budge. "You don't need to do this," John said. "This is about you and me, isn't it?"

Chester smiled. "Of course it is, my sweet scavenger bird, but it's nice to hear you say it." The robot beside Chester moved closer, and he took an array of wires from a machine it carried and placed them on the Broadcaster. Each wire had a circle of tape on the end to hold it on. "Amplifier," Chester said conspiratorially.

Pronto frowned. "So your big plan is to... what? Make all the capes in Capeville more powerful?"

"Yes, essentially, that's right. Very good. Caesar sent us to Capeville to rot for reasons that eluded me. I tried to figure it out for years. It's not really his style, you know, a project of this scope and moral questionability. Moving all the capes to an interment camp? It's not like Caesar. But then I thought one day... what if the Black Vulture hadn't burnt to a feathery crisp on that bridge? This is precisely the sort of answer he might come up with. The best way to remove the cape problem for all those humans might be to put us in a ghetto in the middle of the ocean."

The Pacific stood nearby, his wetsuit glistening in the rain. "Silence! You know nothing about what you are --"

Chester looked at him, painfully unhappy with the interruption. "Shhhhh. I believe I was talking to Mr. Vulture. In fact, all the rest of you can move away ten steps. Mr. Vulture has a chance to stop my plan. The rest of you might displease me and cause me to blow up the bridge. Go along. Shoo. That's it. Good boy. Go on, all of you. Excellent." He turned his attention back to John. "Where was I?"

"You started thinking, despite the fact that no one has heard from him for fifteen years, that maybe the Black Vulture was alive."

"Right! So a few years ago I started some little experiments. Some things that I knew would upset him if he was out there. I started harassing your family, for instance."

"Why would the Black Vulture care about my family?"

"Oh, I don't know. The Black Vulture always liked your father. The Flying Squirrel. You know he was the Black Vulture's sidekick, right? I thought if the old bird was still alive he wouldn't like me constantly sending trouble to your family, which I've done for, oh, three years or so now. Sending Hydra to kidnap you was, I admit, a bit desperate. But that Vulture has been so silent."

John put his palms against the force field, trying to get a closer look at what Chester was doing. He was attaching something to the Broadcaster. "How does giving everyone stronger super powers upset the Black Vulture?"

"He wants to keep the capes out of decent society. The threat of Caesar's power is what keeps them here, in Cape Ghetto. If their powers become stronger, some of them will try to escape." He pressed a button and a golden beam shot straight up, through the force field and pierced the dark clouds. For a moment everything turned golden in a monstrous flash, like lightning. John turned. Powers were flaring up in the night. Eyebeams and lightning, holographic projections and flames burst out. A mountain of ice was forming at the bridge's entry. "It may take some time to control their new power levels."

"You're insane. You're going to destroy the bridge with their powers."

"Oh no, not at all. I packed the bridge with explosives. Today's explosives are so effective. I have enough to destroy the whole bridge in a package no bigger than a carry-on suitcase. I wouldn't destroy everyone by using super powers." He shrugged. "I'm a traditionalist." He turned a knob and the chaos on the bridge increased. Capes were rising in the air, trying to control their powers. Pronto disappeared, running so fast that John didn't even see him leave, just a shimmering and then... gone.

Jupiter Girl shouted, "Vulture, there has to be a way to get inside that force field! You have to turn it off!"

"Hee hee hee. You'll be inside it soon enough." He held up a black box about the size of a shoebox. "Here's part two. It's a power dampener. Without the circuit breakers. Like I used on your kitty cat earlier."

"But that turned off her powers and knocked her out!"

"Yes. I thought, well, Vulture might be unhappy to see everyone get more powers. But maybe he'd like it if I turned them all off. It's a stronger solution than a ghetto." He attached the black box.

John shouted down the bridge, "Get everyone who's flying onto the ground now!"

Pronto appeared for a half second and grinned while saying, "JohnIfoudnthebombIjustneedto --"

The power wave from Chester spread out like a wall. John was knocked to the ground, and powers arced and sparked and flared and then, like spent matches, burned out. Capes fell from the sky, and everyone with a power collapsed like piles of dirty clothes, limp, boneless, done. John ran to Pronto and felt for a pulse.

"He's alive," Chester said dismissively. "I'm saving the murders for the big fireworks at the end."

Jupiter Girl and her father were still standing tall. "It's okay," she said to John, lifting him to his feet. They both took on their native forms and stomped close to Chester's force field. "You'll have to turn that off eventually," Jupiter Girl said. "And when you do...."

Chester grinned. "I'll turn it off right now. Watch this. Right now I have it set so that nothing can get in to the bubble but I can send things out. Like so." He flipped a penny through the force field. It bounced off King Jupiter's nose. He didn't flinch. "You have may have noticed when I had the force field covering the bridge it let things in (like rain water) but wouldn't let things (like poor Frank Hydra) out. It's just the flip of a button." He pressed a button and a force field appeared around the Jovians. They both hammered against the inside with their fists but they couldn't get out. Chester set the force field device on the ground beside them. "Uh oh. Trapped inside. So sad. Don't worry. When the explosion goes off it should destroy the force field projector just in time for you to be barbecued. Hooray!" They slammed their many fists against the field but it didn't budge.

John ran toward Chester, ready to flatten him, but Chester held up a small black box with a red button. "Ah ah ah, my little hatchling. One press and the whole bridge goes bye-bye."

John stood near him, chest heaving. Chester put his arm around John's shoulders. "Look at them. Isn't it beautiful? All the colors of their costumes lying next to each other all down the bridge? I think it's beautiful. The death of the capes."

"No. Not yet. I'm still a cape."

Chester looked over his pince-nez at him. "Are you? For them 'cape' means power. For us, it's a fashion accessory." He started picking his way through the unconscious bodies. "Come on then. I still need to give a speech about my plan, and then rave about our history together before I kill you. It's traditional for you to get to see the prisoners while I do it." He paused and waited for John, who stood, unmoving, beside Jupiter Girl and her father. "Do you want to see your parents?"

John reached toward the force field but Jupiter Girl shook her head violently. It was one-way. If he put his hand inside he wouldn't be able to get it out, and who knew what Chester would do then. "I'll beat him, K'reth. I promise." She quickly shifted into her human form and leaned close to the barrier. He couldn't hear her words, but he read her lips. "Go get him."

John gave her a thumbs up and followed the villain through the battlefield, stepping carefully over the unconscious heroes and villains on the ground. Chester said, "You know, I'm surprised Caesar never showed. He could have wiped this all up in no time." John didn't say anything. "And the Black Vulture has been oddly silent. Maybe you really are all that remains for me. Pity." He stepped over a cape dressed in white with a black skull on her chest. "I love the symmetry of killing all the capes with an exploding bridge, just the same way I killed the Black Vulture."

"What is your obsession with the Black Vulture?"

"Oh? Don't you know? I created him. He's my baby."

"He's your baby?"

Chester wagged his finger at John. "Not my baby, exactly. But my creation. I'm Frankenstein, he's my monster. I'm Rubik and he's my cube. I'm Lucas and he's my Star Wars." Further along the bridge a giant metal dome sat, hunched like a turtle, blocking the path. Metal rungs were scattered over it, and John figured they could climb over it if need be, but the Jester opened a door and they went up a small gangplank and inside.

Game Master sat behind a large metal column, fifteen feet in the air. John's parents, Gecko and Lightning Cat were still in the metal stocks, and they looked up at him expectantly. John held up his wrists, showing them that he wasn't captive.

Chester said, "As you can see, your friends are all fine. Go ahead and say hello."

John crouched down in front of his parents. His father's left eye was swollen shut. "Vulture?" he asked.

John grinned. "It's your son."

Both his parents' faces clouded with concern. His mother asked, "Are you okay?"

"I'm fine. I'm going to beat this guy."

"Did your grandfather give you that outfit? I'm surprised. I never thought...."

"No," John said. "It's a long story. I found the Nest, though, Dad, and G3 has been helping me out."

"G3?" his mother asked. She and his dad exchanged glances. "I haven't heard that description in a long time. I thought he was... decommissioned."

"No. He's fighting a virus right now, though, and pretty useless. Hopefully he'll be up and running soon."

"I'm sorry we've been lying to you all these years, son."

John didn't know what to say to that, so he said, "I wish you had told me."

"We thought it was safer if you didn't know."

"It might have explained a lot of things. Why you forced me to do martial arts class, or why you were so neurotic about screening my friends." He put his hand on his mom's hand. "It seems like lying isn't the best way to protect someone."

His mother smiled slightly. "And yet there you are, wearing a mask."

"Like father like son," John said.

John's dad reached his hand out, and John moved back to him. He pulled him close and said, "John, listen. The Vulture could never forgive Chester, not really, and it gave Chester power over him. Son, you can't make the same mistake. Whatever happens here, whatever happens to us, don't let him have power over you like that."

"I don't understand. What do you mean the Jester has power over the Black Vulture?"

His mom said, "John, we're sorry. Sorry we lied to you. We did it for the best reasons, but they were still lies."

John looked at their hands, reaching to him out of the stocks. "I don't know what to say. I never thought you would lie to me, and I might need some time to figure out how to trust you again."

John's dad nodded, biting his lip. A tear rolled down his face. "Of course, son, whatever you need. We love you."

John hugged his father's head. It was awkward with him in the stocks, but he did his best. And then his mom. "I love you too, both of you."

"Tick tock, little feathered friend," Chester said from across the room. "I'm getting bored. Finish your goodbyes."

John turned. "I'm saying hello, not goodbye."

The Jester dismissed him with a wave. "Whatever. I'm going to kill them once I'm done here. If you want your last words to be *hello how are you* then so be it." They stood there staring at each other, John flexing his hands into fists. Chester clapped his hands. "Chop, chop. Talk to the other two and let's go."

John moved on to the Gecko. Before he could say anything, the Gecko spoke quietly and quickly: "There's a green button on the Game Master's console that frees us. If you should happen to find yourself up there."

"I'll do my best."

"I know it. Good luck, BV."

He came to Lightning Cat, and started to lift his hand to her face, but she shook her head. "I'm building up a charge," she whispered. "And he's watching you. Let's do this."

"Cat, if anything happens –"

Cat shook her head again, and a flicker of blue light danced across her forehead. "If anything other than you beating Chester happens, I'm going to be seriously ticked off at you."

John laughed. "Okay. I wouldn't want that."

"Time's up." Chester stood, leaning on his cane, a tiny smile on his face. "Have a seat, Black Vulture." He motioned grandly to a small wooden chair beside a table. "I'd like to tell you a story." He let a long breath of air out. "It started a long, long time ago, when I was a simple murderer. I killed a woman, mostly as a joke, you know, and it turned out she was the wife of a policeman."

"As a joke?" John couldn't believe it. He knew something was wrong with the man, but this only confirmed it, deepened his concern. He looked back at his parents. His father looked pale, and his mother had a look of contempt on her face. "You're sick."

"Don't interrupt. It wasn't anything personal. Anyway, the courts found me innocent. They couldn't prove I had done it, even though I had, and so I was set free. But the policeman, he knew it was me. He knew it. So he started following me around, wearing a mask, sticking to the shadows. Telling me he was watching me. Started leaving me notes, trying to intimidate me. Oh, the attention was so glorious! I couldn't believe someone was taking notice. So, I started playing little games with him. Leaving him notes. Telling him what I would do next. Giving him chances to stop me. I started calling him my 'Black Vulture' because he was always hanging around, waiting for death." Chester laughed. "He spent years trying to stop me. He would catch me, put me in jail, maybe foil a plot now and then. And after a while he really became the Black Vulture. And I became the Jester. The prankster. The jape. It's all a play, you see? It's all for him. He's my audience. I like him to see the clever things I do. He named me, you know? I was just a regular guy. He's the one who called me the Jester. My name was Scott Jennison. He meant it as an insult, like he didn't take me seriously. So, all of this?" He spun around, pointing at the dome. He hit a button that made windows open, revealing the unconscious capes outside. "All of that?" He pointed at each of the prisoners. "All of them? I did that all... for you. Because I created your predecessor. And he, somehow, created you. We belong together. I can't be who I am without you."

John looked to his father, amazed at the story. It didn't quite add up, and he wondered if it could possibly be true. His father, in the stocks, just nodded wearily. John considered this carefully and said, "How could a police officer have enough money to get all the equipment the Black Vulture has? It must be millions of dollars worth of stuff." "Oh, I don't know. I've wondered that too. You know what else is strange? The police officer I mentioned to you? He died in the Kane Bridge incident. Yes. He was helping some people off the bridge and KABOOM. All gone." The Jester scratched his head. "You know I crippled your grandfather, too. He was a big fan of the Capeville idea. So I guess that's partly my doing, as well. Me and Caesar, working together to make this city." He cackled at the thought.

John jumped up. "It's time to end this, Jester. The Black Vulture is dead. There's no reason for any of this."

Game Master shouted, "Chester, there's a proximity alert. We have five craft inbound!"

Chester jumped up and down, clapping his hands with glee. "Craft time!"

John used the distraction to punch Chester in the stomach. Chester bent over, winded, and John shoved him toward Lightning Cat. Sparks shot from her face, scorching Chester's back, and he fell over, smashing into the floor. John jumped on him and yanked the detonator from his hand.

"My dear boy," Chester said. "I can't believe you haven't learned this by now. But it's on a timer."

"It's the Fighting Fifty-Five!" John shouted to the Gecko. "Captain Anytime is on his way!"

Game Master groaned. "I'm deploying our drones and sending the robot soldiers out onto the bridge to neutralize anyone who causes us trouble."

John ran up to the podium. Game Master backed away, not one for physical confrontation. John hit the green button. The Gecko leapt out immediately, headed for Chester. Chester threw a dampener at the Gecko, but the Gecko dodged it and grabbed Chester with his extra sticky fingers. Chester whipped a vial out of his pocket and sprayed it in the Gecko's eyes. Mace. The Gecko screamed and let go of the thin man. Chester ran down the gangplank and out onto the bridge.

John skid down the plank after him. "Chester! It's not too late. You can stop this. You're in retirement, remember?"

Chester laughed at him and jumped on a platform connected to the dome. It was about the size of a sled, with a long set of handlebars coming out of one end. Chester pressed a button and it lifted slightly from the ground. He leaned toward the edge of the bridge and it started to drift that direction. "Goodbye, Black Vulture. Once I'm safely away I'm going to destroy the bridge with you and everyone else on it."

"Oh no you don't," John shouted, and he ran toward the mobile platform. Chester piloted it to the edge. It dropped momentarily when he took it off the bridge, but rose again, bobbing on the air currents. John ran full speed, without pausing, heading straight for the edge. The platform was moving away from the bridge, but John knew his only chance to possibly catch it was to jump as far as he could. He leapt up on the side rail, still going full speed, crouched down and launched himself over the side. Everything seemed to go into slow motion. The bridge fell away from him, and far below small white caps churned on the water. John stretched himself out to full length, every centimeter needed, his arms straining, his fingers extended so far they hurt. He didn't think he would make it, but a powerful gust of wind boosted him a tiny bit farther. He wondered, just for an instant, if it was Caesar's doing.

The tips of his fingers brushed the top of the platform and he hooked his thumbs under. He swung precariously beneath the platform, and his sudden weight tipped it backward. Chester spun out of control, the platform headed back toward the underside of the bridge. It hit the side of the bridge, throwing Chester over the side and rolling onto the pavement. John hit a girder with his ribs, and it snapped him nearly in half. He barely managed to grab the girder. He pulled hard, trying to get onto the bridge, but he couldn't get the leverage. He could see the top, could see the capes laid out on the ground. In the distance he could see his parents and Lightning Cat and Gecko fighting the robot soldiers. Chester was picking himself up from the ground. John's hands started to slip. He knew he wouldn't survive the fall. He scrambled desperately to get a better purchase with his hands, but he was slipping toward the sea.

Chester grabbed his forearms. "You're not quite ready to fly, little hatchling. Give it time." He dragged John back up to the surface of the bridge. John rolled onto his stomach and was about to push himself up when Chester delivered a quick rabbit punch to the base of his neck. John gasped and fell to the ground. Chester leaned in close and said, "This isn't over, my feathered friend. Assuming you survive the explosion, I'll be back. Maybe three months, maybe three weeks, but I'll be back. And knowing your secret identity... why, that opens a whole new set of wonderful games we can play." Chester kissed him on the side of his forehead. "Sweet dreams, my prince." He laughed maniacally and ran for the other side of the bridge. "Three minutes, Black Vulture, before I mix all these capes together!"

Three minutes. John struggled up, his neck and arms burning with pain. The other capes were starting to stir. People were moving, at least. Three minutes. Maybe those who could fly would be able to carry a few others off the bridge, but there was no way the whole bridge could be evacuated in time. Across the bridge, the Jester was stepping into a harness attached to a bungee cord.

"No," John said, and he got to his feet, swaying. He ran across the span, dodging the bodies on the ground. One of the robot soldiers stepped between him and the Jester. John rolled onto the ground, dodging the robot, popping up behind it and still running. Chester was climbing up on the rail now, the bungee cord trailing out behind him. John put on an extra burst of speed and jumped, tackling Chester and carrying them both out over the water. Chester was laughing harder than John had ever heard. They fell, and John quickly wrapped his arms in the Jester's harness and his legs around the Jester. When they hit the bottom of their fall it nearly wrenched him from Chester, but he held on desperately, and they bounced, headed for the top again, and then came, slowly, to a rest, three quarters of the way to the water.

A speedboat was popping across the water, headed toward them. John shook his head. "All this technology you've stolen and you use a speed boat to escape?"

Chester grinned. "I'm a traditionalist."

"I figure we have two minutes more, Chester, and those steel girders start raining down on us. I'm not going to let you escape that."

"Oh, I'm going to escape, Vulture. Don't worry your pretty little feathers." He smiled lovingly. "I'm thinking I'll start by hunting down every single member of your family."

Pronto shouted at John from the top of the bridge. He said he was going to pull the bungee up. John shouted, "No! The bomb! Two minutes!" Pronto shouted and disappeared again.

A loud roaring came from the bridge. Chester and John both looked up in time to see Game Master's dome lifting out over the water, headed for the mainland. "Plan B is in effect," Chester said happily. "He's going to go release his robot soldiers in San Francisco and declare war in the name of the capes. Shouldn't be long before the entire United States military blows up our island."

Captain Anytime's Fighting Fifty-Five were on the opposite horizon and headed in fast. Maybe they would get here in time? Or maybe they would get here just as the bridge exploded. John said, "This really is about the Black Vulture, isn't it?"

"Of course, my boy, of course. Without him I'm nothing."

John grabbed his mask and disconnected. He dropped it and let it fall into the water below. He looked at the Jester, his mask drifting on the waves. "I'm John Ajax."

"I know your secret identity," Chester said dismissively. His hand went to the release for his harness, his boat beneath them and off to the side. His henchmen were shouting for him to come down. One and a half minutes to go.

"No, Chester, look at me." The old man looked directly into John's eyes, and John released the cape from around his neck. "I'm John Ajax. It's my only identity. I'm not the Black Vulture. He's dead. I will never put this costume on again."

"You can't do that," Chester said. "Who ever heard of a high schooler retiring? It's just not done."

"I can. I just did. I swear to you, I will never wear this costume again. And without the Black Vulture, you're not Chester the Jester. You're just Scott Jennison."

"Don't call me that!"

"And, Scott? You're going to jail. Not Chester. Scott Jennison."

"No!"

"Thirty seconds, boss!" One of the henchmen on the boat below.

"You have to let me go, Vulture," Chester said. "We can both go. I'll save you so we can play this all out again, over and over."

"No. I'm done. Scott, listen to me... I forgive you. I'm going to make sure you end up in prison, but I'm not going to try to get revenge. I'm not going to hold a grudge against you. I'm not going to give you that kind of power."

"Ten seconds!" The boat turned, sending up a wave of spray. It moved away from the bridge.

Chester sighed. "Good help is hard to find. No one is willing to die for their boss these days." Six. Five. Four. Three. Two. "Goodbye, Vulture."

An enormous explosion came from out over the water, and the blast sent them rocking and spinning on their bungee cord. The Game Master's flying dome had black smoke roiling from it. It faltered, then plummeted to the water, sending up an enormous wave. John laughed. "Pronto moved the bomb instead of trying to defuse it. Ha. Ha ha ha."

"You let your friend be the hero? He stops the bomb while you hang on a rope?"

"I told you, I'm just a kid. John Ajax."

Chester scowled. "You're worse than the original Vulture. Oh! You make me sick! How can I be the Jester if you refuse to be my audience?"

"You can't, Scott. You're done. The Black Vulture is dead."

"Then we'll die together," Chester said viciously, and a small knife sprung from his sleeve into his hand. He jabbed it into John's side. John gasped, his grip on Chester loosening. "I'll send flowers to the funeral."

John peeled away from Chester. He saw faces hanging over the rail above, watching. Then he was falling, a gushing trail of red following him like a comet's tail. He felt the impact in his back and ribs, the water hitting him like frozen fists. Above he could see Chester, twisting in his harness. Everything blurred. He saw someone diving off the side of the bridge, hurtling toward him. Then he saw green, murky green everywhere around him. He felt something smash into his chest, knocking the last of the air from his lungs. Then, only darkness.

CHAPTER 19

THE GREATEST SUPER HERO TEAM IN THE WORLD

His hospital bed was in the Vulture's Nest, alongside the wide windows, and when he opened his eyes there was so much sunlight reflecting off the white surfaces it was as if someone had blinded him. He could see his city down below, and it was safe, the bridge stretching toward civilization like a white ribbon. He turned his head, looking into the Nest, and saw his grandfather, dour frown on his face, sitting in his wheelchair. When he saw John, his eyes lit up and he smiled. He reached a wrinkled hand out to John and squeezed.

"Grandpa?"

"Hi, John. I'm glad you're okay."

"But how?"

"Jupiter Girl jumped in after you. Lightning Cat let her out of the stasis field and she immediately flew to help you. Captain Anytime brought you here, thinking it would be better than the hospital, and he was right. I came up immediately, and G3 and I patched you up in no time."

"You? I don't understand."

His grandfather's eyes crinkled at the edges and he laughed merrily. "You haven't figured it out yet? I'm the original Black Vulture."

John sat up in the bed, shocked, and a pain shot through his side. He fell back, gasping, and his grandfather put his hand on his shoulder, holding him down. "Easy, John, easy." He cleared his throat and looked out the window. "In fact, fifteen years ago I woke up in a bed just like this one."

"I don't understand."

"We were on Kane Bridge, and Chester was about to blow it up. I had alienated a lot of my friends by then, and family, too. I was so focused on making Chester pay, it had become an obsession. The bridge was about to explode and in the distance I could see the blurred shape of a runner. I knew it was Rolling Thunder, coming to try to save the day, but he was too late. Too late to save everyone, too late to stop the bombs. He had time, he said, to save one person. He had to run so fast that he broke my ribs, and the concussion of the bomb threw us hard enough that when we hit the ground it broke my spinal cord. I had lost my grip on Thunder. On a lot of things."

"You had to stop being the Black Vulture."

"Yes. I had been about to retire in any case."

"Why?"

John's grandfather looked away, embarrassed. "Because you were about to be born, John. I had a lot of regrets by then. Your grandmother died because I was the Vulture." He held his hand up when John started to speak. "Which is a story for another time. I can't talk about that yet. And your father, I had only spent time with him growing up if he lived on my terms, if he tried to be a cape. I realized... I didn't want to lose you, too. I wanted to watch you grow up, and not as some toddler super hero. I desperately wanted you to live a normal life. So I left some convincing clues that a police officer I had worked with, who died on the bridge, had been the Black Vulture."

"Then why did you live in Capeville this whole time? Why didn't you live somewhere closer to us?"

Grandpa put his hands over his face and rubbed it. "After the explosion... I was angry. Not just at Chester. Angry at the capes. Angry that they, that *we*, allowed this to happen. Kane Bridge was only the most recent example. Most of all I was angry at myself. I had crushed all of life into this little black box, this one goal of trying to stop criminals. I had missed the joy in life. Missed my son growing up, missed so many things. I wasn't going to miss my grandson." He sighed and looked off into the distance. "I tried to convince everyone to be done with the capes, but no one listened. So I started outing them. One by one by one. I invented the idea of the Rubicon Protocol. I sold it to Caesar, who signed on for reasons of his own. And soon I built a world for you... a world without capes, where you could live in freedom, not have to fight giant radioactive lizards or madmen. But it required that I stay here. That I... monitor things."

"Monitor?" John thought furiously through the clues. The maps in his grandfather's house. The retirement home being circled. The unilink transporter being in his house, John being chosen as the successor to the Black Vulture. It all fell into place. "You're the shadow director of the Regulars."

"Yes. A few years ago I approached King Jupiter. He was always one of our more pragmatic members. He forgave me for my meltdown, for the book, for Rubicon, for everything. He suggested I run the Regulars anonymously, thinking – no doubt correctly – that some of our membership would refuse to come under my leadership."

John shook his head. "So all of this... my discovering the doomsday device and stopping Chester... that was all part of your plan?"

"Not exactly. I had hoped you would draw Chester out, that if you went around dressed like me it might get us some information. I didn't mean for you to get so heavily involved. I certainly didn't expect you to be in harm's way. I didn't expect you and your friends to perform better than the Regulars."

"That's because we're the greatest super team in the world," Pronto said, leaning against the wall, a goofy smile on his face. He appeared at John's side in a moment. "Welcome back to the land of the living."

Lightning Cat came charging into the room, sparks flying off her as she shoved Pronto out of the way and wrapped her arms around John, hugging him tight. A warm feeling moved through John's entire body, right out to the tips of his fingers and toes. He lifted one arm and put it around her.

Pronto said, "Looks like you have a serious case of static cling!" Lightning Cat stood up and punched him in the arm.

Jupiter Girl came in, followed closely by her father and John's parents. "You've been waiting all morning to use that line, Pronto."

"So? You can't waste a good line."

John grabbed Pronto's arm. "You saved all the capes, Pronto. That makes you some sort of super hero's hero."

"And I broke the sound barrier. At least twice." His face fell. "My dad says it doesn't count until I can do it in front of him, though, so I guess I'm still Pronto. Although my dad did say that moving the bomb onto the Game Master's ship was, and I quote, 'a work of genius.'"

"Speaking of parents," John's dad said, and he and John's mom pushed their way through the crowd and sat on either side of his bed. "We're so proud of you, son."

John frowned. "Proud of me, but you're going to tell me that it's too dangerous and I'm not allowed to be a cape anymore?"

John's dad laughed. "Son, I started wearing a cape at age ten. Why do you think I was called the 'Flying Squirrel'? Does that sound like a name an adult would choose?" He exchanged a look with his own father. "Besides, did you know that when we carted Chester away he insisted that we call him Scott? That's never happened before. And the Pacific pulled Game Master out of the drink, too. Clean up took a while but I think we got everyone who was helping Chester out, including Hydra."

His mom squeezed his forearm. "Honey, after this week, you can decide what you want to do. But if you're going to be a cape, there will be conditions." She looked around at all of the teens in the room. "You're all going to need training. We're retired. But we can teach you some of the things you need to know. We'll be your teachers. This is non-negotiable."

The Gecko snorted. "I don't need any training."

John's dad smiled at him. "I noticed in the re-telling of the tale that you got captured a lot, Gecko. And I'm sure your uncle would agree that some training might be helpful."

G3 entered the room. "My patient needs rest. His vital signs are strong, but clearly he is tired."

John's mother kissed him on the forehead, and, to John's embarrassment, so did Jupiter Girl. Lightning Cat gave her a dirty look. Jupiter Girl didn't see it, but John did, and Lightning Cat marched up to his bed and kissed him on the cheek, a small spark shocking him. They all filed out of the room. After they all left, G3 turned to him.

"I am sorry for the deception involving your grandfather. He released me to share certain information with you. He informs me that all secrets may now be revealed. Any question you ask, if it's in my database, I will share the answers freely."

"Thank you, G3."

The robot nodded its manikin head slightly. "My pleasure."

"One more thing, G3. I need you to go through all the equipment and remove the Black Vulture logo from all of it. The vehicles, weapons, costumes, everything."

"Then you won't be training to be a cape, sir?"

John smiled at him. "Yes, I will. But as John Ajax. The Black Vulture is dead."

"Very well, sir. I am glad you are safe." G3 glided out of the room.

John turned slightly so he could see Capeville out the window. He felt a momentary pride looking at the bridge stretching out from town, whole and glimmering in the sunlight and John knew that was, at least in part, because of him. Him and his friends.

Pronto appeared by his side again, carrying Gecko. He set him down. "Hey, we snuck back in after the tin can left."

John grinned. "Good. We have a lot of planning to do."

Pronto gave him a deadly glare. "Before we go thinking up team names, though, John, you need to know that Jupiter Girl is mine. You can't go kissing her all the time."

John thought of Jupiter Girl and Lightning Cat and all the changes of the last few days and felt only a happy, warm confusion. He didn't know if he could stick to the deal, but Pronto was his friend and he would try. "She's too old for me, anyway," John said with a grin.

Pronto gave the Gecko a cold stare. "How about you, sticky fingers?"

The Gecko shrugged. "Justice is my girlfriend."

Jupiter Girl and Lightning Cat snuck into the room, as well. They formed a loose circle around him, his four friends. They didn't say anything for a minute, then they all broke out in silly grins. "This is going to be awesome," Pronto said.

John said, "There's still a traitor in the Regulars. We have to figure out what happened to that giant robot, and how Cat's dad is a part of that. And I suspect that Chester wouldn't have been able to do all of this without some help, maybe from the Golden Dragon. It's going to be dangerous."

"It's going to be fun," Pronto said.

John held his hand up over his bed. "Who's in?"

Lightning Cat put her hand on his. "So long as my dad doesn't ground me for eternity when I get home, I'm in."

"Me," Jupiter Girl said, and she smiled at John.

Pronto quickly put his hand on hers. "You know I'm in."

The Gecko looked thoughtful, but he put his hand on top. "We're going to need help," he said.

Pronto laughed. "Then it's official. The greatest super hero team in the world is open for recruiting."

Everyone put their second hand into the pile, and there were grins all around. John felt a rush of affection for them: the speedster, the girl with the electric personality, the Jovian, the sticky-fingered superhero. It was the beginning of something new, something amazing. John turned his head, just for a moment, and saw Capeville, shining in the distance. "No," John said. "Not a team. The Regulars were a team. It was a business. They were colleagues, and it didn't end well. Not us. No matter what happens, we're together. The five us. We're family."

The grins, if it was possible, got wider, and they dog piled onto the bed, hugging each other and laughing and John's side hurt from the pressure and the laughs but he didn't care, not a bit, and they stayed like that, together, talking about their adventures, until the sun washed Capeville orange and the stars pierced the gathering dark.

THE END

CAPEVILLE: THE DEATH OF THE BLACK VULTURE

EPILOGUE

The torches outside his cell guttered and failed. For perhaps one thousandth of a second they failed. His consciousness stirred. He reached out with his mind, probing the outer limits of his prison. Still strong. But the torches would fail, as they had half a century ago. As they had six times in the millennium prior.

He felt his followers calling his name, working the ancient rituals. He followed their cries and for the first time in a decade he felt awareness of the outside world. Great power had been spent on a bridge, only moments ago. The surge came from dark intentions, had been intended to kill. But it had failed. Some misguided servant of light had scattered the darkness, had crippled it.

He recognized the scent of the light. He pulled his hood back, testing the stale air. Yes. It was familiar.

It was fresh and young, but the light had the smallest whiff of his greatest enemy. Caesar. No matter. He had blotted out fresh young lights more than once, and would do so again.

Rise, he called to his followers. *The world must feel the points of our daggers again.*

His followers trembled. As well they should. They asked him, dared to ask him, to whom they should give the daggers.

The children, he told them. *We always begin with the children.*

He sought the light on the bridge again. He closed his burning eyes and studied it carefully. There were five lights, not one, small but bright. Young. Inexperienced. Brave.

He would enjoy destroying them. Snuffing them out, one by one. But first he must build his army. He must send his followers out with the knives. The League of Daggers would rise like smoke from a funeral pyre. The stench of death would be in the nostrils of every servant of the light, and before they died they would bow and kiss his ring.

The torches which kept him in his cell flickered again. Longer this time. Nearly twice as long.

The skin around his teeth pulled back, and he grinned.

Father Corpse felt the darkness increase.

COMING SOON!

CAPEVILLE

THE LEAGUE OF DAGGERS

FROM THE
RUBICON FILES

THE AUTUMN TIGERS

A Chinese super team

THE AVANT GUARD

A team of super heroes who deal with the strange and inexplicable, protecting the Earth from madness and bizarre evils. Their current lineup includes Avant Ghost, Ready Maid, the Situationist, and Captain Dada.

AVANT GHOST

This perpetually young woman and member of the Avant Guard doesn't seem to age. She's also transparent and intangible. She appears to be from the 1920s, but little is known about her other than her commitment to justice and the melancholy sadness on her face.

THE BLACK VULTURE

A street level vigilante feared for both his strength and his intelligence. He was a founding member of the Regulars. He died in the explosion at Kane Bridge (see Chester the Jester).

BRASS KNUCKLES

A ten-foot tall cyborg made of brass, gears and steam hoses. He was built in the 1800s and through careful attention has managed to stay functional. He's a criminal with hundreds of years of experience.

CAESAR

The most powerful superhuman in the world. Caesar has been mysteriously absent since the passing of the Rubicon Protocol.

CAPTAIN ANYTIME

Founder of the Fightin' Fifty-Five, Captain Anytime built his unique aircraft, the Flying Donut, himself. He doesn't have any powers, but he's the best pilot in the world. You can ask him and he'll tell you himself.

CAPTAIN DADA

His nonsensical pronouncements rarely make sense, though his powers of "Surrealist vision" seem to be triggered by nonsense phrases. The surrealist vision appears to be a type of incapacitating illusion. A member of the Avant Guard.

CHESTER THE JESTER

The Black Vulture's greatest nemesis, a show-man who sees crime as performance art. He exploded Kane Bridge, killing the Black Vulture. Chester immediately turned himself in to the authorities, claiming he was "entering retirement."

CHRONONAUT

A time-traveling gentleman with a strange sense of humor and a penchant for "adopting" interesting people from across the timeline to take them on odd, sometimes silly adventures. He calls them the Time Skippers.

DOGFACE

The result of government experiments into canine soldiers, Dogface is not only a talking dog, he's also a grizzled war veteran.

DR. DYNAMO

A scientist completely devoted to experimentation and invention. Sometimes he fights with the heroes, sometimes against, all depending on his own inscrutable preferences. Many of his experiments are dangerous, if not immoral.

FATHER CORPSE

A horrific and deadly enemy of the Regulars who has been imprisoned in a magic dungeon for many years.

THE FIST

Raised in the jungles of South America, the Fist's left hand is as hard as diamonds, and he uses it to punish evildoers.

THE FLYING SQUIRREL

The Black Vulture's one-time partner and one of the more popular capes, he retired just before the incident at Kane Bridge.

THE FOREIGNER

Charles Andu is Lao Wai, the Foreigner, the greatest practitioner of Mystical Arts in the last several decades.

THE FOX

One of Black Vulture's villains, a human trafficker and gang lord.

FUNDAMENTALIST

A member of the villainous team, The Populace. He has the power to persuade people using only his voice, and to create enormous fear in those who choose to disobey him.

G3

The android AI and caretaker for the Nest, Black Vulture's secret HQ.

GAME MASTER

Uther Sanrio makes games, and he has consistently used those skills to break the law... mostly bank robberies and death traps for super-heroes. After the Rubicon Protocol, Game Master amassed an enormous fortune with his video games, primarily the Tread Battalion series. He's a crafty and dangerous villain.

THE GECKO

The current Gecko is the third to hold the title, which has been passed down through his family (his uncle was the original, his father the second). He takes his secret identity and his crime fighting very seriously.

THE GOLDEN DRAGON

The greatest evil mastermind of them all, and Caesar's arch nemesis.

THE GOVERNOR

A massively powerful android who functions as an intergalactic lawkeeper. He was nearly destroyed in the civil war on Mars and has since dropped from public view.

HYDRA

Frank Hyrda is a villain who multiplies whenever he experiences pain.

ICE BOX

One of the Black Vulture's villains, perhaps best known for the "Extinction Event" when she attempted to bring a new ice age into being.

JOLLY RHODA

With her trademark outfit of white spandex with a black skull and crossbones on the chest, Jolly Rhoda strikes fear into the hearts of all thieves and crooks. She has the power to highjack the voluntary functions of those around her, giving her a sort of sophisticated mind control.

JUPITER GIRL

Although she is Jovian, Jupiter Girl has spent most of her life on Earth. Since Caesar disappeared years ago, this teen girl is possibly one of the most powerful beings on the planet: super strength, flight, shape shifting and telepathy are some of her powers. Her true name is Byon'g ana K'reth.

KITSCH

A member of the super villain team The Populists. She can cause vertigo and manipulate emotions.

KING JUPITER

A Jovian who came to Earth many decades ago and has adopted this planet as his own. He considers the Regulars his extended family, though Jupiter Girl is his actual daughter.

LIGHTNING CAT

The more she moves, the more electrical charge she builds up. She's an expert level gymnast.

MASS CULTURE

A villainous bodybuilder who can change the mass of things (or people!) around him. A member of the Populists.

THE MIGHTY FLEA

After buying a mysterious totem at a flea market he gained the proportionate strength and jumping ability of a flea.

MS. UNIVERSE

A genius level intellect who uses technology from the future to fight crime.

THE MUCK

A monstrous creature made of garbage who lives in the sewers and tunnels beneath Capeville. He has no patience for law breakers, though his sense of justice is sometimes alien.

NETWORK

A woman with the ability to speak "telepathically" with any complex machine.

THE NINTH STREET REGULARS

The premiere super-hero team, most often called "the Regulars." Disbanded.

THE PACIFIC

One of the seven children of "the Deep," the Pacific is the only one who sees fit to interact with the world above water. He was a founding member of the Regulars and has been the main ambassador from the Sea Folk.

PERCEPTA

Nothing is hidden from Percepta. A member of the (now disbanded) Regulars and married to Wise Owl.

PRONTO

The fourth fastest person on Earth, after his dad and brothers. He can't quite break the speed barrier. Or keep his room clean.

READY MAID

When it comes to brute strength, not many can stand up to the Avant Guard's Ready Maid!

ROCKET COWBOY

A cowboy with laser pistols, a rocket for a horse and a habit of speaking his mind.

ROLLING THUNDER

The fastest man in the world. He's a first generation immigrant from China. His three sons are all super fast as well: Thunderstorm, Thunder Fists, and Pronto. Founding member of the Regulars.

SEA DRAGON

Lance Stewart was once a member of the Regulars, until he committed a horrible crime and was caught by Rocket Cowboy and convicted. He's immensely strong, and his powers require him to breathe water for at least seven hours a day.

SHADOW WOLVES

Enormous wolves made of shadow who inhabit a strange in-between land of darkness. There is a dimensional gateway to their territory under the streets of Capeville.

THE SITUATIONIST

A member of the Avant Guard. His powers and abilities change depending on the situation he is in.

WISE OWL

No one knows his powers or abilities, but he has a way of being in the right place to help people in trouble. Married to Percepta.

One of the things I love about comics is the enormous overlapping casts, and the small comments in one story that pays off in a big way somewhere else. I'd love to see most of these characters make bigger appearances in the future. (I love the Avant Guard a lot!) Write me and let me know who your favorite is!

CONTACT MATT

Feel free to send me notes, questions or fan art at:
matt@capeville.net

I'm also on twitter (@mattmikalatos), Facebook (facebook.com/mikalatosbooks) and Instagram (mattmikalatos). Or, check out my website at www.mikalatos.com or my podcast at Storymen.us.

Thanks for reading!

IF YOU ENJOYED CAPEVILLE YOU MIGHT
ALSO ENJOY MATT'S FANTASY NOVEL,
THE SWORD OF SIX WORLDS.

THE SWORD OF SIX WORLDS

MATT MIKALATOS

VALIDUS SMITH HAS THREE GOALS. STAY ALIVE.
SAVE THE WORLD. FINISH HER HOMEWORK.

WWW.SIXWORLDS.COM

ACKNOWLEDGEMENTS

A million thanks to my kids, Zoey, Allie and Myca, without whom this book wouldn't exist. You're my real heroes! I love talking about this book and these characters with you. To my wife, Krista, for her support and encouragement along the way, and of course for listening to me expound about my favorite obscure superheroes (like Rainbow Lass!).

To JR., Amanda and Clay. If I were forming a superhero team you all would certainly be on it. Thanks for your feedback, friendship and for encouraging me to keep going.

To my early readers, Josh Alves, Brock Eastman, and C.J. Darlington. I'm so thankful for your insights!

To my editor, the amazing Lisa Parnell.

Wes Yoder, the incomparable super agent and dear friend. Thank you!

Kevin Summers, who did all the formatting for both the ebooks and the print book.

Mike Corley, cover artist extraordinaire, who went above and beyond designing character looks and giving long, gushing, fanboy speeches about how great the book is. Let's have some more of that! One day we'll be able to do the heavily illustrated "Holy Grail Edition" we both want!

Alex Shvartsman and Jake Kerr, thank you for your incredible advice and friendship. I don't think I would have given this whole thing a swing without the two of you cheering me on and explaining how to do it!

And, of course, to Shasta Kramer, who gave me the name "Lightning Cat" from her own superhero name. Meow! Much aloha to you.

Last but not at all least, many thanks to those who most supported my comics habit as a kid: Pete and Maggie Mikalatos, Joe Field of Flying Colors Comics, and Shane Rosenberry. You're the best!

And thanks to you, for reading to the very last word.

Join the Capeville newsletter and be the first to read the next words! http://tiny.cc/capeville

CPSIA information can be obtained
at www.ICGtesting.com
Printed in the USA
LVOW01s2311130217
524179LV00008B/89/P